JUICE!

JUICE!

A NOVEL

ISHMAEL REED

DALKEY ARCHIVE PRESS | CHAMPAIGN AND LONDON

Library of Congress Cataloging-in-Publication Data

Reed, Ishmael, 1938-
Juice! / by Ishmael Reed. -- 1st ed.
p. cm.
ISBN 978-1-56478-637-1 (pbk. : alk. paper)
1. Press--United States--Fiction. 2. African Americans--Press
coverage--Fiction. 3. Celebrities--Press coverage--Fiction. 4.
Simpson, O. J., 1947---Trials, litigation, etc.--Fiction. 5. Crime
and the press--United States--Fiction. 6. Politics and
culture--United States--Fiction. 7. Satire. I. Title.
PS3568.E365J85 2011
813'.54--dc22
2010050132

Partially funded by the University of Illinois at Urbana-Champaign
and by a grant from the Illinois Arts Council, a state agency

www.dalkeyarchive.com

Cover: design and composition by Danielle Dutton, illustration by Ishmael Reed

*For Drs. Mary Gray Patton and James Jae-Jong Chang,
my coaches Drs. Pierre-Damien Mvuyekure, Sämi Ludwig, and
Reginald Martin, and in memory of Vincent Reed, Jr., Our Prince*

"I want my nigger."

—Huckleberry Finn

Fox News Channel's Shepard Smith asked O. J. Simpson if he would take a lie-detector test. "I'm not going to be some dancing monkey for you guys," Simpson said.

—AP Online, June 8, 2000

FOREWORD

Otter, Rabbit, Snakes, Bat, and me, Bear were getting older. Late sixties, early seventies, but because we were in the arts we were still producing though challenged by a younger generation and their manifestos in which we were dismissed as part of an old school or, as one writer with a penchant for redundancy put it, "fading anachronisms."

Some day if he is lucky, he will reach our stage in life. We'll see if he manages to survive the gauntlet formed by diabetes, or Parkinson's Disease, or the Big C. See if he can live from six months to six months awaiting the results of his PSA tests. How will he experience the sadness that comes when visiting hospitalized friends like I felt when visiting Bat at that nursing home? He'd gone to the bathroom in his gallery thousands of times, but this time he opened the wrong door, and instead of the entrance to the toilet, he opened the door to his apartment, took a few steps and fell. You know those old Blues songs about one's "good-time friends?" His good-time friends abandoned him. Later, after he'd recovered, he was being escorted to his gallery after returning from his job as a part-time heckler at the Nuyorican Poet's Café's slam poetry competition. The escort abandoned him at the bottom of the steps. He made it up halfway to the gallery only to fall again, this time injuring his shoulder. Let the young bloods try to encourage other friends awaiting transplant organs or being told that a balloon can substitute for a bladder or that their triple bypass resulted in an infection.

Alonzo Mourning knows that feeling. He had a kidney transplant. Maybe Shaquille O'Neal too. Playing through aches and pains. They were saying in 2009 that he was too old to play basketball, but there he was giving some game to the Phoenix Suns, a survivor in a time when the younger players were regarded in the words of Charles Barkley as "pit bulls." Where entering the paint might put you on the receiving end of a double flagrant. In 2010, he was still "throwing the hammer down" for the Cavaliers, even though he'd slowed down.

Shaquille's story was almost as persistent as the O. J. story. The need for O. J. was insatiable. Even though he had been captured or entrapped as some would say, people were still making money from his career. In 2010 O. J. was still providing people with a gold mine of opportunity. Take Thomas Riccio who set up O. J. like the FBI set up Marion Barry. What is the link, you say? Riccio informed the FBI that he was going to lure O. J. into an entrapment by suggesting that a memorabilia collector was in possession of property that belonged to him. The American media, a sort of spare all-white jury, ignored the FBI's role in the Las Vegas entrapment. As the *New York Times* reported on September 23, 2008:

> The man who set up the hotel-room confrontation that led to armed robbery charges against O. J. Simpson testified Monday that he had received at least $210,000 from several news organizations, including ABC News, in exchange for interviews, photographs and parts of an audio recording he had secretly made of the events.
>
> Those fees included $150,000 from the celebrity gossip website TMZ.com for excerpts of Mr. Riccio's audio recording, as well as $15,000 from ABC News and $25,000 from *Entertainment Tonight* for what Mr. Riccio said were interviews about the confrontation. In the audio recording, Simpson is heard saying "nobody leaves this room" loud enough for the all-white jury to convict him, but even the FBI couldn't vouch for the authenticity of the tape.
>
> But spokesmen for ABC News and *Entertainment Tonight* said the payments were not for interviews but for other materials. A spokeswoman for TMZ.com said the website doesn't comment about how it acquires material.

Riccio isn't the only individual who is cashing in on O. J. Gossip about black celebrities is the new form of bread and circuses, while more serious offenses are ignored by a media that serves the corporate world. For example the manufacturer of a diabetes drug called Avandia was exposed by a Senate report to have caused tens of thousands of heart attacks. The manufacturers of the drug were aware of the toxic effects of the drug but had it distributed anyway. Corporations are individuals according to the Roberts court, but, unlike human individuals, they can get away with mass murder by paying a fine.

O. J. has made more money for those who have commercialized his cases than all of the slaves in Virginia made for their "masters" in a decade, and like those slaves, O. J. is broke while the new masters, the corporations that were able to sell their products off his back, are rich.

Of the film *Obsessed* which toppped the box office in 2009 despite hostile reviews, Stephen Holden wrote for the *New York Times*: "The movie's most disturbing aspect, of which the filmmakers could not have been unaware, is the physical resemblance between Mr. Elba and Ms. Larter to O. J. and Nicole Brown Simpson. It lends *Obsessed* a distasteful taint of exploitation." During the first weekend after hitting the screens, it grossed 28 million dollars, not a penny of which went to O. J. On April 7, 2010, he vegetated in prison while the Associated Press reported that people tried to cash in on the clothes that he wore when he was acquitted of murder:

> The tan Armani suit, white shirt and gold tie that O. J. Simpson wore on the day he was acquitted of murder have been acquired by the Newseum in Washington, D.C., for a display exhibit on the "trial of the century," the curator of the museum of news said Tuesday.

"For us, it's a piece of news history that we will include in our collection of objects relating to the trial," said Carrie Christofferson, the curator who was involved in negotiations to obtain the suit.

Fighting Over O. J.'s Acquittal Clothes

But who am I to point a finger? O. J. has provided me with a gold mine of opportunity also. In fact the image of gold plays prominently in the case. Goldman, the murder victim's father, Golden, the Los Angeles coroner, and Denise Brown. Nicole's sister. She has been called a *gold* digger (like me). When she had a dispute with the Goldmans about who would profit from the book *If I Did It*, in which with the help of a ghost writer Simpson proposes some hypotheticals about how the murders might have taken place, Denise said that she realized why the word gold appears in Goldman's name. Sydney and Justin, the children of O. J. and Nicole, are sometimes referred to as "golden." These golden children, Sydney and Justin, whose welfare those members of the "general public" were so concerned about, have become adults. The "general public," mind you, vote for politicians who send black children, who are not so golden, to homeless shelters.

PART 1

1

None of my Rhinosphere buddies, Snakes60@, Rabbit64@, Bat68@, or Otter73@, would have ever predicted that by June 2007, I'd be sounding like Shaquille O'Neal of 2004, because up to that year, I was like Rasheed Wallace. A team player. A minor Egyptologist. A man who drew technical fouls (called "Rodmans," after Dennis Rodman) and suspensions for criticizing those who, in my mind, delivered unfair calls against me and my brothers. How did the *Times* put it after the Los Angeles Lakers were blown away in 2004 by these ragged upstarts, these Motown Hood Rats: "Teamwork Thumps Star Power." Not always. I found that out the hard way, backing loser after loser all for the sake of the team. The brothers. The Fellas. But now I'm like Shaquille O'Neal. He said after the fifth game Lakers defeat, "It's going to be a funny summer. Everyone's going to take care of their own business and everyone is going to do what's best for them." Call it enlightened self-interest, pragmatism, or taking a page from Michael Jordan, who said, "To be successful you have to be selfish, or else you never achieve." Before, if I were a basketball player, I would have shared the ball with my fellow teammates. Like Steve Nash. That was then. Now I was going to be like Allen Iverson, a ball hog. I was definitely going to get my three-pointers, teamwork or no teamwork. I was going to avoid the paint and depend upon perimeter shots. But with this award, I was like somebody who hit a clutch, buzzer, beating three-pointers from the opposite end of the court.

Esther and I are lodged in a suite down the hall from one that was once occupied by General Douglas MacArthur. He used to watch the Friday night fights here. This is a famous New York hotel, the one every travel site advertises with these words: "Since 1893, our name has epitomized the quintessential luxury hotel experience. Each spacious, individually decorated guestroom and suite offers a rewarding union of timeless elegance and up-to-the-moment convenience, luxurious comfort and classic sophistication." You know the one. How did I get here? The wonderful buffet we had a few hours earlier, attended by some of the most distinguished members of my profession, the speeches from my colleagues, people who up to now considered me a troublemaker, an iconoclast, a gadfly, a witch doctor and even more derogatory things. They were all singing my praises.

Ever since the backlash on the judgment in the O. J. criminal trial, I had been in a rage. So were my e-mail companions of The Rhinosphere. We agreed that this was because the other jury, seeking profits from a marketing strategy called the Racial Divide, had muddied the waters.

Since that 1995 verdict, the Jim Crow media jury has been attempting to double-jeopardize, triple-jeopardize, and quadruple-jeopardize O. J.

Unlike the jury in the criminal trial, where evidence had to be examined, the media could play fast and loose with the facts and were doing so even twelve years after the trial. It comes down to this: who do you believe, some of the leading scientists and forensic experts in the country, or Bill Maher, who couldn't even begin his 2009 season without a reference to O. J. Simpson? Simpson began as a football player; now his name is included in the testimonies of patients who pay two hundred dollars per hour to psychotherapists. (Tiger's name too.)

During one point in the criminal trial, one of O. J.'s dreams was entered into evidence. How many dreams has O. J. entered? And in what role?

Snakes, who was not considered a hothead like me, Rabbit the filmmaker, Bat, and Otter agreed with supermodel Naomi Campbell that with the O. J. case all black men were guilty by proxy. (In 2010, Ms. Campbell is O. J.'d over whether she received a diamond from Charles Taylor, the former dictator of Liberia. Mia Farrow disputes Ms. Campbell's testimony. When Ms. Farrow wrote a book critical of Woody Allen, she was dismissed as a flake even by female critics. With her contradicting a black woman, she will probably be believed.) That was how we all felt in 1995. Rabbit had even said that I'd gotten diabetes because I'd spent all of that time before the tube, obsessed with the O. J. case.

But since I received the news of my good fortune, my blood sugar had returned to normal. At first I was reluctant to sell out a brother, but my family, Esther and Hibiscus, gave me an ultimatum I couldn't refuse. And you know, it was all for the best. I was no longer fretting about every setback in Michael Jackson's cases. Alan M. Dershowitz's book asserting Mike Tyson's innocence, published in 2004—I would have ordered it from Amazon immediately. Not anymore. Kobe Bryant? Maybe the prosecution meant well when they refused to go along with the judge's request that a member of the defense team be present when they examined his "victim's" DNA. What did I know?

And O. J. as late as 2005, they were still trying to trap him, the tenth anniversary of his acquittal for the murders of Ron Goldman and Nicole Simpson. But of course, he outwitted Greta Van Susteren, one of those whose career was made by being connected to the case, and he totally demolished Catherine Crier. Escaping their verbal traps.

Even though a number of books had been published asserting O. J.'s guilt, perhaps the vilest and most racist, I had thought at the time, had been Jeffrey Toobin's *The Run of His Life*. But hey, maybe Toobin was right when he said that blacks supported Simpson because they are divorced from reality and shouldn't be patronized or "patted on the head." Toobin was a graduate of Harvard Law School and an editor of the *Harvard Law Review*. What the hell did I know?

But even after the decisions rendered by all-white juries in Santa Monica and Las Vegas, conspiracy theorists cling to O. J.'s innocence, no matter how flimsy the evidence for such a position might be. Like the following flimsy evidence, noted by CNN:

MAY 4, 1995 – Blood taken from beneath Nicole Brown Simpson's fingertips could have come from someone other than her accused killer, O. J. Simpson, a prosecution witness said Thursday under cross-examination.

Greg Matheson, chief forensic scientist at the Los Angeles Police crime lab, conceded that according to scientific literature offered by the defense, the blood was inconsistent with a genetic marker in the blood of either O. J. Simpson or his slain ex-wife.

But, hey, maybe Matheson is wrong. Maybe he can't see "obvious evidence" when it exists right before his eyes. Maybe we should rely upon Dan Gerstein, who, appearing on MSNBC December 26, 2008, to comment about the problems of an impeached Gov. Rod R. Blagojevich, under fire for allegedly offering to sell President Obama's vacated Senate seat, said, "if it were a movie it would be 'Mr. Simpson Goes to Washington.'" He said, "The Government was using a strategy from the playbook of the Simpson defense team: create a circus as a way of distracting from the obvious evidence." Why don't the forensic scientists Wecht, Lee, and Matheson see the evidence as obvious as this commentator who has no training in forensics? Or Bill Maher? These scientists are probably wrong. Whom should we believe? The talk show hosts, members of the same fraternity as Maher, who said that the winter of 2010 proved that global warming is a myth or the overwhelming majority of scientists who were warning us about the consequences of climate change?

In addition, while engaging in the usual sarcastic and vicious comments about O. J., the media were very respectful of Dr. Henry

Lee who still, ten years after the murders, insisted that bloody shoe prints belonging to two pair of shoes, showed up at the crime scene. Not one pair. (But in 2007, they got him, accusing him of pilfering a fingernail, evidence in the Phil Spector case, who, like O. J., is accused of killing a blonde, but no one called his trial "the trial of the century.") Cyril Wecht, the Los Angeles Coroner, also subscribed to the two-killer theory. Experts Lee, Peter Neufeld, and Barry Scheck claimed that the DNA evidence used in the O. J. trial was corrupted. "Garbage In, Garbage Out." The *New York Times* reported on February 4, 2009:

> Forensic evidence that has helped convict thousands of defendants for nearly a century is often the product of shoddy scientific practices that should be upgraded and standardized, according to accounts of a draft report by the nation's pre-eminent scientific research group.
>
> The report by the National Academy of Sciences is to be released this month. People who have seen it say it is a sweeping critique of many forensic methods that the police and prosecutors rely on, including fingerprinting, firearms identification and analysis of bite marks, blood spatter, hair and handwriting.

But the Media jury said that the blacks on what they constantly and mistakenly call "The Black Jury" weren't persuaded by the reasonable doubt presented by the O. J. defense team. They were into paying back the police for Detective Mark Fuhrman, even though they didn't hear all of the information about Fuhrman's racist leanings as revealed through a series of tape recordings. Both Toobin and the late Norman Mailer, writing in *New York Magazine*, said that blacks are incapable of rational thought. Like members of many other species, blacks operate on the basis of instinct, they were suggesting. Blacks were non-Cartesian. (They don't think therefore they ain't.)

2

On June 19, 2004, Larry King did an anti-O. J. show that included Denise Brown, Fred Goldman, Detectives Tom Lange and Phil Vannatter. Denise, who, like her late sister, has dated mobster hit men, said that she was launching a show about domestic violence. Kim Goldman, Fred's daughter, encouraged people to spit on O. J. were they to cross his path. Fred Goldman, Goldman's father, accused the late Johnnie Cochran of setting race relations back one hundred years. While this used to bother me so that I would shake my fist at the TV, and uptick my blood sugar and blood pressure, I have been cured. The fact that Tiger Woods still misses fairways and has to make miraculous shots out of the rough, doesn't affect me the way that such misses did in 2004. (Making miraculous shots out of the rough might be the image of what black men in the U.S. have to do in order to succeed.) Hell, just like Rabbit said when he and I met for the first time. Tiger is worth so much money that he can't even do ads for Buick anymore, because most people would associate him with a Lexus. And Roy Jones, Jr.? If it were 2004, I would have been in a funk for weeks, my blood sugar monitor telling me to "eat a snack" at watching the great Roy Jones, Jr., getting knocked out. Twice. But things changed for Tiger when he was outed as a serial philanderer in 2010. At that point, all speculation about his racial identity was cleared up. As Wanda Sykes put it, it was his black part that bought the Cadillac and the Asian part that wrecked it. Ben Armstrong, my colleague, said that white women should be grateful that somebody still wanted them. White men were tired of them and taking up with Asian women who served beer to them and their friends while they watched football and encouraged them to go to strip clubs and have affairs. (Of course, I disagreed with him.)

And O. J.? In 2007, he was doing well. Parrying with the hosts of talk shows who wanted to pump their ratings. His children had grown up in his care, even though I think Gloria Allred tried to get them removed from O. J.'s home. (In 2007, Ms. Allred was lawyering for one of Britney Spear's bodyguards and arguing that her children be taken away. She wanted Michael Jackson's kids removed from his custody. She's Lilith of the legal profession. And her daughter, Lisa Bloom—what's the word I'm looking for? On Court TV, she welcomed the 2008 Las Vegas show trial of Simpson with "alacrity." A second generation black male basher.) It's 2007 and O. J. can take care of himself. A one-man growth industry. Like in the old days, making more money for others than for himself. A gold mine of opportunity for Jeffrey Toobin, authors Chris Darden, Faye Resnick, Ben & Jerry's Ice Cream, Utility Wagons, and the breeders of Akita dogs. I'm not complaining. I'm getting my cut. Without O. J., I wouldn't be here. Enjoying these swell digs. How did I, the last man to believe in O. J.'s innocence, come to be dwelling in a suite located in the Waldorf-Astoria? A lot has happened since that day in 1994 when we heard that O. J.'s wife, Nicole, and Ron Goldman, a waiter and some say drug courier operating out of the Mezzaluna restaurant, had been murdered in Brentwood. For me it all began during a vacation in Hawaii.

3

JUNE 1994

I'm convinced that dreams arise from a slough within the psyche.
They have something to do with the flow of fluids within our bodies. With Diabetes 2, I'm very conscious of blood arriving at its
anatomical destinations. My slough becomes stimulated by the
sound of ocean waves colliding with a beach. I wish that there
were a better way to explain it. Whatever the reason, being near
the beach washes out the accumulation of debris lodging within
my mind. Many years ago, I needed a drink from time to time.
Nowadays I need two drinks. The Pacific and the Atlantic. They
calm my hypertension and my hyperglycemia.

Every time I hear the banging of the waves a dream rolls out.
Bad dreams: snakes, rats, dead people. It's as though my soul is being laundered. By the time I leave for home, I'm less anxious. I'm
no longer making the six o'clock run to the Turtle Bay Hilton to
buy the mainland papers. I'm away from the fax machine. Online.
Away from that monkey on my back, television. I'm always channel surfing from C-SPAN to CNN. Not here.

My wife, Esther, and my daughter, Hibiscus, spend a lot of their time shopping, while I wait in the car. "I'll be back in ten minutes" means forty-five minutes to them. When we're not shopping for groceries at the Food Fair, we eat out at some of the restaurants between the beach houses and the Turtle Bay Hilton. Sometimes we might go to one of the hotels in Waikiki. The Sheraton, where we can sit out on the veranda and watch the swimmers and ocean liners. It resembles the main house of a large plantation. They perform the hula here. The poet Kathryn Takara is especially adept at moving her hips to the movement of the waves. We've decided that everywhere Americans go, there is a Waikiki. A brassy commercial strip of restaurants, shops, bars, and tattoo parlors.

Sometimes, the Americans come to our part of the island in buses. (We're in Laie, staying at the Malauki Rentals, in a duplex on the beach.) The tourists arrive at the Polynesian Cultural Center which features a show with pretty mixed-race young people rowing in and out of a stadium in boats while singing and dancing. A little slapstick is added for the entertainment of the audience. Occasionally, a male rower pretends to have fallen into the water and the crowd erupts into uproarious laughter. This must be an example of Mormon humor. We are told that as a condition for their hiring, the natives have to convert to the Mormon religion.

A woman as big as Pele, the volcano goddess, says that the thin women are put out for the tourists, but the heavy women know the hula. They can shake that thing. The Polynesian people we see, heading for the Mormon's Food Fair, have a casual style. They were no match for the Anglos, who invaded these islands, searching for sugar. Many of the natives are dark skinned and have those full features that we associate with some African faces. Possibly descendants from a migration that began on the east coast of Africa, but some University of California anthropologists contend that the Polynesian people are of Chinese origin. Upon seeing pictures of Hawaii's early monarchs, however, it occurred to me that I have relatives who look like them.

Critics of Afrocentrism can recognize the facial features in a police sketch as belonging to a black man, but when these features appear on the face of a Hawaiian monarch or on that of a Pharaoh, the identity of this royalty becomes subject to all manner of esoteric hair splitting.

Hawaiian music is different. It's as cool as green tea. More sugar for the ear. Their ocean has a personality. It performs. It changes colors as oceans do, as seas do. I heard a woman say on the radio that the Mediterranean has such a navy blue tint that the term navy blue must have been coined with the Mediterranean in mind. Formerly we were able to swim near the compound without fear, but now sharks are approaching the shallow waters near the land. There is a scarcity of fish, their food supply, and so they're after another source of food. The natives are devoted to sharks and are said to even have worshipped sharks at one time. Legend has it that the Pearl Harbor disaster happened because the harbor was built on the skeleton of a shark. The shamans warned the Navy not to build it there. Am I digressing? I've been accused of that. But since 1994, many subjects have been connected to O. J. no matter how strained the connection. There is, however, a legitimate connection of O. J. to sharks. More later.

After a week, the wastes accumulated from dealing with everyday life on the mainland—road rage, kitchen fights, bills—have about emptied from my head, and I have lost my combative masks. My frowns, which are my part of my armor, disappear. I begin to go cold turkey on espresso. I'm losing weight. And I'm cleansing my colon. I'm sticking to my nutritionist's recommendation for treating my Diabetes 2. Weighing things. Avoiding foods that are white. White rice. White flour.

First we hear that O. J.'s ex-wife, Nicole, and a friend have been slain in the Brentwood section of Los Angeles. This is the first time that I have ever heard of this place. Later, when I go to Hollywood in connection with one of the periodic nibbles for film rights to my sixties cartoon *Attitude the Badger*, the limousine driver tells me that a neighborhood we're driving through has been taken over by people from Central America. He didn't seem too pleased.

Besides, I hate football. Oh, I'll watch the final Super Bowl game, but football games always revived those memories. Humiliating memories of being ridiculed in high school for not going out for football, like the cartoonist Art Spiegelman who was ridiculed when a kid because he was bad at baseball. I was too busy trying to imitate Daphne du Maurier when the model of my peers was Deacon Jones. I thought that football was childish. Artless. The jocks who I knew in high school were vain and stupid. But all of the girls were after them. At the time, I was undergoing a transition from being a nerd to becoming hip.

My only connection with O. J. is that for our Hawaii vacation, I rented a gray Subaru station wagon through Hertz. I always thought that O. J., running through the airport for Hertz, was not dignified. It reminded me of poor Jesse Owens who, even after embarrassing Hitler at the 1936 Olympics, had to return to the United States and race with horses for a living. Oh, there is another connection. O. J. played with the Buffalo Bills. I like Buffalo Wings, a recipe invented by a Buffalo black man though a woman, who cooked at the Anchor Bar in Buffalo, one of the showcases of Buffalo bebop, which had a strong Italian American bent (there's a direct line from the brass of Giovanni Gabrieli to that of trombonist Frank Rosolino), gets all the credit.

Sometimes, when I need a little comfort food I sneak over to the Big Fat Chicken restaurant and indulge. All of this stress is a little overwhelming for a strict diabetic diet to attend to. I sometimes take my chances and pray that the reading before breakfast isn't too high. Little did I know that the media would get into the black man's head with O. J. in the same way that Dennis Rodman got into Alonzo Mourning's head in the 1997 NBA games and the way that my lancelets get into my fingers. All except my blogger companion, Otter. He is prescient, a gift he says that he inherited from his mother, a clairvoyant.

Naomi Campbell, a jet-setting glamorous black model, was being interviewed. She's a defiant one alright. A descendant of one of these really black-skinned beauties who would spit in the Overseer's face as he flogged her. Slash the master's throat as he tried to rape her. Rabbit says that in his opinion she's the most beautiful woman in the world. He fantasizes about her bangs. Her soft eyes. The way her smooth shining brown body appears beneath a fur coat that hardly covers it. He says that if you tasted her she'd probably taste like plums. She made a remark in an interview on April 29, 1995, the day that Mayor Giuliani remarked, a remark that he later denied having made, that he'd like to see all of the poor people leave New York. The cultural decline of New York that had begun under Ed Koch, Puerto Rican removal, and black removal, was being continued by Giuliani. From the musical *Shuffle Along* to the Salsa, New York's cultural industry has always profited from the underclass. She said that in the American subconscious, O. J. Simpson represented all black men. Including me, I suppose. She was right. All of us in The Rhinosphere were O. J. We were Rev. Eugene Rivers's "Zulu Nation." Old men out of step with the New Order. Trying to fend off change with spears, clubs, hand axes, javelins, halberds. For whom a blackberry was something edible. This was on a show called *Positively Black*.

O. J. was taking over my life. The O. J. story got its hooks into me ever since it was announced on Hawaii television that O. J. had not surrendered and was a fugitive. That killed my vacation. Not only did he have to kill two white people, but a blonde. A blonde born in Frankfurt. In the hierarchy of white women, blondes are at the top. Brunhilde. She is the trophy that white men, for whom the home of Western civilization is Scotland, are vowed to protect. When the press characterized the Simpson trial as the trial of the century, in a century in which the Nuremberg trials had occurred, were they saying that one blonde is worth more than all of the victims of the Nazis? That this trial was more important than tribunals for the murderers from Serbia and Rwanda? If he'd been charged with killing a black woman, the press would have made very little of it. The day after former

Senator Bob Kerrey, now New School president, confessed to ordering the murder of women and children, Bernard McGuirk mentioned the murder of Nicole as being more important than the atrocities committed by American soldiers in Vietnam. In the middle of that week, Howard Stern, whose set displays a photo of O. J. and Marv Albert, mentioned Nicole's diary. Now you know if Nicole is worth more than all of the victims of the Nazis, this blonde has to be worth more than all of the women in Asia. The face that launched a thousand lips on talk shows and in gossip columns. If O. J.'d been charged with killing a brunette, not as much fuss would have been raised. If he'd killed somebody Jewish? Remember the preppie murder? Robert Chambers killed Jennifer Levin and the press used the stereotypical image of the Jewish woman as the consummate tease (a Nazi stereotype, and one that was floated about Monica Lewinsky) and the society guy not only got off lightly, but appeared on TV simulating the strangling of the victim.

This incident has been forgotten. And nobody did a Jim Lehrer NewsHour essay claiming that her murder meant that evil had re-entered American society—had it ever left?—as they did when they cited the Central Park rape (black and Hispanic defendants), later found to be innocent. During one broadcast Kathleen Sullivan, who hosted the O. J. trial for the Entertainment Network, said that many of the network's viewers saw O. J. as Satan. (In 2008, Barack Obama was associated with the Beast of the Apocalypse by religious nuts.)

Rabbit thought that the movie *The Devil's Advocate* was signifying on the O. J. defense team. Satan being the ultimate client for lawyers who will do anything to get a client off. (In 2007, after O. J. was arrested for, according to him, entering a collector's room in Las Vegas, to retrieve some memorabilia belonging to him, Pat Oliphant drew a cartoon of the late Johnnie Cochran, phoning O. J. from Hell.)

I asked two white brunettes why there was a premium on blondes in the West and they said that this was a question they'd been asking themselves every day. Nicole Simpson, on top of being a blonde, was a Nordic type. She didn't go to Hell. She went to Valhalla.

4

JUNE 1994

I've broken my media fast. I'm back to Hilton's Turtle Bay (the final scene from *Don Juan DeMarco* was shot here), buying newspapers, trying to keep abreast of every new detail. I'm wearing dark glasses, because I want to escape the stares of the white tourists. They think that I did it. They think that I'm O. J. and my wife, a "white woman," is Nicole. Shortly after the murders, Bat, of The Rhinosphere, a salon keeper, and central figure in a Loisaida literary cult, e-mailed that he was walking down the street with a white woman in New York's Alphabet City and someone yelled out, "Hey, O. J." I guess this is what Bob Lee meant when he said that racists have a tendency to pluralize individuals. O. J. is all black men rolled into one. After a skinhead shoots a black woman on a street corner in Boulder, Colorado, a white man calls C-SPAN's *Washington Journal* and says that though he doesn't condone what the skinhead did, he can understand the resentment that the skinhead felt. The caller brings up O. J. as though the two events are connected. The shooting of the woman and the O. J. case.

My Jewish wife looks Cuban, but in this country she's considered white. And so these white tourists at the Turtle Island are probably thinking that my relationship with her is the same as O. J. Simpson's toward Nicole's. That there's a 911 tape with her voice on it. Or am I being paranoid? Possibly.

5

JUNE 17, 1994

The night that O. J. was on the famous white Bronco run, Esther, Hibiscus and I were having dinner at a restaurant that had been converted from a sugar mill. All day, I had been nervous and worried about O. J. Wondering if he was all right. Thinking that if he really killed Nicole, whether it wouldn't be better for the fellas, for me, were he to kill himself. Like in that passage from Richard Wright's *Native Son* where two black guys are talking and they decide that it would better if Bigger Thomas, an escaped murderer, were arrested so that the heat on them would let up.

We picked at our meals. I listlessly ate shark, small potatoes, and spinach. I didn't touch the white wine or the salad. I was watching my portions, which is what my dietician says I should do, with my Diabetes 2 and all. I'm watching everything that I drink and eat. Twice a day, I have to check my blood with a glucose monitor. It controls my life. The role that sugar plays in my life as well as in history should not be underestimated. One historian even speculated that the root cause of British Imperialism was a sugar rush. Rum. Tea. Greeners tell us that if we run out of oil the world might have to be run on sugar. Brazil is way ahead of that score. Fueling their cars with sugar.

When my blood doesn't fill the little white circle on the box, I get the message "Not Enough Blood." I sometimes think that the little box is laughing at me. I'm supposed to avoid stress. I'm a black man and I'm supposed to avoid stress. Let me run that by you again. I'm a black man and I'm supposed to avoid stress. I was neither hungry nor thirsty. I'm watching O. J. and Al Cowlings inside this white Ford Bronco, a scene that even upstages the NBA finals. It's the 1994 NBA finals. The Houston Rockets vs. the New York Knicks. Hakeem Olajuwon, a Muslim from Nigeria, emerges from the games a star. First player to be named NBA regular season MVP, NBA finals MVP, and Defensive Player of the Year in the same season. For collectors of stereotypes, the television scenes are a bonanza. Two black athletes, one of whom is a criminal suspect, followed by a phalanx of police cars sharing a split screen with black basketball players. This Bronco chase, which will become as iconic as Rev. Wright's sermons.

The fact that Patrick Ewing breaks the record for the most blocks occurring in a game is overshadowed by the white Bronco being pursued by the police with O. J.'s fans staked out along the way, on bridges and road shoulders. What a bizarre conjunction. I feel dreadful. O. J. says that he wants to go to Nicole's graveside and commit suicide by blowing his brains out with a Magnum. Part of me says, yes, yes, please do. But this is a brother. Am I so concerned about my own safety that I wish that a brother who is a suspect in the murder of a blonde kill himself rather than put the rest of us in jeopardy by our being associated with him? Giving the enemy ammunition to harass us with their demonic media equipment forever. Naomi Campbell is right. When they do O. J., they're doing us.

When Esther and Hibiscus try to get my attention, I tell them to shush. I'm fixed on the TV screen. They shush me back. These people I'm living with have never heard of the Victorian era when wives and daughters let the man sit at the head of the table and carve turkey and lay down the law for the household. Have his spouse and daughter fetch his newspaper, slippers, and pipe. The scenes in my household would not inspire Norman Rockwell. I'm not good at carving meat. (I'm no O. J. Simpson. Just joking.) They've not read Gertrude Himmelfarb. She says that all of us modern people should adopt Victorian values. So black people should be Victorian. Hope that doesn't include anti-Semitism, Gertrude. (But then again, would I want to dine wearing a three-piece suit and tie like James Mason and Claude Rains in the movies, wearing a suit even at home?) I catch them snickering at me. And Hibiscus is always signifying on my expanded colon. The dietician says I have to lose weight or else I might have later complications. This is what diabetes patients are always looking forward to. Later stages. Amputations. Kidney dialysis. Blindness. I admit that I look like an overweight Marlon Brando in *Don Juan DeMarco*.

On the screen, Al Cowlings and O. J. are being greeted by hundreds of people cheering for O. J. Wishing him well. We watch as the Ford Bronco, followed by a battery of police cars, heads toward his Rockingham estate. There are tense moments before he decides to surrender. I'm tight in the stomach. Cramps. After that, the press shows O. J. shifting on his feet and rolling his eyes as he is arraigned by the police. Why did he allow himself to be interviewed by the police?

Why did his lawyer, Howard Weitzman, leave O. J. to the mercy of the LAPD? Gloria Allred says that O. J. confessed to having committed the killing to Weitzman and this is why Weitzman wouldn't handle the case and why Robert Shapiro had to be called in. Since the late eighties, Gloria Allred has been running rampant over the reputations of black men including Clarence Thomas, Mike Tyson, O. J. Simpson, and Michael Jackson but, in 1997, when she dares to come to the aid of a woman who accuses Marv Albert of assault, the same white commentators, who tolerated her outbursts against black men, called her the Don King of the legal world, and an ambulance chaser. In 2008, wouldn't you know, she appears on the BBC leading a group called PUMA, ex-Clinton supporters who are opposed to Barack Obama. The president should tell his Secret Service to watch Gloria Allred lest she try to kidnap Malia and Sasha.

When I returned to the beach compound from my walk on the beach, among ancient fishing nets, jellyfish, and dead stingrays, during which my thoughts riffed about like a Jazz solo, Esther and Hibiscus were asleep. Checking my e-mails, I found one from Sebastian Lord, manager at KCAK TV, asking me to send in a cartoon about the O. J. case by FedEx. Jonathan Kraal, the president of KCAK, was demanding a full court press. Every department would focus on O. J. Twenty-four-hour O. J. The station would tell the eyeballs that Koots Badger, my cartoon character, was on a vacation. I didn't even have to think. I had to stand up for the brother and not submit some cartoon that would play into the hands of the enemy. I got the idea from the report that a policeman, upon hearing that O. J., a black celebrity, might be involved in a double homicide, said, "Oh, Boy." Besides, I was thinking of the way that the police manhandled Virginia Saturday, who was fired by Kraal, the network's CEO. How I just stood there with a doofus look. I was thinking of my own run-ins with the police. The insults that Bat, Rabbit, Otter, and even Snakes had experienced all of our lives. I was well, thinking like my old alter ego. *Attitude the Badger.* They used the cartoon to end the following evening's news, but I could tell that Simon Fansworth the anchor didn't approve of it. Frowned and shook his head on camera. Shrugged his shoulders and made no comment about it, which was part of the format. His engaging in some clever banter about my drawings. He reported some gossip from the trial. He was wearing a dinner jacket, one of four that he owned, and often bragged to the staff that after being ousted from the horsey set for exposing the unscrupulous financial dealings of a blue blood, he was welcomed back because of his contacts with insiders connected with the O. J. case, insiders cultivated when he was writing screenplays in Hollywood. He was a much-sought-after guest at parties because of the O. J. gossip. Says he has a deep throat on the inside of the prosecution team. He was becoming a sort of wandering troubadour, going from party to party to deliver the goods to the parasitical rich—people who live on interest, dividends, and insider country-club tips on the stock market. People who have nothing else to do but spend their days on three-hour lunches and partying and talking about O. J. in between selecting drapes and buying jewelry from the collections of European royalty. Otter says he was in New York receiving an award for his translations of Bashō when his editor took him to a trendy place called Michaels, a restaurant located next door to an umbrella store, and he saw Fansworth there. Bowing and scraping before celebrities as they entered. Rabbit said he reminded him of the scene in the movie *The Elephant Man* where the freak is pouring tea for his guests. But hey, who am I to point fingers? The whole country is enveloped in an O. J. craze. Anyway, later, on Princessa Bimbette's show, the white callers expressed their outrage at the cartoon.

After awhile, I got tired of Hawaii with this O. J. thing going on. I couldn't sleep. I was irritable. It was also part of my Diabetes 2 diagnosis. Being irritable. Snapping at Esther and Hibiscus at the least provocation. (And of course, they snapped back.) My whole body felt like an abscessed tooth. Caused by neuropathy. The Hawaiian landscape became boring. The ocean and the sun were beginning to resemble scenes in those velvet paintings that you used to buy at Woolworth's. We no longer drove up to Waimea Bay for a longer walk than the one available at the Mokule'ia. Hibiscus pouted and slammed things when I announced that I had to get back to New York. Esther expressed her annoyance in a different way. Silence. She made you feel like something cold and dark but this was war and I had to be at the front, armed with my erasable color pencils and paper. Esther called O. J. a murderer. Hibiscus said that he was a jerk. A jerk and a creep he may be, I said, but he was my jerk and my creep. On the plane home, we dined in silence. I was one of the lucky cartoonists who could still manage first class.

Esther and Hibiscus were upset that their vacation had been interrupted by my concern for a person whom Hibiscus called "a stupid jock." They were not as willing to make the sacrifice on behalf of a brother man in harm's way as I. In fact, they were calling him names that I couldn't repeat in civilized company. Though Esther had gone to a fancy college, she grew up in the streets of Detroit, the notorious neighborhood of Dexter Davison, in one of these poor Jewish families (yes, hundreds of thousands exist, according to Michael Lerner). Came from a stock of Russian women. The kind of women who gave birth in the fields, handed the newborn to a daughter, took a swig of vodka and went back to work, so the family story went. That's how her family put it around the dinner table when she was growing up. That's the story they told. And Hibiscus. She attended a rough community college before attending one elite university in the Northeast and so she was known to say things like "motherfucker" when she got mad. These two didn't take no shit. With my newfound energy which as in the old days stemmed from rage, on the flight home, I composed another cartoon while they were asleep. This cartoon would get me some notice. I loved it. It was like the old days in the East Village. The days of *Attitude the Badger*. I was putting some kick back into my art. My cartoons about the LAPD were considered rowdy by some.

6

Alan Dershowitz: . . . Policemen are trained to be cool. They're professional witnesses. The Mollen Commission in New York, after reviewing thousands of hours of police testimony, said, police perjury is rampant in the courts, but lawyers can't get at the perjury unless they can confront the witnesses with their words . . .

Nancy Snyderman: You're telling me that police departments tell their detectives that it's okay to lie?

Alan Dershowitz: Not only do police departments tell their detectives it's OK to lie, they learn it in the Academy. They have a word for it. It's called, "testilying." And they do it coolly, and they do it in a way that they can't be broken down unless you can confront them with their own words.

—Alan Dershowitz on "Testilying," from *Reasonable Doubts: The Criminal Justice System and the O. J. Simpson Case*

New York, March, 1994—Undergoing downsizing, and being threatened by right-wing congressmen, our "progressive" television network had decided to go commercial. A number of people were let go, but I had been kept on. My cartoon, *Attitude the Badger*, had attracted a following among progressives who practiced their diction by listening to BBC broadcasts and formed lines around the block to gain entrance into ice-cream parlors, and Indies. They included former hippies who loved *MacBird!* in the '60s, but insisted that their kids learn *Macbeth* in the '90s. Alumni of Woodstock, who lectured the younger generation about their morals. I guess you'd call them neo-liberals. Coffeehouse liberals who would later elect Bush by voting for Nader. Everybody was let go except for me and a few others. Strange. For some reason, the new owner of KCAK, alternative television, Jonathan Kraal, who had taken over this formerly government-supported, viewer-sponsored network, kept me on. He wanted his station to appeal to high-school teachers, dot-commers, and MBAs. I have nothing in common with these people. I sign my cartoons "Bear," a pen name I'd been given by an Indian named Leslie Laguna. (My real name is Paul Blessings.) The old types were offended by some of the changes Kraal made. Adding a sports announcer. Ending the coverage of the Cuban Revolution. Dropping the drama and literature departments. No more Geronimo Pratt. Ending a number of feminist programs. Adding a sportscaster, Ben Armstrong. Adding a lot of food shows. (One whole show was devoted to cheese.) But what really outraged some of the former "progressive" viewers was the hiring of Simon Fansworth, a failed mini-series writer; recovering alcoholic and drug addict who spiced his broadcasts with scurrilous observations about the private lives of celebrities. Rumor was that Kraal was paying him millions. During the criminal trial of O. J., as the anti-O. J. cameraman did close-ups of the audience, Fansworth's facial editorials competed with Kim Goldman's.

As I said, for a cartoonist, I was lucky. The '90s were a bad time for cartoonists. Of course, I, like many black Americans in my class, had to pony up some ass. Had to make compromises. Kraal held a series of interviews with the personnel of the station. Some emerged from these interviews with glum faces, shortly afterwards, emptying their desks and bidding their former colleagues goodbye. Then it came my turn. He confronted me with one of my cartoons, which showed Badger addressing a rally of badgers and pledging that "we will never be driven underground again. Nor shall we burrow in the holes of others." He suggested that I change my character into a charming curmudgeonly old Badger, Koots Badger, a harmless crank and paranoid out of touch and still under the impression that Badgers were being pursued by hunters. I told him that I had to think about it, but then I returned to the small apartment that Esther, Hibiscus and I shared in Brooklyn (we could no longer afford Manhattan), assessed our income, debts; I agreed to the deal that Kraal offered. Unlike those few cartoonists who were syndicated, I would only have to submit one cartoon a week. My income would increase significantly. I would have a downtown studio in addition to a four-bedroom condo near the Beacon Towers. All of this was surprising to me. I knew that Sebastian Lord, the station manager, didn't approve of this arrangement.

It was reported by the American Editorial Cartoonists that many cartoonists were losing their outlets. (Some were losing their lives, too. After being fired by *Penthouse*, a young comic book editor, George Caragonne, "Captain Marvel," committed suicide on July 20, 1995.) Full-time cartoonists were becoming "a frill." Many were being "killed by dwindling readership and growing electronic competition." As a television cartoonist, I was part of the electronic competition. To squelch the criticism that came after the firing of some people of color, at the insistence of Kraal, those of us who were kept on were given bonuses. Whether the black president of the network, Renaldo Louis, had objected to their dismissals is not known.

Kraal was smart. He knew that he could deflect criticism about the lack of diversity in his operation if he put a black man at the top, even though he had no power. Renaldo. He was a man who kept his thoughts to himself.

The Harlem Populist, an uptown paper, had accused those of us remaining at KCAK, especially Renaldo, of being lend-lease bloods and worse. One scribe even referred to us as journalistic Buffalo Soldiers, after those sad black men who joined the Manifest Destiny, which, in the Southwest, among Native Americans, is likened to Hitler's call for a greater Germany.

With my bonus money, this Buffalo Soldier went to Hawaii. Just in time because a media watchdog group threw up a picket line in front of the Kraal Towers building. They joined the lesbians, gays, Native Americans and Latinos, New Agers, and the ecologically-minded who were already picketing Kraal Towers for laying off the hosts of their favorite programs. The blacks were outraged over the firing of young Virginia Saturday, a popular black reporter. She had been fired for complaining about the changes that had occurred at the station, ignoring the memo that warned the station personnel of airing the station's dirty laundry on the air. Kraal had barred her from the station, but she showed up somehow getting past the security on the ground floor. She refused to pack up her things and leave as ordered. I won't forget the day that the police came to the station and arrested her. They were bending her arms behind her back and she was struggling. They came by the place where I and some others were standing. The cop smirked at me and at Virginia's struggling. I won't forget the contemptuous look that she gave me for the rest of my life. I thought that she was going to spit in my face. I definitely wasn't one of these proud black warriors that Tremonisha Smarts, the black feminist playwright, was always writing about.

The protesters were joined by former KCAK subscribers who were outraged over this new format and the commercialization of a television station that had been founded by a left-wing group, headed by a man who had fought with the Abraham Lincoln Brigade during the Spanish Civil War. These people, now in their nineties, were some of the most vocal of Jonathan Kraal's opposition. They accused the new owners of "dumbing down" and "union busting."

The gay demonstrators were upset about the hiring of Sebastian Lord, whom they regarded as a gay turncoat, a right-wing lap-dog, and one who benefited from the Stonewall revolt, yet was critical of militant gays. The Native Americans objected to the name of Kraal's baseball team, the New York Apaches. They found the New

York Apaches' mascots the most offensive. Two monkeys dressed as Indians with headdress and all, named Geronimo, and Sitting Bull. Maybe there would have been sympathy for these protestors in the '60s. These were the '90s. Also, such demonstrations were being dismissed as exercises in "political correctness," a phrase that the right, never ones for original thinking, borrowed from the left. And elements of that entity known as the general public was comfortable with bigotry. Their resentment led to the rise of rabid-mouthed talk-show hosts. They greeted John Rocker warmly, when he returned to baseball. He was suspended for putting down a whole bunch of "identity groups," as they are called. They embraced Mark Fuhrman, a man, who, during the O. J. criminal trial, was revealed as a cop who was capable of planting evidence.

Andrew Johnson, who helped restore the Confederacy, was now a noble tragic figure who had risked impeachment for the sake of principles. Confederate gangsters and murderers Jesse James and his brother, Frank, of Quantrill's Raiders fame, were back in the saddle. Between Abu Ghraib, a president who couldn't pronounce it, and guests of the *Jerry Springer Show*, where members of the white underclass, hidden from the public by a press that accommodated whites, were in full view. These scenes and facts were all you needed to know about the United States of the '90s.

7

On Friday, Sept. 29, 1995, a talk-show caller asked Gloria Allred why she and Marcia Clark, feminists, embraced Mark Fuhrman when they knew full well that he belonged to something called Men Against Women, a misogynist outfit that made life miserable for policewomen. She equivocated. Ms. Allred had been brought on to denounce Mike Tyson and Clarence Thomas in the past, but she's soft on Fuhrman. Very soft. While Louis Farrakhan is condemned by Congress for hatemongering, Fuhrman, a Nazi and someone who actually beat up some Jews, according to Johnnie Cochran, is embraced by John Gibson and Geraldo Rivera when he comes out with a book about the murders in Greenwich, something Dominick Dunne has already covered; Fuhrman accuses the Greenwich authorities of moral corruption. Okay?

Lord summoned me to the station. I should have gotten an inkling of what was in store from the signals I got from Princessa Bimbette, the diminutive brunette who was given a morning show during which she tore into black male celebrities. Football stars engaging in brawls outside of strip clubs, etc. When I walked into the elevator she was standing there. Garfield closed the door and prepared to ascend us to our respective floors. "Hello, Princessa," I said. She stamped her right foot, folded her arms, and, looking toward the ceiling, showed the whites of her eyes. Garfield said, "Ms. Bimbette, the man is talking to you."

"Just take me to my floor. That's what you can do for me," she snapped.

"Yes, Ma'am," Garfield said. When we arrived at her floor she almost ran from the elevator.

"What the hell is eating her?" I said.

"She was so mad at you for some cartoon that she asked Lord to fire you." Garfield, like those blacks consigned to the lower rungs of the employment ladder, knew the goings-on in the higher rungs of those places where they were employed.

When I entered Sebastian Lord's office, I found that Garfield was right. Lord started to strut around the office as he scolded me. "This cartoon is worse than the one about the police. I'm not going to run it tonight. The fucking phones have been ringing off the hook about the last one. What do you have against the police? I mean we'd just as soon publish cartoons by Emory Douglass. Your people are the ones who need the police the most. Besides, O. J. entertained the police in his home. He and the police were very close."

"It might be that you have a different experience with them than I. These cops may have been guests in his home, but I know my cops. You and the white commentariat are either willfully lying or you live in an America that's radically different from the one that blacks, Indians, and Latinos live in. What would be these policemen's motives they always ask? You mean to tell me that none of those white men was upset about Simpson being with this blonde woman with this trophy body? Have you ever heard of the Algiers Motel incident? During the Detroit riots, some white cops found some black men with white women at the Algiers Motel and executed the men. You should read John Hersey and Michael Harper on the subject—"

"Princessa and some of the other station's women were so offended by this new cartoon that they are threatening to quit if you're not fired." He didn't even hear me.

"What?"

"This cartoon of yours. Here you have O. J. sodomizing this female figure. That's supposed to symbolize America. It's much too frank. It has no subtlety."

I was ranting and raving for nothing. This was the kind of guy who could sit through *Die Meistersinger* without snoring. Liked baking pies. Had posters of Maria Callas and Colonel North on display in his apartment. Considered himself a new black. Some blacks, Latinos, and Asian Americans had problems with gays and most of the violent hate crimes against them were committed by young white men. Gays have had problems with them too, problems about which Marlon Riggs and Barbara Smith and Audre Lorde have written. I wasn't surprised to learn from David Brock that closeted homosexuals had been in on the drafting of the Reagan strategies, which left millions homeless. Is he correct? Closeted, self-loathing gays in on drafting polices that were hostile to gays, blacks, and the poor?

Governor Ronald Reagan of California became angry when columnist Drew Pearson reported prior to the *Time Magazine* of November 10, 1967, that a ring of homosexuals surrounded the Governor:

> Pearson had charged that two members of Reagan's staff were involved, that Reagan had kept them on for about six months after first hearing about their proclivities and that he finally dismissed them, not for moral reasons but because right-wing supporters had objected to the pair's relatively moderate political views. In his best purple prose, Pearson claimed that an all-male "sex orgy" in a Lake Tahoe cabin had been attended by the two staff members, a part-time athletic adviser to Reagan, two sons of a state senator and a Republican campaign consultant.

Another "homosexual ring" ring was uncovered in the Reagan and Bush White Houses on June 29, 1989, by Paul M. Rodriguez and George Archibald of the conservative *Washington Times*:

> Homosexual prostitution inquiry ensnares VIPS with Reagan, Bush "Call boys" took midnight tour of White House . . . A homosexual prostitution ring is under investigation by federal and District authorities and includes among its clients key officials of the Reagan and Bush administrations, military officers, congressional aides and US and foreign businessmen with close social ties to Washington's political elite, documents obtained by the *Washington Times* reveal.

One of the ring's high-profile clients was so well-connected, in fact, that he could arrange a middle-of-the-night tour of the White House for his friends on Sunday, July 3, of last year. Among the six persons on the extraordinary one A.M. tour were two male prostitutes.

Federal authorities, including the Secret Service, are investigating criminal aspects of the ring and have told male prostitutes and their homosexual clients that a grand jury will deliberate over the evidence throughout the summer, the *Times* learned.

Reporters for this newspaper examined hundreds of credit-card vouchers, drawn on both corporate and personal cards and made payable to the escort service operated by the homosexual ring. Many of the vouchers were run through a so-called "sub-merchant" account of the Chambers Funeral Home by a son of the owner, without the company's knowledge.

Among the client names contained in the vouchers— and identified by prostitutes and escort operators—are government officials, locally based US military officers, businessmen, lawyers, bankers, congressional aides and other professionals.

In 2010, an antigay Tea Bagger was shouted down when he made antigay remarks at a conservative conference, which proved that gays were welcome in places where blacks were subjected to the most racist disparagement. In Dominick's novels about the rich, gays are members of this class as well, while blacks are absent. There was a rumor that Ronald Reagan was gay. In 2010, Schwarzenegger, who loved his yacht-owning buddies—who had kept the mentally ill on the streets, where Ronald Regan left them, and who now wanted to cut off social programs entirely—expelled home-care workers who served the sick and handicapped; Ted Olson, who was opposed to Civil Rights, Jerry Brown who as Oakland Mayor vowed to break black political power, and Rudolph Giuliani, architect of the notorious stop-and-frisk police actions and who lived with two gay men, all supported gay marriage described by "progressives" as The Civil Rights issue of the twenty-first century.

According to his wife, Nancy, Ronald Reagan was in such a poor state in December, 1999, that he couldn't put a complete sentence together. Some said that one of the African "saints" who had accompanied blacks on the crossing had "fixed" him for those policies, but I wasn't joining in on the speculation. Hell, at my age, Alzheimer's could happen to me. Soon.

"First of all, O. J. is not sodomizing the figure, but calling a play. I wanted to show how this O. J. case has energized America. That's why I called it 'Juice.' You don't know anything about football."

He was dressed casually and in good taste. You could tell that his clothes were expensive. A black velvet sports jacket and tailor-made jeans, silk shirt. His eyes could have been plucked from the North Sea, they were so blue. He was one of these guys who was crazy about *Brideshead Revisited*. A Judy Garland fetishist.

"Looks as though you're sympathizing with this murderer." As a black journalist you hear a lot of remarks like this from your colleagues. I'd found that the best way to deal with it was to ignore them. Eat shit.

"Though the media are making bucks out of O. J.'s problems, he's the one who's giving them the juice. Calling their plays." I stood up and got into his face. "He's a trickster like the Coyote tales, the animals in the Joel Chandler Harris stories. As for his being a murderer, aren't we suppose to hold people innocent until proven guilty?"

"Okay, smartypants. You're suspended for thirty days. A lot of our viewers are calling up and complaining. They're saying that you're taking this racial stuff way over the top and it's about time someone called you on it. I guess I have to be that someone. You'll still be paid and you can have access to your office. After the thirty days are up, we'll discuss your future around here, if there is one." He then grinned. A grin that was mocking, and hateful. I had tried to play it down the middle. Drawing Koots Badger who didn't represent anybody's race. A creature out of step with his time. A fading anachronism. Someone who doesn't recognize freedom when he sees it. Doesn't realize that the dogs and the hunters have been called off. Thinks that hunting season is all year long, etc.

I got up and left but not before engaging in a stare down with Sebastian.

"You blacks might have been big now in the twentieth century, but gay, lesbian, and transgender issues are those that will dominate the twenty-first. After all, gays were oppressed two thousand years before blacks."

"Yeah and some of them were emperors, kings, and popes. And during the slavery period, which side do you believe that white gays were likely to be on? The slave driver or the slave? Oscar Wilde, your icon, was pro-Confederate. Must have been the whips." He turned red.

As I left his office I was wondering why I was being kept on when others who had higher ratings had been let go. Suspended instead of being fired. Was it because my being on the staff deflected criticism that Kraal was a bigot who hated black journalists? Also, I still had a core of loyal followers, but that could end. Look at Stan Mack. His following didn't prevent him from being fired in July 1995 from the *Village Voice* by Karen Durbin. I had to get out of this business. Launch my painting career. I wonder, did George Harriman, the founder of black cartooning, have days like this?

8

I arrived in New York from Bison, New York, with hopes of becoming a painter. That didn't work out and so after a few years of struggling I tried my hand at cartoons. The painting could wait.

A publisher of an underground newspaper asked me to do a cartoon. My first attempt. That's when I came up with a series called *Attitude the Badger*, after all, what better representative for the underground culture than the Badger, which spends time digging holes and when out of holes, occupying those of others. Constantly pursued by hunters and their dogs, who represent the establishment and authority.

Attitude the Badger was based upon a poem I'd read. It was written by John Clare (1793–1864) and it was about this badger who had to use all of its waking hours fending off enemies and grumbling about the situation of badgers in a society dominated by hunters and their hounds. When the '60s counterculture and black Power movements failed, the people who could afford to subscribe to cable were no longer interested in *Attitude the Badger*, a radical, a symbol of underground culture.

No longer will we have to flit from holes to holes

The cartoon figure was right at home with *EVO*, The Velvet Underground. Marion Brown. Umbra. Fair Play For Cuba. The Summer of Love. Stanley's and The Annex, Tompkins Square Park, but that was then. This was now. And because the station went commercial, I had to transform *Attitude the Badger* into Koots Badger, inspired by Ralph Ellison's model of seeking a crossover audience by getting rid of the black Nationalist hero, Leroy, from his novel. If Ellison had kept a black nationalist as a hero in his book, he would never have been voted the best novelist of the postwar period by hundreds of literary critics.

Unlike the old underground and viewer-sponsored days, Kraal had to appeal to his advertisers. And so rather than go broke, I went postrace, that is, I put the pain of the Badger in the background. I reinvented Badger.

Instead of the anti-establishment protestor, who walked about the Lower East Side dressed up like Lenin in Zurich, where he lived on Spiegelgasse in 1917, a street where stood a cabaret in which Hans Arp and Tristan Tzara launched the Dada movement in 1916, the new Badger was a clawless, harmless old curmudgeon who was always threatening individuals and institutions with his cane. I had shelved the militant Badger and replaced him with one less threatening. Koots Badger was born. A paranoid cartoon figure who heard the barks of nonexistent hounds.

I was, well, becoming universal and mellow, which meant that middle-class white people were beginning to appreciate my cartoons as well. One critic said that I was "Beyond black and white." I had been invited to join the Millennium Club—the dream of all cartoonists—the cartoon elite, which consisted of one hundred members, the first black man. They had been attracted to my article in *The American Cartoonist* in which I chided those black cartoonists who were hung up on the past and unwilling to enter the world of the postrace harmony and sunlight.

Avenues A and B, these dingy ethnic walks of the '60s had become uptown and touched with a funky glitziness. The places where artists and writers frequented in the '60s, drank pitchers of beer, and got into fights had become singles bars. The Puerto Ricans who owned these streets in the '60s had become subjected to ethnic cleansing, and so had the sixty thousand blacks who once lived here. Now there were glitzy hotels and three-million-dollar condos.

Some of the posh hotels on Houston were as pricey as the Waldorf. Avenue A resembled a gigantic student union. Like Bleecker Street. Tenements in which Chinese families had lived for decades were being infiltrated by young whites, the Children of Reagan, who complained about the smells from Chinese cooking, their leaving their doors open while eating noodles, their talking loud in the hallways, their refusal to say hello.

There was a place on East Third called Mama's that resembled the old family-styled restaurants of the '60s, but at most of these places you had to shell out a lot of dollars for two dinners. Mama's prices were reasonable. I usually went for the couscous and vegetable dish.

Now I had a whole floor full of supplies with a skylight. I was near my other children, the fax, phone, Xerox machine, and drawing materials. The whole screed. When I finished my cartoons, a messenger would come down to the studio and pick them up. Once a week I would be driven to Kraal Towers.

9

I enjoyed Robin Williams' performance in *One Hour Photo* so much that I viewed it for a second and third time. Williams plays a bachelor photo developer who becomes attached to a white suburban family. He's crazy about it and has selected this family as his. As you know there comes a moment in movies about serial killers when their pursuers break into the suspect's home and find that he has built a veritable shrine to his deeds. Newspaper clippings that report his exploits. Maybe some lighted candles. Photos of the person or persons he has stalked or murdered. In this movie, the scene takes place in the home of the character played by Robin Williams. The camera cuts away to a wall to which he has been pasting photo prints of the family for many years. The character has become sick about this family.

Pretend that the Robin Williams character represents many Americans and someone finds the wall of their secret obsession. It would be plastered with photos of O. J.: O. J. in a football uniform,

O. J. running through the airport, O. J. and Nicole entering a stadium with Nicole's arm in his. Their biracial children, Sydney and
Justin. Johnnie Cochran trying on a knit cap. (What is it with
black men and the knit cap? A knit cap that goes with a navy
jacket. Remember the Susan Smith sketch of the black man who
she said had kidnapped her children? In the sketch, the black
man was wearing a knit cap.) This obsession with O. J. is not
only fed to the masses by twenty-four hour cable news, but in
the highest circles of the government. When the man whom in
The Rhinosphere we call The Boer, G.W. Bush, appears before a
press dinner, during the last week in March 2007, a film is shown
before the President and the First Lady in which O. J. is seen as a
passenger in the now infamous Bronco. Donald Rumsfeld cited
O. J. in a joke during a Pentagon briefing even as he planned the
murder of thousands of Iraqi citizens. Cluster bombs. Degraded
uranium. One blonde is worth more than all of the casualties in
Iraq? Rumsfeld had O. J. on his mind. Speaking of a war initiative
proposed by Rumsfeld, The *New York Times* columnist Maureen
Dowd brought up O. J. when quoted in *Global Policy Forum*, May
29, 2003, about the war initiative. She likened it to "O. J. [Simp-
son] vowing to find the real killer."

Not only is the political and journalistic sphere obsessed with
O. J., but O. J. shows up in the literary world. Scott Spencer is
thinking of O. J. in his book *A Ship Made of Paper*. Among the
twenty references to O. J. is this one: ". . . some of them are putting groceries on the table by writing a lot of damn foolishness
about O. J. Simpson." In the film *City by the Sea*, released almost a
decade after the trial, scriptwriters have O. J. on the mind. There's

reference to the shoe evidence in one of the character's speeches. As Johnnie Cochran said repeatedly before his death, no invoice has ever been found tracing the purchase of Bruno Magli shoes to O. J.

And what became of some of O. J.'s pursuers? Those who tried to hunt down the man, who, in their minds, killed his blond trophy wife? Geraldo Rivera's assignment as war correspondent was a disaster. First, he gets into trouble for telling a worldwide audience that he was broadcasting from the site of some Marine deaths in Afghanistan. It turns out that he was hundreds of miles away from the site. Next he is ousted from Iraq for giving away troop positions. And Dominick Dunne, a Truman Capote wannabe without the formidable literary chops, and the man who greeted the verdict in the criminal trial with the famous dropped jaw, and who made a good living talking shit all about O. J.? Like a vulture who lingers about a piece of meat until the scavengers get done, he is present at the 2008 O. J. trial.

He tells a reporter that this is a bad time in his life. He has incurred the wrath of Robert Kennedy, Jr. Kennedy says it's Dunne's rumormongering and that of Mark Fuhrman, national hero, that led to the conviction of his cousin, Michael Skakel. (In 2002, Dunne had to settle out of court for suggesting that Congressman Gary Condit "frequented Middle Eastern embassies for sexual activity with prostitutes, and during those times, he made it clear that he wanted someone to get rid of [Sandra] Levy." So says Wikipedia. In 2009, it was announced that an inmate in a California prison had murdered Ms. Levy, but it was too late for Gary Condit, whose reputation had been trashed. Dunne paid an undisclosed amount to settle that lawsuit in March 2005. On August 26, 2009, Dunne died as a result of liver cancer.)

Nancy Grace, whose comments about O. J. were so savage that she became a television star, is exposed as a liar and someone who harassed a woman to the point that she committed suicide. The relatives of Ms. Grace's murdered fiancé dispute her claim that she is a crime victim because her fiancé was killed while "walking through a minority neighborhood." And Jim Moret, cheerleader for the Goldmans? His career is on the skids. (But in 2009 he makes a brief comeback when some gossip shows spread scurrilous rumors after Michael Jackson's death.) He's gained a lot of weight and now does gossip chores on *Inside Edition*. And Eliot Spitzer, who thought it funny that O. J.'s home was razed? He wasn't Governor of New York for long before he got involved in a scandal having to do with his security guards. Later, he had to resign over soliciting call girls. This is what people in California call "bad karma." Yet, in 2010, he's hosting TV shows while Kwame Kilpatrick, who, like a number of white politicians, lied about a relationship with a mistress, is given such a stiff sentence for parole violation that there are gasps in the Michigan courtroom.

10

Rabbit, Snakes, Bat, and Bear (me) are our Rhino names. Our blog is named for the observation made by the Jazz poet Ted Joans that the situation of a black man is like that of the rhino. Here goes the rhino, lumbering through the rain forest, minding his own business, when suddenly he is ambushed by his enemies. Netted by poachers. Removed from his Aboriginal surroundings. People believe that rhino horns are sources of sexual potency. They feel the same way about us. But the younger generation would prefer seeing us in a rocking chair on the porch of a rest home, swapping stories about the 1960s like Koots Badger.

Rhinos are not news junkies because the news entertains them, but because, like the Jews and gypsies of Europe, they have to be aware of their enemies' movements, lest they be caught off guard like the Cherokee, or recently the Afghans, who were going about their daily chores when assaulted from bombs dropped from thirty-five thousand feet. As the character Salman, the father, says in Wajahat Ali's play, *The Domestic Crusaders*, we must be aware of what our enemies think of us. Lest we be taken by surprise. Droned. All of them have passports—Rabbit, Bat, and Snakes and Bear. (But given the complexity of their DNA, where would they go? Africa, Europe, or a Native American reservation?) Every morning, when they communicate about the news, it's not just engaging in high gossip, but like those retired generals who stand before those maps on TV. Placing dots. It's like they're tracking troop movements. They interpret the news like Mort Sahl and Dick Gregory. They "read" the news like the Rastafarians. Like with my diabetes, which I'm required to track. There are good days and bad days. Take December 27, 2001. The grievances, their enemies would say, bitching, began to appear as soon as I sat down at my blue Mac laptop to rhino (a verb). Now, in the old days, over-sixties guys like us would sit on a stoop swapping stories about sports, music and all of the women who had succumbed to our charms (we'd be lying). Or if we were Puerto Rican telling tales in some Lower East Side club or Italian American, dressed in white and spinning yarns while playing bocce ball, but with cyberspace we can do the same thing without facing one another. I prefer it that way. A typical exchange:

SNAKES: I told Bat that Jordan shouldn't have tried a comeback. Look what happened last night. He scored less than double digits for the first time since 1988. A career low.

BAT: Give him time. He's rusty after giving into his fantasy of becoming a baseball player. Granted that he ain't no spring chicken and maybe his legs have gone, but look what he did to the Knicks last week.

SNAKES: You can't measure things by the Knicks. This year, they're incompetent. Ever since Van Gundy left. These old men don't know when to quit. Whether it be sports or politics. Look at Giuliani. Tried to stay on for another term.

OTTER: They played that farewell speech on television over here. Somebody called him Mayor of the world.

BEAR: Mayor of my ass. Frankenstein-headed motherfucker. The speech was bizarre. See him pacing up and down, thanking God for the microphone going on at one point, and making weird connections.

BAT: Yeah, but they got the message. Whenever he said homelessness, crime, and welfare they knew that he was talking about niggers.

BEAR: Look how I busted up these niggers, he was saying.

BAT: There were only a few black people in the audience. A bunch of these silly-assed arrogant wonks, bureaucrats, and his Gestapo police.

OTTER: You always go over the top.

BAT: You over there in Tokyo. It don't affect you. Me and Bear are in New York. Did you hear? They racially profiled one of The Boer's secret service men. An Arab American.

OTTER: They made him get off the plane.

SNAKES: They'll do Condi next.

OTTER: No they won't. The Boer will call a state of emergency, one of those pilots prevented her from getting on the plane. She's his main squeeze [the blog calls W. Boer, because the Rev. Eugene Rivers, the man whom the GOP tried to anoint as black leader, accused other black leaders of using Zulu tactics].

BEAR: They use her to embarrass Colin. Whenever he tries to take an initiative, she cuts him down. Like he said there might be some room for some Taliban in the new Afghan government. She undercut him just about as soon as he said it on one of these white-boy Sunday shows. Said the proposal was ridiculous.

BAT: You need to do a cartoon about it.

BEAR: I don't think so.

BAT: Do Giuliani?

SNAKES: Have you thought about asking O. J. to send you some cash. You've been his greatest defender.

BEAR: Sebastian Lord suspended me, but I'm still getting paid.

BAT: They're missing an opportunity. All the other media are cashing in, why did he suspend you?

BEAR: They didn't like the police cartoon. Kraal is pro police. Says that they stand between civilization and the jungle.

BAT: Why did you have the police with four arms?

BEAR: One to harass a suspect, one to take a bribe, one to hold his phone, and one to hold his pet's leash.

OTTER: An armadillo, why an armadillo?

BEAR: If you eat a half-cooked armadillo you're inviting a case of leprosy. Police corruption is leprosy on the soul of America.

SNAKES: I got that. But what did that have to do with O. J.?

BAT: It didn't hook up for me. The armadillo part.

BEAR: Upon hearing that he was arrested one of the cops said, "Oh Boy."

SNAKES: That was not the only problem. The police failed to obtain a warrant to enter Simpson's residence; they also failed to notify the coroner's office in a timely fashion.

BAT: What's so unusual about that? They do that to blacks and Hispanics all the time.

OTTER: But O. J. is a celebrity.

BAT: So. There's a report that the LAPD was spying on celebrities.

RABBIT: Probably peering into how people were having sex and jacking off to the scenes.

OTTER: Think they're spying on those Scientology freaks like Tom Cruise?

RABBIT: I went to see *Vanilla Sky*, this movie that ripped off a movie called *The Game*. There's a scene where this novelist says to the character played by Tom Cruise: "You're in O. J. land." Now this movie is about a guy who has paid to be kept alive and so we don't know whether he's dreaming or whether he's living or whether the Penelope Cruz character is real or not. So what is meant by "O. J. land?" What do Ashcroft, Imus, the *WSJ*, and others mean when they invoke the characters from the trial in order to justify military tribunals? Saying that if you brought the terrorists here they might be defended by someone like Johnnie Cochran, meaning that someone like Johnnie Cochran could get bin Laden, their O. J. terrorist, off. I can just remember how a caller into C-SPAN's *Washington Journal* put it: "You bring bin Laden over here and within six months he'll be down in Florida playing golf with O. J." And so, just as President Clinton became President O. J., Osama bin Laden has morphed into O. J. The O. J. terrorist. My dentist tells me on Jan. 25, 2002, of a cartoon which asks, "How does bin Laden look without a beard?" and the answer is "O. J." In other words, the murder of one blonde is worth over three thousand people murdered at the site of the WTC. One blonde.

RABBIT: In John Carpenter's movie *Ghosts of Mars*, everybody, even Pam Grier, has hots for the blonde. Everybody that is except for Chuck D., who plays the protector and the nurturer of the blonde. In one scene he even offers her Hattie McDaniel type services. Sews up her wound after she has been injured—by the way, Bear, I'm worried about you. You see that picture, *A Beautiful Mind*? You're going to be like that character. The guy gets an obsession about the Russians planting an A bomb and starts reading things in magazines and newspapers—codes that aren't there.

SNAKES: I saw that movie. They break into the guy's garage and he's got all of these clippings that he has decoded. That's going to be like Bear.

BEAR: You guys may think I'm crazy, but who do you think they're after when they do O. J.? All of us.

(We're telepathic. How did Snakes know that I had that image in mind? One of America as a serial killer obsessed with O. J.?) Richard Wright and his circle entertained French women and tourists with their clever, often put-down banter in the Café Tournon over cognac and cigarettes. The white expatriates gathered at Harry's and Shakespeare & Co. bookstore. We have an Internet chat room. Less expensive. No romantic entanglements. We don't even have to leave the house.)

11

June, 1999—Their TV networks do specials on the fifth anniversary of the killings. It's a one-sided rant in which all of O. J.'s enemies are hosed down, deloused and brought before the tube to denounce the football player for the umpteenth time. They won't let O. J. go as long as he can be used to contain blacks. Like the Stoner Rebellion, Nat Turner's uprising, and the actions of bad niggers like Gabriel gave them the excuse to punish African Americans in Georgia, Virginia, and New Orleans. They end their millennium reviews in their newspapers and magazines, a white-power exercise without the Wagnerian sound track, by bringing up O. J. and his crime. They will be on O. J. for the next century.

Denise Brown, who still has the tastes of an escort, is brought on "A&E" to testify about the wickedness of O. J. But in November of 1999, while appearing on the *Larry King Show*, she's unable to explain why the Nicole Simpson Foundation, which she heads, spent only three hundred thousand of the eight hundred thousand dollars it took in on battered women. Was O. J. right when he accused her, during Fox TV's O. J. Outrage Week, of pimping her sister's death? Geraldo has Daniel Petrocelli on, whom you would think was Thurgood Marshall and Clarence Darrow combined when all he did was avail himself of a civil jury, sixty-five percent of whose members believed that O. J. was guilty even before they were seated. Peter Arenella wasn't the only legal mind that commented about the unfair rulings by Judge Fujisaki. *USA Today* reported on February 6, 1997, that "Some of the rulings by Fujisaki during and before trial clearly constituted 'gross' legal error, said Peter Arenella, a law professor at the University of California at Los Angeles."

Right wing blondes, attired in Nancy Reagan red, are on television comparing the case of Bill Clinton with that of O. J. Simpson. The men who run the networks prefer blondes even to the Connie Chungs who won't cause a fuss like the brothers and sisters are inclined to do. Wonder whether Clinton, whose inaugural speech was shared by split screen with the announcement of the O. J. civil verdict, imagined that he would be O. J'd next. Merchandised by Neutron Jack, one of those who capitalized on the O. J. case. After one blonde, Laura Ingraham, appeared on the cover of *New York Times Magazine* section, attired in a leopard-skin miniskirt, her career was made. The fact that she clerked for Clarence Thomas excited the depraved voyeuristic who probably masturbated to the fantasy of Ms. Ingraham sprinting around Mr. Thomas's office in a leopard-skin miniskirt, and, you know, bending over file cabinets and stuff. In Nov. 2000, in the *International Herald Tribune*, Ingraham can't even comment on the presidential impasse in Florida without mentioning O. J. She basically says, "Hi. My name is Laura. And I'm an O. J.-holic." Me too.

Maybe both O. J. and Clinton are coyotes. The coyotes defecate and urinate on the traps set for them, which just about describes what O. J. and B. C. did to their pursuers. In 2007 the Goldmans go after O. J.'s Rolex watch only to find it's a fake. They talk about the O. J. defense and the O. J. presidency. They're right in one sense. Key moments of both cases are dominated by all-white juries. In the civil case, O. J.'s fate is placed in the hands of twelve whites, half of whom are women. The kind of people who are afraid to enter closed spaces with black men. The House Judiciary are white men whose style is that of a former time. They could have been cast in the 1930s by Hal Roach. They groom their hair with Wildroot Cream Oil. They are like a Model-T Ford chugging down a country road to Clinton's Mercedes, tearing up the Autobahn. Their faces are like those appearing in the 1940s ads for Gillette razor blades. They're the kind of people who once traded baseball cards and shot marbles. One of them has his hair cut like Alfalfa in the *Our Gang* movies. Another one, Lindsay Graham, barks into the microphones like the character Spanky. He resembles Spanky, played by actor George McFarland. The round chubby face, the eyes, even the manner of speaking. Clinton's four-hundred-dollars-per-hour lawyers have them for breakfast. O. J. them. My partners and I can sympathize with them. These neo-Confederates and their craving for lost causes. We too, have gotten outclassed like the Zulu. But their style makes a comeback with The Boer, the kind of ruler who came in during the last stages of the Roman Empire like the one whom the barbarians made wash a horse, while they laughed.

Because they see too deeply, the black intellectuals and artists who make people "anxious" die young. Their immune systems are slowly eroded through stress. The women intellectuals get breast, lung, and colon cancer, and lupus. When half the best African American male novelists over fifty get together, it's like a convention of the American Diabetes Association. My cartoons don't have the depth of their observations, but I got it too. Physical lynchings are rare (though in 2007, three white boys hanging a noose on a tree in Jena set off a wave of noose sightings, one even showing up on the door of a black professor's office at Columbia). They get to our insulin. The pancreas is shot. Those with Diabetes 2 are most likely to have plaque accumulating in their brains, the trigger for Alzheimer's. When Simpson's lawyers file to appeal the decision in the civil case, on July 11, 1998, the TV southpaws, who serve the Left Handers, engage in their sadistic pleasure. CNBC even runs comments by Marcia Clark and Petrocelli, both of whom have become rich from being associated with the Simpson case. Another lawyer and professor on the same show almost apologizes to the pair for having to point out where Simpson might have some justification for the appeal of the civil jury's decision, the Double Jeopardy gamut, Goldman's "proper jury." The American media, instead of a court of law, tried O. J. On the same night, on the *Larry King Show*, a British journalist is chided by American correspondents for saying that O. J., like the Ramseys, the Colorado billionaire couple whose daughter was murdered on Christmas Eve, were tried on television.

For years, cable accused Patsy Ramsey of murdering her child; she is eventually exonerated by new evidence that points to another killer. But it's too late for her. She's dead. The Britisher is disconnected from the spirit of the times in America, symbolized by their dredging up that masterful propaganda film, *Gone with the Wind*, which did more to restore the Confederacy than Andrew Johnson, who, wouldn't you know, is viewed as a martyr toward the garbage end of the twentieth century in America. (In 2009, a feminist salutes Scarlett O'Hara for her "courage." She slaps Prissy, one of the African prisoners who does the household work for free. Aren't feminists supposed to be against battery? Could Scarlett and other Mistresses and Masters be accused of receiving stolen property? And what kind of family values does Scarlett O'Hara present? Did she enjoy being raped?)

12

I'm having lunch at one of those trendy East Side restaurants with Ben Armstrong. He's another one of these guys whose brain is ignoring signals that the body it rules has had enough cherry pie. Or as B. E. Levin and V. H. Routh put it in the abstract for their "Role of the brain in energy balance and obesity" in the *American Journal of Physiology*:

> Energy balance and body weight are regulated in short, intermediate, and long cycles that are superimposed on each other. We propose that the brain is the primary center of this regulation . . . Work in animal models suggests that the brain of obese individuals largely ignores signals of excess adiposity from the periphery, keeping the body weight set point at pathologically high levels.

He has a tiny head and his bifocals give him the appearance of a frog. His body is, however, huge. He's a voracious eater, often wolfing down some steak and eggs and then falling off to sleep. He's been raised on a high-fat diet. I once asked him why and he said that fat tasted good. My diet is limited because of my diagnosis. I have to study the ingredients of a meal before eating. I have to watch my sugar and carbohydrates. I have to weigh things at every meal. I was keeping my readings close to normal until I attended a cartoon conference in Montreal where I dined each day on French food. My readings shot up to over 200 and my physician prescribed Glucophage. I had to go to diabetes class. I thought that I knew more about carbohydrates than I thought I'd ever want to know. But there's always something new to learn.

"The word is going around that you were suspended."

"That's right."

"Why?"

"The last O. J. cartoon that I submitted. Haven't you seen it? Princessa got a copy of it and posted it on the Internet."

"Yeah. She says you're here because of affirmative action. Says that the deal you got has spoiled you." I pulled the cartoon out. He paused from his lunch and examined it.

"How would you interpret this cartoon?"

"The cartoon shows O. J. Simpson as a quarterback. He's calling a play and some blonde woman representing the U.S. is about to pass the ball to him. I can see why they rejected the cartoon."

"Why?"

"Because, O. J. was never a quarterback. He was a running back. Gained 11,236 yards. He was seventeenth in rankings among all-time rushers. You may know a few things about basketball but you don't know a damned thing about football."

"That's what cartooning is all about. I have to blow up a situation in order for the viewer to detect the irony. I don't have to explain it to you. You're a sports announcer. You guys carry on like you're on acid. You're always hyping and exaggerating. Yet, nobody is talking about suspending you." I remembered the line in the classic study of cartooning entitled *The Art of Cartooning* by Roy Paul Nelson: "What sets the cartoon apart from other art forms is exaggeration. A cartoon screams, while an ordinary drawing or painting whispers."

Fair and Balanced

"So why don't you tell them that you made a mistake?"

"That's not the issue. They're saying that the cartoon shows O. J. sodomizing America. Princessa is riling up her idiot fans. Telling them that I'm disloyal and congratulating Lord for banning the cartoon. She even called me a Maoist because the woman in the cartoon is wearing pigtails. She says that's the favorite hairstyle of the Chinese Cultural Revolution."

But he didn't hear because by the third sentence he was laughing so hard he was turning heads.

Finally, he settled down. I asked, "Don't you think you're going to offend Kraal when your pro-O. J. book is published?"

"Everybody is getting mileage out of this O. J. thing. Why should me and O. J. be the only ones broke? Shit. Everybody and his brother is making money off of this thing. O. J. and this white girl. I'm definitely gonna get mine."

"But how can you write a book about O. J. when you only interviewed him once? How can you have the audacity to entitle a book "The O. J. That I Knew"? Isn't it disingenuous for you to receive a hundred-thousand-dollar advance to write a book about a man you only met once?" Some of the white commentators who hated Johnnie Cochran ridiculed his use of the word disingenuous.

"Yeah, well what about this woman, Susan Forward?"

"Susan who?"

"You know. That psychoanalyst who interviewed Nicole Simpson only a couple of times. Not a day goes by when she's not on television. She even wrote a book.

"He ought to kill a couple of people each year. Be good for the economy. Only kidding," he said.

Not only are the television networks improving their ratings, but they're selling t-shirts and O. J. games. They have a t-shirt depicting O. J. as Jesus Christ, wearing a crown of thorns. Can you imagine how the executives at Burger King, McDonald's, Ford, Bentley, Bloomingdale's, Bruno Magli, and Ben & Jerry's must feel? All of this free publicity for their products. During the course of the trial, their products are mentioned to millions of possible consumers. KCAK was drawing big advertisers. Speaking of the devil, Renaldo Louis, President of KCAK, Sebastian Lord, and Jonathan Kraal, the owner, walked in at that moment. Heads turned. The three marched toward our table. Lord and Kraal nodded and kept going. Renaldo paused. Renaldo didn't mingle with the black staff. He was a symbol of the postrace African American. A new class of black Americans. Young theologians, intellectuals, entrepreneurs, and artists. Louis was one of these people who was a journalist first, and an African American way down the list. He spent a lot of time lashing out at people on welfare and preaching self-reliance and discipline. Always quoting his grandfather, a successful judge in Trinidad. A black man who went about wearing a white wig. He was the kind of guy who got invited to Bill Clinton's birthday parties. He was taking all of the flak from the station's former listener sponsors, sixty-five percent of whom shopped at gourmet supermarkets. A watercress-and-brie crowd that was uncomfortable with the station's new format and were beginning to drift, offended by the commercial direction of KCAK under Kraal. Behind his back, his white colleagues called him a Ken Barbie, a pretty boy. A chocolate bar. Godiva chocolate. He had good hair. "How are you fellas?" he asked. A smirk accompanied the question. We both nodded.

"Bear." He said my nickname with a sarcastic smile. "What happened? Are you going to return to Koots Badger? Those O. J. cartoons are, well, hostile. We got a lot of complaints from our advertisers."

"It was Lord's idea. He told me to put Badger on vacation and do some O. J. cartoons since other media were making so much money from O. J.'s 'antics.' That's the word he used. *Antics.*"

"Yes, but our spin is that he's guilty. Didn't you get the memo? That's why Princessa and Fansworth's ratings are high and yours are at the bottom. And I'm surprised that Lord put you up to it. He doesn't know that you still harbor attitudes from your old Greenwich Village days." He sneered.

"East Village," I corrected him.

"Boy, are you a fading anachronism. Like my mom. Sugar Hill's last Garveyite." One of Kraal's bodyguards gently reminded Louis that Kraal was awaiting him.

"Yes, of course." He grinned. "Well, Ben, what chance do you give to the Raiders this season?" But before Ben could answer, the bodyguard took hold of his elbow and moved him in the direction of Lord's table.

"Wonder what those guys are up to?" I said.

"Renaldo is their new golden boy," Ben whispered. "They've never forgotten Max Robinson's example. And Bob Teague who went out and wrote a book, putting NBC's business in the streets. He said that when a woman was hired by NBC in the old days, the hiring manager would pat his crotch and instruct the women that they had to keep 'down there' happy. And Gil Noble, a troublemaker. And Earl Caldwell. He's suing Zuckerman over at the *Daily News.*"

"You remember Max, the way he got out of hand, in their eyes. Snubbed the Reagans. Since then they've screened the number-one black newsman. Louis's views are no different from those of Lord's. We thought that Lord, being gay, would side with us. He's further right than Kraal. As for Renaldo, they don't respect him. They laugh at him behind his back. I heard Lord, Fansworth, and some of the others laughing at him. Ridiculing his abilities." They continued talking about Michael Jordan's return to the Bulls from baseball and the poor performance in the first few games of his comeback and they had some discussion about Darryl Strawberry's most recent problems.

Kraal had hired two bodyguards who traveled with him wherever he went. They were positioned inside and outside the restaurant. This was because of the kidnapping of Lim Burger, the radio shock jock with whom Kraal had been dining a few months before. Kraal had been trying to lure him to KCAK. Burger had said on the radio that the way to get rid of Haitian immigration was to fumigate the island of all of the subhumans and convert it into a casino. He'd said that Martin Luther King's birthday was a black day on the American calendar. He said that the appropriate way to celebrate King's birth date was for everybody to rent a hotel and have an orgy. When Indian protestors had set up a picket line outside of the station where he worked, he said that if the Indians had been exterminated there would be no protest against the New York Apaches, the name of Kraal's team, because none would be around to carry a sign, and he scolded the murdering pioneers for not finishing the job. He was found wandering about a deserted street in Brooklyn. He said some men wearing buffalo masks had tried him for promoting hate crimes and found him guilty. They didn't reach the sentencing stage because one of the men who was supposed to guard him fell asleep and he escaped.

He said that they were going to negotiate with Skull and Bones, which held Geronimo's skull. They were also going to demand that the mascot Native American names be discontinued. One conservative columnist for the *Anglo Saxon Explainer* sighed that New York had become so politically correct that if you said "lonch" instead of "lunch," La Raza would be on your ass.

The restaurant patrons stopped dining as Kraal's loud and vulgar voice shook the establishment. From our tables, we couldn't hear what he was saying. He glared at Renaldo Louis, who withered under his gaze. We joined the customers, the waiters, and even the cooks, standing in the doorway, all staring at Louis. One of his bodyguards went out of the restaurant and returned with two middle-aged black men, but they were dressed young like Carmelo Anthony. They were carrying skateboards and dressed in the fashion of the hip-hoppers in *Source* magazine. Blink blinking. Jewelry, cornrows, tattoos. Both were carrying basketballs. It occurred to me that the hip-hop generation was entering its middle age, but their appearance might suggest a fashion of arrested development or maybe I was just an old coot. They were accompanied by a man who was later identified as their agent, Jonah Steele. His face bore the colors of a skin rash. As he tramped by the table, we got a whiff of his unpleasant body odor. He was breathing heavily as he took each ponderous step. Sweating. Dirty collar. Food spots on his clothes. Black greasy hair. The two called their group Lizard Brain. Their hip-hop rivals were called "Leaky Condoms."

"What the fuck is going on?" Ben asked.

"Beats me," I said.

We kept talking about sports. You know, the usual. Whether Sugar Ray Leonard's use of the bolo punch was effective. Shortly after the entrance of Kraal and company, I glanced over at the table and saw that the two men were dining on hamburgers, french fries, and sodas. The group seemed to be in animated conversation. Suddenly, Kraal looked in Louis' direction and said something like, "I don't give a flying fuck what you think, asshole." Louis was grinning like Dr. Lakshmanan Sathyavagiswaran, the Indian coroner who had to clean up the thirty mistakes that Dr. Irwin Golden, LA coroner, had made while conducting autopsies of Goldman and Nicole Brown. The Indo-American bowed and scraped before the white men on the prosecution team. Eager to please them. Grinning and grinning. Finally, the two men were laughing so hard that they were holding their sides. One man couldn't catch his breath and the other man had to slap him on his back. Renaldo Louis rose and angrily left the restaurant, almost knocking our table over leaving Lord, Kraal, and the two black men, laughing. It didn't take much of an imagination to figure out who was being laughed at, but we wouldn't know the reason until later. The night that Jagid and Jagan inaugurated a show called *Nigguz News*.

13

APRIL 1995

Everybody is making money from O. J. Even those involved in the serious arts who boast about their "standards." A director at San Francisco's American Conservatory Theater goes to some lengths to explain that it was only a coincidence that A.C.T. was presenting *Othello* during the trial of the century, which makes Nicole Simpson the victim, Desdemona, but unlike Desdemona, the tabloids and the defense team hint that Nicole isn't so pure. The Othello image is used frequently in connection with the trial. (Once, during an Ira Reiner and Dominick Dunne discussion of the O. J. case, an ad for Laurence Fishburne's *Othello* ran during the commercial break.) Amy Tan, already the subject of criticism from Asian American writers for exhibiting Asian American misogyny for the entertainment of whites, strikes out for new territory. She drags O. J. Simpson into her opera *The Bonesetter's Daughter*. To avoid the protesters, I sneaked back into the building through one of its back entrances and got on the elevator that would take me to my office. Garfield Harrison was operating the elevator. His nose was almost as large as his face and his eyes looked as though they were enjoying an inside joke.

"This is America gettin' its retribution."

"What?" He must have read my thoughts. He was a small and hunched-over bald black man whose uniform was always clean and whose shoes were always shined.

"I say this is America gettin' its retribution. The people of the world want to get next to America. All they need is some shit and some fuel. Everybody got that." The TV had announced that fertilizer had been used to make the bomb that destroyed the Federal Building in Oklahoma City. "Don't you have any sympathy for those people who were blown to bits in this tragedy? Many of them were black and what about the children?" I said.

"The children must suffer with the wicked, like in the Bible. God is showing his angry wrath to America. Paying them back for the treatment of colored folks. More planes will fall out of the sky. More buildings will be blown up. They all up in arms about that dead white baby whose picture was on the cover of the newspapers, but what about these poor black children who going to starve because of this pharaoh, Newt Gingrich." I found it hard to visualize Newt Gingrich as a pharaoh.

"These are the last days of America all right. The handwriting is on the wall. The country's wickedness is going to bring about its destruction and this bombing in Oklahoma is just the beginning. And look at all these white chirren blowing up their classmates to kingdom come. Dead Indians and slaves are whispering in they ears. Telling them to do that." A white man got on the elevator. Garfield's blink rate became normal again.

"How are you, Mr. Spitz?" The white man in a suit and tie and with shining hair smiled widely.

"Well, hi Garfield. Hey, thanks for those theater tickets. *How To Succeed In Business* . . . It was a knockout. My date enjoyed it."

"Don't mention it, Mr. Spitz." Renaldo had recommended that they go automated as part of Kraal's downsizing plan, but they kept Garfield Harrison on. Was it because he did more than operate the elevator? He had an ingenious way of remembering forgotten anniversaries, birth dates, obtaining tickets to shows, flowers for dates. With the tips and the interest on loans, the old man was drawing thousands of dollars more per year than his regular salary. The station's accountants were recommending that Garfield be let go, and an automatic elevator be used, but for some reason, Jonathan Kraal was keeping him on. It was as hard to figure his staying on as it was my being retained.

Back downtown, I entered my studio. I spent an hour at the board but nothing came. I turned on the TV. They were broadcasting a memorial service from Oklahoma. I couldn't get into the service. There was some nice singing from a white choir and a children's singing group was thoroughly charming. A white singer tried to do a soul spin on Eric Clapton's "When You See Me in Heaven," accompanied by a guitarist. It was sincere, but tepid. Then this sister got up and belted out "America the Beautiful," and "God Bless America" and I put my head on the table and wept. Thinking of all of those children and the parents holding teddy bears in their arms where their children should be and the blacks and whites comforting each other. Thinking about how untreated racism was destroying the country. Regardless of my cynical and sometimes grotesque cartoons, deep down I was a patriot. Every time I hear the "Star-Spangled Banner," that ugly piece of noise, derived from an old Irish drinking song, I get goose pimples. I break out. Even though the line, "Bombs bursting in air," had an inappropriate ring in light of what happened to the Oklahoma City Federal Building. Garfield would say that the ghosts of murdered Oklahoma Indians caused this. Timothy McVeigh and his followers insisted on their second amendment rights, and terror for them meant that Jews and blacks were in a position to take their guns away. They were arming themselves for a coming race war. Forming militias and stashing weapons.

I didn't know that Senator Joe Biden had it in him. Speaking of the growing white militia movement, he gets on *Meet the Press* on April 30 and says that if Farrakhan and his people were marching around the Michigan woods in uniforms, the paratroopers would be landing. Sen. Orrin Hatch is asked whether Mark of Michigan, a militia member, should be condemned by the Congress that condemned Farrakhan and Khalid Muhammad. Hatch evades the question, but later his comments against the man painted as the white O. J., Bill Clinton, are harsh. So are those of Henry Hyde who once defended an abortion clinic terrorist. Later, *Newsweek*, which does a cover story on O. J. that many find foul, racist, and offensive, does a positive cover portrait of the bombing suspect, Irish American Timothy McVeigh, showing a picture of him smiling. Victoria Toensing, a Reaganite and an anti-O. J. commentator, who wears a steady, tight, nasty smile, like Charles Grodin's, and who described F. Lee Bailey, O. J.'s lawyer, as a "tough jerk," says that before judging Timothy McVeigh we should hear the facts, yet she's on CNBC every other night carrying on about O. J.'s guilt. (Timothy McVeigh was finally executed on June 11, 2001, and some in the media saluted him for quoting *Invictus* and facing his death stoically. He died with his eyes open.) One day he might draw as much praise as Mark Furhman, Jesse James, Robert E. Lee, Bernard Goetz, John Wilkes Booth. Give it time.

Charles Grodin improves his ratings with a vituperative exchange with Alan Dershowitz, in which Grodin breaks out into slobbering babble about how the whole damned LA Police Department would have to have been in on the conspiracy to frame O. J. even though the LAPD coroner contends that it could have involved only two people.

Feeling that he's on to a good thing, he repeats the line every night. "The whole damned police department would have had to be in on the frame-up." For this outburst he is rewarded with a profile in the *New York Times*, which has made up its mind that O. J. is guilty. But in 1998 his show is dropped by Neutron Jack because he's accused of spending all of the time criticizing the corporate world, and expressing despair about homelessness.

How many people have been maimed and condemned to an early death by the corporate world? General Electric, whose stockholders benefit from the high ratings that O. J. brings, this multimillion-dollar slave auction, is accused of polluting the Hudson River. They dispute the findings. G. E. demands that its own examiners, its own dream team, be brought in to examine the river's contents. Nobody knows the names on this dream team. None of the talk shows, which G. E. owns, criticize this dream team.

14

Assistant LAPD Crime Laboratory director Gregory Matheson said that it was wrong for crime scene technician trainee Andrea Mazzola to use the same swatch on several blood samples in Simpson's Bronco and that it would have been better if she collected more evidence. He also said she made a mistake when she rolled up a section of the car's carpet because blood from one area could have been spread to another area.

Court TV criminalist Andrea Mazzola is obviously hiding something. She can't recall her testimony from two days before or from five minutes before. The same experts who hounded Rosa Lopez, a Latina, who says that she saw Simpson's Bronco parked near his Rockingham estate when the murders were supposed to have been taking place, is pummeled by the pro-prosecution media, because she says that she can't remember events that happened ten months prior to her testimony.

On May 10th we get some more good news. Some DNA mixed in with O. J.'s, found on the steering wheel of the Bronco, is said to belong to a fourth party. I felt so good that I decided to take my wife and daughter out for dinner. I opened the door to our condominium. The place had been redecorated. I hadn't seen them since the beginning of the trial. Except for some trips to Kraal TV Network and to Mama's for my morning espresso run, I was secluded. Sequestered like a member of the jury in the O. J. trial. The view, looking out over the East River, was still awesome. The sounds of Django Reinhardt's sensuous and lush guitar were coming from my daughter's room. This was odd. I was used to her playing Boys II Men, Salt and Pepper, Tupac, T.L.C., The Notorious B.I.G. And this loudmouthed woman rapper who seduces audiences with her call for a return to "African values." I needed some answers. My wife walked in. She was carrying some groceries from D'Agostino's. She seemed shocked to see me. But then she recovered. She had a few more gray hairs. I embraced her, but I could feel some coolness between us. She stiffened. Her eyes always reminded me of those of Vermeer's model for "Girl with a Pearl Earring."

"What's going on? You don't look the same. What happened to your hair? What did you do with my studio?" I asked. I followed her into the kitchen. She began to calmly remove the items from the bags. Nothing I liked was on her shopping list. But there was Geritol. Ben-Gay. Denture powder. Metamucil.

"I thought you'd moved out. We haven't seen you since we returned from Hawaii. Then you come breezing in here, asking me a lot of questions." She didn't look away from the groceries. She was beginning to put them away. All on designated shelves, boxes, and in crystal containers. She was very Swiss about things like that.

"It's been that long? I've been working. Trying to help out O. J. The station is biased against him. It's hard to get anything that's objective through. White people can write and talk about his guilt and make millions. They won't let us say anything and there have been reprisals against blacks who even question the railroading that the brother is getting. This faggot named Sebastian Lord."

"I wish you wouldn't talk like that."

I ignored her. "He was brought in by Kraal when he took over. The guy suspended my cartoons. We had an argument."

"Why aren't you doing anymore Badgers?"

"Not with this O. J. thing going on. The brother needs all of the few blacks who are in the media to support him. At KCAK the deck is stacked against O. J. Simon Fansworth, Lord, Princessa Bimbette and Raquel Torres, this right-wing Latina are all against him, and Kraal and Renaldo Louis. Only Ben Armstrong and I are standing up for this martyr to the corrupt racist criminal justice system. And Lord, this fucking Tory British import. He even wrote a piece putting down KCAK TV in the London papers when he visited home, saying that he's surrounded by Yankee incompetence, and Kraal has still kept him on."

"You care more about O. J. than you care about your family."

She hadn't heard me. "That's not true. Where's Hibiscus? Since when has she taken to Django Reinhardt, Bizet?"

"She's away at college. She got into UC Santa Cruz."

"What?"

"I called you but you never returned my call. She's in her fall semester."

"Well then who is playing that music?"

"My dad."

"Your what? What's he doing here? He said he'd never set foot inside of your house, after you married me."

"His course in Babylonian Astrology was eliminated. The state of New Jersey is cutting back on such courses."

"Didn't he save any money?"

"He didn't get his pension. He was dismissed for moral turpitude. She was a nineteen-year-old blonde."

"What about his savings?"

"He lost his savings in an Arizona land scam. Something happened to him after Mom died."

"How is that *my* problem? You're asking me to share a house with someone who hates me. How could you? All of those shitty letters that he'd send about you, me, and the kid over the years. Went through some kind of religious ceremony, reading you out of his life. Because you married a black man. Don't you remember?"

"He's my father. What am I suppose to do? Let him sleep in the streets? Don't get excited. It's bad for your diabetes. I'll bet you aren't eating right. When are you coming home? I miss you!"

Just then her father left my daughter's room. He was wearing a bathrobe. He shuffled past us without saying anything. The man was reeking of alcohol. He was hobbling, wheezing his way over towards the bathroom. He was stooped over as though he had dowager's hump. He was coughing and sweating. Momentarily, we heard huge explosions of flatulence coming from behind the door of the toilet. I didn't have the heart to continue quarreling with her. That would change a few minutes later when I entered my study.

"Esther, come here." She entered the room.

"What the fuck has happened to my room? My drawing board and supplies. Pencils, erasers, paper. Whose books are these? And these maps of the universe. What are they doing here?"

"My dad's. They're his astrology books."

"That does it," I said. I got my coat and left, slamming the door behind me. I took the train down to the studio. Crowded out of my own home. Of course, I loved Esther. But in time of war, my job was at the front.

1 5

I'm a survivor all right. After generations of ancestors working in the fields, factories, cleaning homes and offices, my generation had a chance to go to school, read books, attend plays, and do desk work just like W. E. B. wanted it. Like an old time Talented Tenther, I even had a season ticket to the opera. Only falling asleep once. During Wagner's *Die Meistersinger*. I think it was the droning, lumbering trombone score that did it. Besides, like millions of my contemporaries, I'm fond of gazing and staring. This "sedentary" lifestyle got me in trouble with glucose, which one geneticist has said we should avoid more than the snakes we were originally programmed to fear. A bakery display of cake, muffins, and cookies is like a nest of cobras to me. They should invent a candy bar for diabetics called The Grim Reaper. How did I know that sugar had a dark side? If I die before my time, it will be due to sugar. Not snakes. While my ancestors wrote songs about a life so bitter that they couldn't wait to be hastened to another world (how did that song go? "No more weeping and wail-ing"), a sweet life might be the death of me. I could blame it on O. J. Everybody else does. O. J. has become a metaphor for things wrong with culture and politics. Like the 2000 oil crisis that came that August. It's because people were buying these utility wagons. O. J. began this trend. You of the Millennial Generation don't remember Rita Hayworth, the actress, do you? She was in a movie where she sang the song "Put the Blame on Mame." Put the blame on O. J. O. J. caused my diabetes and everything else that went wrong in the '90s. Because of O. J., I had to satisfy my cravings for sugar in other ways. Johnny Hodges' alto, Freddie Roulette's syrupy "Sleepwalk." Sugar for the ears. French Impres-sionism. Sugar for the eyes. Maybe Rabbit is right. My Diabetes 2 got worse from sitting before the tube for hours at a time and not getting enough exercise and ballooning up to two hundred pounds. Loading up on peanut butter sandwiches. Huge muf-fins. Cookies, candy, and chocolate and yes, using coupons for Happy Meals from time to time and listening to people on tele-vision blaming O. J. when things go wrong. O. J. O. J. this. O. J. that. O. J. O. J. O. J. When I'm in Santa Fe, Esther tries to get me to go to the Santa Fe museums. Get O. J. off my mind. Why go and stare at pottery and landscapes when I can watch this crisis that's been taking place all day. I'm a news junkie. As Jeffrey St. Clair says, "I don't want to miss anything." People like me would rather watch bulletins than contemplate an eclipse. Though I must admit I had to take a second and third look at the work of Francisco Sanabria's work. His stunning "At Gloria's House" and "Before Departure."

They won't let O. J. go. We're a few years into the twenty-first century and they still won't let go. The story clings to the American imagination like a swimmer clinging to a life raft among white sharks who smell blood in the water. (Thirty years from now no one will understand this image, white sharks having become extinct by then.) As an aspiring painter, I know all about Winslow Homer. The O. J. story, which began in the twentieth century, had spilled over into the twenty-first.

16

Blogger Bat's profile says that he is a Lower East Side art entrepreneur; he is surrounded by interns, young white women mostly from schools like Sarah Lawrence and Barnard. They run errands for him and manufacture his magazine, *Getting Along*, and manage his gallery. They're volunteers. Idealistic. Some of them from France and other countries, who've signed up to become interns. But when they arrive in the States, they become no-shows and spend most of their time sightseeing. The directors on his board keep changing. Members of one tried to oust him. They thought that because he was blind he'd not be privy to the private e-mails they were sending to each other in which they were discussing how to dispose of him. Confined in his own home, which he had made available for their "art." They discussed whether they should even confine him to his bedroom. Young white women have poetry readings in which they read poems about holding mirrors to their vaginas and discovering their vulva, or whether one should kiss their partner after having oral sex, while in Africa women carry water all day, or in the Middle East, women are forbidden from looking directly into the eyes of a man or in Cambodia children as young as eight are forced into the Sex Trade and tell their customers, white Johns from Europe and America, that they know how to give good head.

Some of the interns come from wealthy households, but when he takes them to cultural events, he has to pay for all of them at the door from his university pension and Social Security. They plot against him, but he always unveils the plot. His blindness has blessed him with other gifts. He is like Tiresias. But as Paul Mooney says, do the niggers appreciate it? He responds to some weak papers at a Paris conference without notes. A degreeless street intellectual embarrasses the scholars who present papers on Chester Himes. People who have spent half their adult lives on college campuses. Do the niggers appreciate it? When he returns home, Brooklyn's Frantz Fanon College fires him. A blessing in disguise because even though he is often beset by problems and misfortunes he is now the most powerful art personality on the Lower East Side. Professor Bat. Did I say misfortunes? A premature death of his son. A self-styled Yippie co-investor in the townhouse which houses his operation, he ran off with a hundred thousand, which, without Bat's knowledge, was borrowed against the house. A former lover played the same trick for another hundred thousand. She became enthralled with a Haitian who started a fire that destroyed a manuscript that he'd been working on since the '60s. Yet he doesn't feel sorry for himself. He sits on a beat-up couch, munching on takeout food, and receiving visitors and phone calls from the international avant-garde.

One version is that critics called playwright Otter a puppet master so much that he decided to study the real puppet theater. I tried to tell Otter that white critics have accused black male writers of hostility, anger, ranting, and bitterness for over one hundred years when they try to write honestly about their situation in the United States and that when they accuse a writer of creating puppet-like characters or cartoon characters, it's usually about their annoyance at the way white characters are drawn. One critic went as far as to suggest to Charles Chesnutt, whose characters were "well rounded," stick to black characters. Otter also came under a lot of criticism for his prophecies about the situation of the black male. One could say that Otter is the one who saw O. J. coming. He, like those Jews who foresaw the arrival of a hostile German government, got out in time. He is spared the psychological pressure that black men come under during the O. J. phenomenon, which gives the people with the most numbers (for now, anyway) another opportunity to assault African Americans with more insults and humiliation, such castigation leading to strokes, high blood pressure, heart attacks, diabetes, and early death for millions. Sure, it's The Juice on trial, but his trial becomes a ritualistic mock lynching of all black men, the same way that Willie Horton was used to signify on the brothers. The stress that burns up our nutrients. We the mascots. Just like the Indians are mascots for sports teams who wish to portray a warrior image, black guys are mascots for things like date rape, domestic abuse, sexual harassment, giving people AIDS. One of the many things that Indians and blacks have in common is that smallpox was used as a weapon against them. Bacteriological warfare. Some trace the AIDS epidemic to a Philadelphia smallpox experiment, which used Africans as guinea pigs. But maybe Jeffrey Toobin is right when he says that blacks are in touch with reality and should not be patted on the head.

The crack epidemic that set back African American progress was a case of chemical warfare on the ghettos of America. A way to finance the off-the-shelf Contra operation. Colonel North said that Reagan knew all about it. That's why very few black people showed up at the ugly, tasteless panoply that accompanied the burial of the man. He began the destruction of the University of California, which, before he arrived, was nearly tuition-free. He felt that a higher tuition would "keep out black troublemakers." The job that this actor began on behalf of rich and elderly whites was finished by another hired face: Arnold Schwarzenegger. He gave his yacht-owning friends a fifty-six-million-dollar tax break, the amount of money that would have brought indoors the mentally ill among the homeless from outdoors—where Reagan had cast them. Reagan began his campaign in Mississippi, the scene of the murders of three civil rights workers. Alexander Cockburn wrote:

> The Great and courageous black attorney, J. L. Chestnut, one of two black people in the huge audience, recalled Reagan's crying that "the South will rise again and this time remain master of everybody and everything within its dominion."

Otter says that the Japanese may be racist, but they're cool with it and that for now, he can walk around Tokyo streets at any time of day or night without fearing assault which is more than you can say about a black man walking through parts of Brooklyn, South Boston, or the mountains of Tennessee. He says that he can take out his wallet without being shot. Over there he says it's the Chinese and Koreans whom they hate.

The black author, James Alan McPherson, gets beaten up critically for saying the same thing. That he was more comfortable with the Japanese than with Americans. The white men (folks knee-deep in their own "identity politics"), who once praised the author's Ellisonian stance of universal humanist transcendence, get on McPherson's case when he says that within the last fifteen years, after some insults from members of the mercenary white underclass—people who don't care whether one is a black male Pulitzer Prize winner—he realizes that he's a black man. This particular policeman apparently didn't read the press releases of the Pulitzer Prize committee. The Japanese whom Otter has met are affectionate toward McPherson for his interest in Japanese culture even though McPherson doesn't know the difference between romaji and hiragana.

Rabbit was right. If anything happens to black men in the U.S., people will look back upon the O. J. case as one of the turning points. And now those screenplays by white males about black men, to which he objected in the eighties, look tame in comparison to the stuff that's coming out in post-O. J. America. The National Organization for Women even had to expel the head of the LA branch for racism. Tammy Bruce, who had issues with her father, which, of course, black men have to pay for, referred to first lady Michelle Obama in 2009 as "trash."

Comedian Paul Mooney talks about a typical white entertainment, *The Green Mile*. A black man plays a variation of one of the long-standing black stereotypes. You rub on a black man and you get lucky in bed. (In 2009, a Republican operative refers to Barack Obama as "the magic Negro.") No wonder Ted Joans compared us to rhinos, whose horns are supposed to cure erectile dysfunction.

Rabbit is a filmmaker who has created a number of low-budget films. He can't get distribution and so they go nowhere. He and the rest of us view the imprisonment of our image by outside script-writers, directors, and producers as cultural aggression. They are the Boers and we are the Zulus at the Battle of Blood River.

They are able to turn the reality of our lives upside down. Rabbit mentioned *Clockers* and *Crash*, which, like films starring Jodie Foster and Clint Eastwood, encourage vigilantism; it's the white cops who are the heroes. In *Gone Baby Gone*, Morgan Freeman even revives the Bill Robinson/Shirley Temple duo. There's very little difference between the roles assigned to them and the appearance of black actors in that scene from *Birth of a Nation* in which black legislators drink whiskey, eat chicken thighs, and leer at white women sitting in the gallery. Rabbit supports O. J. like the rest of us, even though he shares our opinion that most black athletes are dopes. Have their autobiographies ghosted by white men. Regularly get into brawls outside of strip clubs.

Snakes is a model of responsible behavior. He is thoughtful. He remembers birthdays. Sends Christmas greetings. He is a man who is often called upon to deliver eulogies at the funerals of friends. Those that he can't attend list him as honorary pallbearer. He will always observe the courtly style of his Southern upbringing. Shoes are always shined. Handkerchief in suit pocket in case some sniffling damsel has to blow her nose or come to tears. He says things like "Yes, Sir" and "Yes, Ma'am."

17

MAY 20, 1995

I'm back at my studio on East Fourth between B and C. I'm in-ternetting. I'm following the case of a Cambodian cartoonist who has been jailed for his depiction of Prime Ministers Prince Noro-dom Ranariddh and Hen Sen as Master Thieves. Hen Vipheak, 28 year-old editor of the *Serei Pheap Thmey* (New Liberty News), was fined five million riel ($2,400) and warned that he'd receive a longer sentence if he didn't pay the fine. We cartoonists have to stick together. I brought his case to the attention of the American Association of Cartoonists. (He was later pardoned by the King.)

They were calling the week ending May 20, 1995, a "bad week for the defense." It did look pretty bad. For the first time I began to believe that O. J. did it. How was he going to explain all of the astronomical odds against the blood drops found at Nicole's con-dominium and at the Rockingham estate belonging to somebody else? Ron and Nicole's blood being present in his Bronco? But hell, then I thought, some of the blood that appeared on the fence wasn't there when the fence was first examined. And what about the sock found in Simpson's bedroom?

I wasn't going to abandon my buddy, O. J. Just as well because on June 23, 1995, the blood evidence was blown away.

Population geneticist Bruce Weir conceded that he overestimated the chances of a match between O. J. Simpson's DNA and DNA found at his home and the crime scenes.

"I'm sincerely sorry and I'm also embarrassed," Weir said during questioning by defense attorney Peter Neufeld. "When I do calculations, I do not consider any forensic implications, and if you are suggesting that I do, I will disabuse you of that right now."

Peter Neufeld asked, "by failing to include the additional pairings in these samples, in these items, which do not exclude Mr. Simpson, the number that are arrived at by you and put on that board are biased against Mr. Simpson; isn't that correct?" "As it turns out," said Weir, "it looks that way, yes." Weir had overstated the likelihood that the defendant's blood was contained in blood mixtures found in his Bronco and on a glove found behind his home.

18

JUNE 12, 1995

Marcia Clark had gotten up and shouted at Judge Ito, who as usual melted under her attack. She accused Johnnie Cochran of calling her hysterical. He didn't call her hysterical, but promised the judge that he wouldn't be hysterical. She took it personally.

Princessa Bimbette and other commentators spent the whole hour saying that Johnnie Cochran should apologize to Marcia Clark. Gloria Allred said that he should apologize to all women. The next day Marcia Clark signified on Bernard Scheck, implying that he had only a half a brain, but nobody asked her to apologize to the intellectually challenged. And when she implied that F. Lee Bailey had a small penis size—"Maybe the small gloves belong to Mr. Bailey"—she said, during one exchange, nobody asked her to apologize to those suffering from penile deficiency. She was referring to the gloves that were found near a wall on O. J.'s property. There was speculation that they had been planted, there being no evidence of their having been dropped by somebody abandoning a crime scene. As Cochran said in the transcript of his closing remarks, answering the prosecution:

> Now, under their theory, at 10:40, 10:45, that glove is dropped, how many hours is that? It's now after 6:00. So what is that, 7 1/2 hours? What's the testimony about drying time around here? There's no dew point that night. Why would it be moist and sticky unless he [Mark Fuhrman] brought it over there and planted it there to try to make this case? And there is a Caucasian hair on that glove!

Ms. Clark believes that since she is a woman, her situation is comparable to that of African Americans, thus allowing her to say things about black men that, in a previous time, would have been considered racist. The highest point in her feminist fantasy occurs when, responding to information that Mark Fuhrman arrested black people merely for being in the wrong (white) neighborhood, Ms. Clark said, equating sexism with racism, that she not only thought it wrong that a person be arrested for being in the wrong neighborhood for racial reasons, but for gender reasons as well. Huh? How often do white women get arrested for being in the wrong neighborhood?

She's like the white women at National Public Radio who go tabloid whenever a black man's reputation is at stake. NPR's Margot Adler reported about the sentencing of Autumn Jackson for her part in the extortion plot against Bill Cosby. A slap on the wrist, considering the fact that she made the threat while Cosby was mourning the loss of his son. Ms. Adler reports that Cosby "had sex" with Autumn's mother. Ms. Adler published a book which says that a black man threatened to rape Ms. Adler if she didn't kiss him. So just as black guys have to pay for all of these black men who've crossed Gloria Steinem and Susan Brownmiller, Cosby and the rest of us have to pay for this guy who threatened Ms. Adler. As long as African Americans are blamed collectively for the actions of an individual or a few, they aren't free.

American Jews who thought that the country was the Promised Land got a real jolt toward the end of 2008 when Bernard L. Madoff was accused of swindling his clients out of fifty billion dollars, raising the worst anti-Semitic stereotypes of the thieving Jewish bankers, just as Richard Price's *Lush Life*, Steven Spielberg's *The Color Purple*, David Simon's *The Wire*, and David Isay's *Ghetto Life 101* raised the worst anti-black-male stereotypes about incestuous, misogynist, drug-dealing black men. The *Times* article of Dec. 23, 2008, said, "Jews feel ashamed by proxy." Join the club.

19

MAY 24, 1995

I was tired of watching the trial, and trying to get some ideas for cartoons. Though the mass media for whom facts are minor inconveniences maintain that Judge Ito favors the defense, the majority of his rulings favor the prosecution. The electronic lynch mob chastises Judge Ito for the DA's losing the criminal case, but, according to Johnnie Cochran, Ito sided with the prosecution seventy percent of the time.

Ito, who had been giving the New York lawyers Scheck and Neufeld a difficult time, let Clark get away with murder, as one expert said.

A Mill Valley lawyer said that Marcia Clark plays little girl to Ito's father. All the little girl has to do is throw a tantrum to get her way.

Rafiki came and got me. I didn't know how long this luxury would be available to me. Once at Kraal's towers, I heard some raised voices coming from the newsroom. Ben was arguing with

Raquel Torres. The one the PR guys in the mailroom called Tokina. Tokina Torres. While the Puerto Ricans and blacks had been subjected to ethnic cleansing by Rudy Giuliani, a notorious cross-dresser, a man whose father once shared a jail cell with the Harlem gangster Bumpy Johnson, Mexican Americans were showing up in New York increasingly.

They were standing in the middle of the newsroom. Everybody was looking up from their computers and following the argument. Among them Princessa Bimbette. She was sitting at her desk, chain smoking and preparing for her show. She was taking it all in.

"I'm just asking for balance, that's all," Ben said.

"I am balanced, you're just on his side."

"I'm just wondering why you always report the prosecution's side of the case, but never the defense's side."

"Could you give me an example?"

"The other day, the defense asked for sanctions against Marcia Clark and you didn't mention it. Cochran got the limo driver to admit that he wasn't positive that the Bronco wasn't parked at the Rockingham address and you reported it without mentioning his qualification. He didn't say it wasn't there. He said that he didn't see it. Besides, some of the guys who worked with the limousine driver said that he was high on pot that night. Maybe that's why his timeline about when the Bronco was parked was confusing."

"You're just sticking with your black brother. Playing the race card."

"You could be accused of playing the gender card by bonding with your white sister. Calling her Marcia. Very unprofessional. The only thing that white women expect of you is to be their maid.

You Latinas still don't get it. They put this 187 up to kick your ass out of the country and you still love white people. They beat up Mexicans at the border and you don't do shit. They insult and laugh at Rosa Lopez and you remain passive."

"How dare you insult me this way. I'll put in a complaint. You blacks are always bitching, always complaining about your victimization. Reverend Eugene Rivers is right. You should work hard like the other people entering this country. You and your Chaka Zulu leaders. Asking for affirmative action—"

"Your ass wouldn't be here if it weren't for affirmative action. Why do you think they made you the coanchor? Because they were afraid to hire a real Latina, somebody unafraid to take a position that wasn't approved of by the Rathswheeler crowd. You and that sinister creep Geraldo Rivera ain't doing nothing but carrying buckets for the white man."

"You're just jealous of Geraldo. His success. And I might tell you that our listeners are complaining that the station has added sports." Ben ignored her.

"And what about your commentary about the defense team introducing race? That they should never have done so. Defending Mark Fuhrman. He said that he was sick of blacks and Mexicans." He got up in her face and stressed the word *Mexicans*. Puerto Ricans were now complaining about a museum that once had been funded for Puerto Rican culture, being turned into a Mexican American museum. Some of the tensions between Mexican Americans and Puerto Ricans were based upon some Mexican Americans holding to the belief that Puerto Ricans had black blood. Of course millions of them also had African ancestry. Otter said that he attended a conference in Mexico and a speaker commented on the African heritage of every South and Central American country except for Mexico.

They kept on arguing. After I picked up my mail, mostly hate mail inspired by Princessa calling me a terrorist and leaking the cartoon that she and others claimed showed O. J. sodomizing the U.S., I went downstairs and called the car service. Rafiki pulled up in about five minutes. I jumped in. He handed me a New York paper. There was something in there about Judge Ito getting tough, which meant that they appreciated the fact that he was shutting up Johnnie Cochran. The *Daily News* had a reporter named Michelle Caruso working for them. She was a white middle-class feminist, which means that black men were the targets of her exercises against the DPD (Dominant Patriarchal Discourse). She gets on the *Larry King Show* and says that she's glad that nine women are on the jury, which means that she hopes that O. J. will be convicted because of the 911 call during which Nicole pleads for her life. She's another one of these white women who believes that she has a common bond with her black sisters on the jury. Boy, is she in for a surprise. What they conveniently leave out when they play the 911 call is that during this incident O. J. doesn't strike Nicole. The most ludicrous part of the one-sided commentary during the case were the middle- and upper-class white men, trying to speculate as to what was on these women's minds. I know these black women who, before the verdict, were always described by the press as "well dressed," and "intelligent," but then, after the verdict, they were accused of succumbing to Johnnie Cochran's "race card." That night I got a call from Garfield. Seems that Raquel's brothers didn't like the disrespectful manner by which Ben communicated with their sister. They decided to defend her honor, their mother's honor, and their country's honor, the kind of instructions that Julio Caesar Chavez's corner used to give him when he was behind on points. Armstrong received a rib injury, a black eye, a non-specific back injury. He's going to be away from work at least for six weeks. He was lucky that he wasn't challenged to a duel, which would have been the case had he insulted a Mexican American woman in Arizona or New Mexico.

20

JULY 24–28, 1995

July was a good month for the defense. The prosecutors kept daring the defense to prove their theory that the police planted evidence. They said that if blood were used from the evidence processing room as the defense claimed, then a chemical preservative called ethylenediaminetetraacetic acid would be present in the control samples. But when the EDTA showed up, they said that there was not enough to have been planted. A CBS affiliate in Los Angeles announced that Nicole Simpson's blood would appear on some socks found in Simpson's bedroom, even before the socks were tested! Shortly before the civil case began, it was disclosed that Detective Philip Vannatter was not only carrying around O. J.'s blood, an event that was declared unusual, but had gone to the morgue and requested samples of Nicole and Ron Goldman's blood. The media made very little of this incident. When the FBI expert Roger Martz takes the stand, he agrees with the defense that there is EDTA on the socks, but, during the lunch hour, the prosecution gets ahold of him. After lunch he changes his story. Martz is later accused by another agent of consistently siding with the prosecution. This constitutes examiner bias. Shortly after the all-white jury in the civil trial begins its deliberations, it is revealed that the FBI lab is as much a cesspool of contamination as the LAPD lab. Agents confess that they are told to lie in favor of the prosecution. Roger Martz is transferred as a result of the scandal and even *Time Magazine* says in its April 28, 1997, issue that suspicions about Martz's performance affects the O. J. case.

> Last week's report also faulted Martz for his testimony on blood preservatives in the first O. J. Simpson trial, saying it "ill served the FBI" and "conveyed a lack of preparation, an inadequate level of training in toxicological issues [Martz's field of expertise] and deficient knowledge about other scientific matters."

One of the country's foremost forensic experts, Cyril Wecht, M.D., J.D., also raised doubt about the prosecution's blood evidence. He wrote that a small portion of a vial of blood, about thirty drops, taken as a sample from Simpson was missing and unaccounted for. The defense claimed that the police had taken this and planted the blood drops on the Bronco and at the crime scene. The blood found at the gate of Nicole Brown Simpson's house, which matched O. J. Simpson's, also contained EDTA. The same was true of the blood samples found on the socks, which matched Mrs. Simpson's blood . . . If there was EDTA—

and I believe Dr. Rieder's testimony that there was—then the blood did not come directly from the person. It was quite possibly taken, stored, preserved, then placed on the socks and the gate, or, in some negligent fashion, contaminated.

Whom does one believe when assessing O. J. Simpson's guilt, or innocence? Dr. Cyril Wecht, M.D., J.D., Michael M. Baden, M.D., Henry C. Lee, Ph.D., or comedians and talk show hosts like Chris Matthews and Bill Maher? The blood evidence is always cited by O. J.'s accusers as proof that he killed Nicole, and Daniel Petrocelli, in what amounted to a mugging of Simpson by an all-white jury, based his case on blood evidence that could have been planted by the police.

There was more bad news for the prosecution in July. On July 27, one of the jurors became ill and the defense presented physical evidence that the police had planned to frame O. J. Simpson for murder. Herbert MacDonell, who was the blood spatter expert, said that there were stains on the socks in O. J. Simpson's bedroom that looked like they had been applied, and they had gone all the way through the fabric. This couldn't have happened if he was wearing those socks. He said the "stains" looked like smears. And the blood came into the sock from the inside, so the blood couldn't have gotten on the sock while he was wearing them. They also looked like balls, which should mean that they were wet when they bonded to the fabric.

Some say that the reason the nurse Thano Peratis, who took Simpson's blood, wasn't called by the prosecution was because he could have helped the defense's claim that the blood was planted. The defense claimed that the nurse's saying that he had taken eight ml of blood meant that some of the blood—1.5 milliliters—was missing. But later, in one of the more farcical events from the trial, the prosecution interviewed the nurse. He changed his mind. The video looked contrived and nobody from the defense was provided an opportunity to cross-examine the nurse. Moreover, Deputy District Attorney Hank Goldberg secretly went to the nurse's home to get him to contradict his previous testimony at both the grand jury and the preliminary hearing.

Nothing can remove my joy on this weekend. Not even Melanie Lomax, yet another pro-prosecution commentator, who has made nasty and hostile remarks about the defense and Simpson since the beginning of the trial, but, like other feminists, black and white, who gave O. J., Tyson, and Clarence Thomas a hard time, she swoons over Clinton, even though feminist theory would read his affair with Monica as a case of a powerful man exploiting a woman less powerful than he. Wasn't there "disempowerment" happening in that case? How does Melanie look? In a famine she would survive about a month longer than the rest of us. Marcia Clark continues to get her way. Judge Ito gives in. Regardless of what *New York Times* reporter David Margolick, another shill for the prosecution, claims, that Ito is against Marcia Clark because she is a woman, Ito constantly gives in to Clark even after he has made a ruling. She keeps arguing and Ito changes the ruling.

The prosecution violates discovery rules by withholding videotape that challenges two crying white women's testimony about Simpson's demeanor at his daughter's dance recital. The video shows a smiling Simpson in contrast to their testimony that he was sullen. When the defense violated discovery rules, Cochran and Douglas were fined (even though Shapiro takes the responsibility).

21

Esther sounded very serious when she asked me to come up to our condo. She said that it was a very important matter that the four of them had to sit down and discuss. The four of them? That Hibiscus had come home from Santa Cruz, and had announced something that she wanted to share with me. As Rafiki drove me across town, his car part of a slow train dominated by yellow metallic mules, he started bragging about Olajuwon.

"Look, I'm not up to it today." What could be so important? And what did she mean by the four of them?

When I entered the condominium, they were all seated. Hibiscus, Esther, and a third person. The third person was a young woman. She was wearing a kind of hairdo that use to upset the NAACP and generations of assimilationists. It was the hairstyle of the pickaninny. In precolonial African theater, this was the hairstyle that actors playing prostitutes wore. She was wearing a bright red dress that matched her bright red lipstick. She was wearing a ring in her nose, another detail that older generations had winced at. Hibiscus was dressed the same way. Given these fashion stances, my wife, who was as hip as they come, looked like Betty Crocker.

"J.B., this is Hibiscus' friend, Karisha. She's a classmate of Hibiscus." He extended his hand to her. She sort of scowled at him and kept her seat. She folded her arms and rolled her eyes at the ceiling.

"I'm not shaking hands with no supporter of O. J. Simpson," she said, moving her neck from side to side. Hibiscus frowned and smiled at the same time. My wife shrugged her shoulders. I looked at my daughter.

"You love O. J. more than you love me and Mom. You're down there in your studio. I'll bet you've built a shrine to O. J.," she said.

"But the brother is innocent; I see it as my duty to defend the downtrodden black male." They laughed. Even Esther.

"That cartoon wasn't cool," Karisha said.

"You had O. J. on the top and the woman beneath him," Hibiscus said.

"And furthermore, you just as bad as O. J. He committed domestic violence, the way I look at it, you used your cartoon to degrade women. As for that first cartoon. The one about the police. I'm tired of you black men blaming all of your problems on *the man* instead of your own evil," Karisha said. She and Hibiscus gave each other a fist bump. Esther smiled.

"How did you know about the 'Juice' cartoon? It wasn't run."

"It's all over the Internet, Dad," Hibiscus said.

"Oh, right?"

"That's right. Nothing can be hidden anymore," Karisha said.

"Look, I didn't come here to discuss my art. What did you call me up here for?"

"Bear," Esther put her hand on mine. "Hibiscus and Karisha are going to get married. Hibiscus got the idea when we were in Hawaii. Down there people are agitating for the right of people of the same sex to get married. And there's a report that Vermont will soon okay marriages between people of the same sex, and California. Isn't that nice?"

"Get married!" I leapt from my chair. My hands started to sweat. My face felt damp. "Get married? What kind of crazy shit is that? What are you talking about?" I started to pace up and down, ranting and raving.

"See, Mom. I told you he wouldn't understand. He's always made homophobic remarks, as long as I can remember," Hibiscus said. Her eyes locked on to mine.

"Homophobe. That's what he is. Brother Cornel is right about you guys," Karisha said. I was enraged like Al Pacino playing Don Corleone in *The Godfather*, the scene where his wife tells him that she's aborted their child because she didn't want to continue two thousand years of Sicilian history.

"How could you encourage such a thing?" I said. From my tone, you could determine that I was upset with my wife.

"Are you all right, Bear? Are you keeping track of your blood? Want some orange juice?" Esther said. Now that I had diabetes, she was always explaining away my anger as being biological.

"That's why he's so irritable," Hibiscus said, glancing at Karisha who grinned.

Maybe they were right, I thought. One of the side effects of diabetes was irritability. During one of my diabetes classes, a truck driver got into an argument with a dietician over the nutritional value of ketchup. He was defending ketchup, she was against ketchup. He sounded a little insane.

"Calm down, Sweetheart. Things have changed, Bear. People are expressing their love in many different ways these days," Esther said.

What's wrong with the old way? I thought.

"We can have children if that's what you're worried about, having grandchildren. The typical patriarchal vanity. Desiring that their line have continuity. There's artificial insemination and both Hibiscus and I can be cloned. The technology is now available. There are experiments now with stem cells. Sperm from stem cells," Hibiscus said.

"Soon there won't be a need for men," said Karisha. Not only did the remark hit me in the pit of my stomach, but the mischievous smile that accompanied the remark froze my scrotum.

"How can you hate gay people who're oppressed even more than black people?" Hibiscus said.

"Who says so?" I asked.

"Henry Louis Gates, Jr., says so," they said in unison. "The world is changing, but you remain behind. I could tell the way that you discussed Sebastian Lord that you wouldn't be prepared for Hibiscus and Karisha loving each other," Esther said.

"Well, they certainly have found a way to exterminate black people. They're using AIDS, crack, lack of prenatal care access, homosexuality, turning the black race into a race of mules." I was shocked at my utterance. I was sounding like a dope. A fundamentalist. What's that guy's name? Rev. Lou Sheldon. Some backward-thinking person.

"Gays and lesbians were oppressed in the West long before the slave trade," Karisha said.

"How many among them were popes and kings?" They started screaming and yelling at me, talking at the same time. Sebastian was unprepared for this retort. It didn't work on these two.

"If you're such a race man, why did you marry me, why didn't you marry a black woman?" Esther said.

"I married you because I loved you, dammit." There was a silence. Even the coldness in Karisha's eyes melted a bit.

"Then why can't you understand our love?" Hibiscus said.

"It's unnatural, that's why. Read your Bible." Me. Telling someone to read the Bible. "Jesus condemns fags on three different occasions."

"Figs, Dad. Figs." The three started really laughing then. Karisha fell off the sofa on to the floor, she was laughing so. Hibiscus doubled up, holding her sides. Why did I go there? No biblical scholar, I. Esther calmed down the scene.

"Since when have you been so interested in the Bible? Besides, they could say that about us. They could say that love between a black and a Jew is abnormal," Esther said. "They once outlawed marriages between blacks and whites."

"Those were marriages between men and women, not same sex, besides since when have Jews become white? If Jews are so white, why don't their fellow whites accept them as whites? Like the Romans, the Germans, the Czechs, the Austrians, the Saudis, the—"

They were interrupted by Esther's father shuffling into the room. The attention in the room turned to him. He was limping. He coughed up something and then swallowed it.

"Gypsies."

"What? What are you saying, Dad?"

"We're not Jews, we're Gypsies. We have Gypsy ancestry—that's why we left Germany. It's about time you knew." Esther's hands flew to her cheeks. Hibiscus had to help her to a chair. Her father dropped another bomb.

"We chose to identify ourselves as Jews when we came through immigration because we felt that it would be easier to be a Jew in America than a Gypsy." The old man coolly removed a Lucky Strike from a robe pocket. He held their attention as he gave the history of his family from their migration from India into Europe to their attempt to live as assimilated sedentary types in German society until the hated genealogical tests were introduced. He said that some of his brothers tried to conceal their identity by joining the Nazi party. At the end of his recital, Esther was in tears. I sought to comfort her as the old man rose and started toward his room. Before leaving the room, he looked at the four of us and shrugged his shoulders. I interrupted him.

"Wait a minute," I said. He turned.

"You said that the Europeans considered Gypsies to be black. That there was even an expression, 'No washing ever whitens the black Gypsy.' Yet you ostracized your daughter for marrying me. Help me with this."

"Look, I don't have anything against you personally. In fact, I think that your cartoons are a riot, but I learned very early what immigrants before me learned."

"What was that?" I asked.

"The road to whiteness runs through Niggertown." He entered my daughter's room and shut the door. Hibiscus was sleeping on an air mattress that had been set up in my study. Soon an aria from

Bizet's great opera could be heard. Carmen singing of the unrestricted freedom offered by the gypsy life.

> CARMEN: Away over there you'd follow me / if you loved me / There you'd not be dependent upon anyone / there'd be no officer to obey / and no sounding Retreat sounding / to tell a lover / that it is time to go / The open sky, the wandering life, the whole wide world your domain / for law your own free will / and above all, that intoxicating thing / Freedom! Freedom!

Would his wife's newly found heritage get him off the hook with some of his cultural-nationalist buddies? Not on your life. For them, both Jews and Gypsies were white. They saw things in black and white. They were Americans. You might call it a cartoonish view of the world, and now this cartoon nation had a cartoon president, The Boer as we Zulus called him, and a clever cartoonist had depicted him as a boy wearing a beanie with propellers on the top. A boy president. It was said that when he left the presidency in 2009, the first thing he did when he got settled in Dallas was to kick off his shoes, have an aide pour him a large glass of Jim Beam, light the fireplace, and finish reading "My Pet Goat."

22

While the media virtually ignored the shenanigans of one of the prosecutors who tried to actually contact one of the defense's experts (a report that Chris Darden attempted to harass a member of the DA's office) is given little coverage by a media, rooting so for the prosecution, beginning in June 1995, this desperate, fiendish prosecution begins to show the "gruesome" autopsy photos.

The Volvo version of *Beavis and Butthead* over at Court TV: Dan Abrams and Greg Jarrett (who, with Charles Grodin, would like to see the jury system abolished and substituted with what? military tribunals?), and the elder Colonel Fred Graham, one of these guys who is probably still trying to argue about whether Lee was a better general than Joseph Johnston, get off by describing O. J.'s reaction to the pictures. The cameraman from GC Productions, Chris Bancroft, zeroes in on O. J., usually after some ghastly photos and exhibits are shown. In Bancroft's hands, the camera is accusatory, indicting. It lingers over the way O. J. looks at the ceiling. Trains his eyes on a calendar. Wipes away a tear. How he rocks back and forth. I decide to do a cartoon about Court TV. The cameraman has made the Goldman family part of the prosecution team. Kim Goldman makes expressions of disgust and wiggles her nose as soon as the camera gazes upon her. She uses her face to make editorials about the defense's arguments. I repudiate Rabbit's remark, and exercise in Rhino rhetoric that every time he sees somebody picking their nose he thinks of her. No compassion at all. The country had lost the civility it had in the eighteenth century when it was beset by maundering savages who refused to become "enlightened," their refusal agonizing both Thomas Jefferson and George Washington.

John Gibson, the newsman who introduces the Geraldo show, talks about Simpson "hiding behind his lawyer, Kardashian," while the autopsy pictures are displayed, when anyone could see that Simpson repeatedly leaned back and looked toward his accusers.

Cochran complained about the camera being fixated on Simpson. Ito, of course, disagreed. He wanted O. J. to witness every cut, lesion, abrasion, etc. Wanted O. J. Simpson's face mashed into the crime scene. The prosecutor and his puppet judge want to show how this nigger cut up this white woman to shreds. Dismembered her and broke her down like Bigger Thomas broke down Mary Dalton's bones. Bigger burned her in the furnace. While the white boys are reporting on Simpson's agony, and focusing upon him, I'm watching the Indian Dr. Sathyavagiswaran who, without having performed the autopsies on the victims, puts forth all of these hypotheticals that are favorable to the prosecution's theories, if you can call them that. The prosecution calls him instead of this coroner Irwin Golden who threatens the prosecution's case by refusing to rule out two killers, a conclusion also reached by Henry Lee. When the defense gets up to argue its case, the puppet judge hurries them along, while this coroner is on the stand for nine days after which Shapiro demolishes his testimony with a few sharp questions. This Indian, belonging to a group considered by Rabbit to be the most Uncle-Tom of all immigrants—the British really trained them—must love the white talk show callers referring to him as "dignified." I examine his tie, which has the pattern of a boa constrictor's skin. I watch how his tongue flicks as he hypothesizes to a member of the prosecution, Brian Kelberg, about how Goldman received his wounds.

One medical examiner calls Dr. Sathyavagiswaran's appearance "ethically despicable" and says he's always called in when the prosecution has screwed up. Though he points out Golden's errors, he was the boss and should have taken responsibility for the errors, this medical examiner says. Appearing on Barbara Walters's show, Fred Goldman says that O. J. is guilty.

I'm wondering how Simpson is going to overcome all of the wailing white women connected to the case. The witnesses from the Mezzaluna Restaurant. Kim Goldman. Denise Brown, who checks her mascara while crying on the witness stand. They're like the Southern white women who complained about black men paying too much attention to them in order to test the readiness of white men to die for them; their successors put pressure on the white male commentariat to do the same for Nicole. By defending her honor, they're defending the honor of all white women. How long will white men be conned into this medieval valor by women who want it both ways: liberation and chivalry, too? Weren't the six hundred thousand men killed during the Civil War, enough? Defending slavery and protecting white women only to be betrayed by them at the end. Richmond women engaged in a binge of party going and hedonism toward the end of the war, while the Confederate white men were dying on the battlefield. In her book, *Mothers of Invention*, by Drew Gilpin Faust, the author quotes the February 1864 *Richmond Enquirer*, which complained about the "season of reckless frivolity that has made Richmond during this winter, a carnival of unhallowed pleasure." How long will white men be chumped? One of the reasons that Ida B. Wells had to leave Memphis is because she said that these white women were lying about black men raping them. In Memphis, the rape hysteria was used against black men who were competitive with white men. Followers of Booker T. Washington were lynched. If, as Karisha said, that women don't need men to reproduce, shouldn't white men and black men, Asians form some kind of club that would be devoted to preserving the male species? Something to think about.

23

I had gone to visit Ben, who was recovering from his encounter with Raquel's brothers. He lived on the Upper West Side in one of those apartment buildings that had a doorman, and an Art-Deco lobby. His place was stacked with so much African sculpture that it resembled what western curators call a museum of "primitive art." Who's primitive, the Greeks and Romans whose work is a xerox of the natural world, or Oceanic and African art in which the artist, like Jazz musicians, improvises upon what the natural world gives them. I was getting tearful, which is what happens to me when I drink scotch, and Ben was trying to console me.

Maybe Esther, Hibiscus and her lesbian lover were right. That O. J. the brother was, well, a jerk. In fact the next morning, suffering from insomnia, in my downtown studio, I turned on the TV set. It was about four thirty A.M. I had been working on a cartoon based upon a remark that Simpson had made to Paula Barbieri, his girlfriend (whom Nicole described as "skinny" and with "big lips").

How could I defend someone who said dumb things like that? I threw the cartoon into the trash. I wasn't prepared to abandon the brother. Ben said, "You just have to understand, it ain't your fault. We're just living through a period that's confused. Take Dennis Rodman, all dressed up like a bride, all this unisex stuff. Men and women sharing bathrooms. You could blame the whole thing on Little Richard and his followers like Prince and M. J. It's not like the time when me, you, and O. J. were kids. Kids and wife get out of hand, you slap them down. Those days are gone forever, and if you ask me, I think it's all for the best. Shit. Just what would have happened had we gone around wearing earrings in the '50s, like these boys, or wore pants with our underwear sticking out. Man, we couldn't have walked down the street without getting ribbed."

"But all of this ambiguity is trying. There are no boundaries anymore. Life is difficult enough without this . . . this uncertainty. Maybe the white boys are right when they say that we should emphasize those things we have in common instead of those things that separate us. What the white boys called 'identity politics.'" I started to bring up his plan about white men and black, maybe Hispanic and Asian brothers, forming some new club or movement to preserve the male species now that fluids necessary for reproduction can be created in stem cells.

"You always wax philosophic when you have a few. But it's not all that simple. The white boys say that because they want the status quo. It's only natural that people want the world to be run by people who look like them. The days when they made all the decisions have come to an end. They're worried. Look, the way I look at it, Hibiscus is going through a phase. You know, she's on this campus and she's hanging out with these trendy women and well, that's what you get for sending her to California to school. What on earth is 'The History of Human Consciousness' anyway? Next thing you know, they'll be teaching crime shows. Sounds like some kind of snap course. People liable to do anything out there. Why Otter said that, before he left for Japan, he was standing in line with a date at a Berkeley theater and he and his date were the only straight couple in line. He said that people were glaring at him." I was ignoring him. My cell phone rang. It was Jonathan Kraal. He wanted me to come to the office. Said that it was urgent. I left Ben's apartment to wait for the Nigerian.

24

My cartoons had been suspended by Lord and there didn't seem to be a great protest against their discontinuance from those who could afford satellite TV. Many were upset about my cartoon, which Princessa or Bimby who had rabble-roused her fans into believing that my cartoon showed O. J. sodomizing a woman representing the United States. They didn't like the caption either. "Juice." Mostly the kind of people who, when a black man passes them on the street, clutch their purses. Rafiki showed up about ten minutes later. I could tell that Kraal had arrived. His Rolls Royce was double-parked in front of the building. The Giuliani no-tolerance policy didn't apply to people of his class. I was looking out over the Hudson River when he entered his office. It had a lot of curvy furniture and abstract paintings. People who couldn't draw. There were photos on the wall in which he was posing with celebrities. A couple of presidents. Movie stars. Hip-hoppers. He entered his office abruptly. Didn't say hello or nothin'. Ignored me. Went over to his desk and started examining papers. He carried a bottle of mineral water. "We're going to start airing your cartoons again," he said, finally, without looking up.

"But Sebastian said—"

"Forget about him. The suspension has ended." He lit a cigar.

"Is that all?"

"We want you to return the harmless old Koots Badger. Get away from the O. J. stuff. Many of our viewers believe that the guy butchered those people. We're going to announce that 'Koots Badger' has returned from vacation."

"No deal. Everybody around here is anti-O. J. The guy is being framed and Ben Armstrong and I are the only ones standing up for O. J. I mean I guess you heard that the hair found on the glove found at the Rockingham estate belonged to a white man and—"

"Look. I'm not trying to convince you. But most of our readers believe that the guy is guilty. So do I. Your cartoons might have been in demand by the old viewer-sponsored crowd, but we're trying to attract a new upscale suburban audience with our product. They get sick of hearing about race all the time. And everybody is glad that we eliminated that black history weekend that was run on this station for years. A lot of crazy antiwhite junk. Conspiracy theorists, especially that nut who called white people ice people. Our gender-and-same-sex audience want to hear about *their* problems."

"Listen, why don't we just call it quits. Obviously, this arrangement isn't working. First Sebastian censors my stuff and then you're telling me that I'm not selling. You're treating me like something disposable. A nigger."

"There you go playing the race card. Don't get your feathers ruffled. People are tired of this Chaka Zulu shit. You should listen to Reverend Eugene Rivers."

"I don't have to take this. Young Brothers are talking about doing *Attitude the Badger* as an animated series. I could always do animated cartoons for the art crowd. It's obvious that I'm wasting my time around here." I was bluffing. I rose to leave.

"Suit yourself." He didn't even look up as I exited from his office, slamming the door. I thought he'd ask me to reconsider. Shit. I really blew it. What was I going to do now? It took me about an hour to gather my things. Once downstairs, I found that Rafiki had already heard the news and told me that he had orders not to give me any more car service. I had to take the subway back downtown. No sooner had I entered my studio than my cell phone rang. It was Jonathan Kraal.

"OKAY look, I'll give you a raise." He sounded urgent. Hyper.

"You what?"

"I said, I'll give you a raise. Just name your price."

"But you just said—"

"Forget what I said." He told me the details of the new deal. Not only would he give me a raise, but I'd only have to draw once a month instead of weekly. Both his detractors and supporters were used to calling him an enigma. That was an understatement. But there was a catch. The O. J. cartoons would no longer be part of the television newscasts. They'd be placed on a blog that the KCAK was experimenting with. That would reduce my viewership. Berkeley Breathed, the Pulitzer Prize-winning cartoonist and children's book author, said that comics would be left behind when newspapers go fully digital. He acknowledged that there will always be graphic humor around, but "the last cartoon character to have been invented that will have been a household name was *Calvin and Hobbes*."

Breathed said his readership was 60 million to 70 million people in 1985, when *Peanuts* had a readership of 200 million to 300 million and *Calvin and Hobbes*, 200 million people. "That will never happen on the Web. Your readership drops to a couple thousand people—maybe, if you're lucky, 10,000."

The Web has a dedicated viewership, he explained, meaning a reader has to type in the name of a strip to go to it that day. "You are no longer a found delight," he said. "You are a dedicated delight. And that's what changes the readership." That night I had a dream that Koots Badger was dreaming that Opus had been killed and that I was now going to kill him. I wasn't going to kill him, only continue his suspension.

25

MAY 14, 1995

The County of Los Angeles's District Attorney's Office. Two suits were discussing the Simpson case:

— You see old man Brown on Geraldo's last night? I could kiss the guy.

— Yeah. Called O. J. a monster and said that it was the defense team that turned him into a monster.

— Said that he was an animal who was eating his young. Great stuff.

— Maybe the defense won't call Sydney. Geraldo said that if they called the Simpson kid, it would do irreparable harm to the criminal justice system in the public's eyes.

— Irreparable? That PR said *irreparable*?

— He went to law school.

— Boy, the Goldmans and the Browns are doing a great job. Going on TV and crying. That Denise is a great crier. Fat Tony said so, too. [*They cackle. Evilly.*]

— Can you imagine. You think that the *Inquirer* is right. That she's fucking Fat Tony.

— Who cares? Those families are doing more to win this case than this fucking prosecution team we're stuck with. Every time they bawl and cry on the talk shows they're influencing public opinion and if we get a hung jury, they're prepping the civil jury that will do the job in sending this nigger's ass to the can for the rest of his fucking nigger days.

— Why do you think that Garcetti decided to try it downtown among the woolies any way?

— He's one of these responsible conservatives. If it weren't for Fuhrman, the guy wouldn't have a case at all. Too bad that Hodgman got sick. Fucking Darden and Clark are blowing it. That McVeigh fellow. I don't agree with what he did. But he's standing up for a whole lot of white guys. They got these woolies and these bitches taking our jobs. As for Garcetti. The guy is half Wetback. Probably has some nigger genes. He's worse than those two.

— Don't look at me. It was this affirmative action shit that got Darden and Clark in here.

— That bitch is on permanent PMS. She's turning the jury off with her outbursts. She's hysterical—

— Shhhhhh. We're not supposed to say that around here. [*They both laugh.*]

— Yeah and that Darden. Said he was sick of law. What a fucking wuss. He says we're giving Marcia all the good direct examinations and he's left with the shit work. Says he's beginning to be hated by his own people. Hates the day he was born to have to defend a piece of crud like Fuhrman.

— Fuck his ass. If it were up to me there'd be no more niggers around here. Be glad when Pete Wilson is elected President. Get these niggers out of our hair.

— Yeah, well if he becomes president, the chief will get a promotion. He plans to ride this O. J. nigger's ass right into the Governor's mansion.

— Well I won't be around for that campaign. Plan to join Fuhrman up in Idaho. Niggers know what they get if they show their black behinds up there. I'm taking early retirement. In the old days, when the guys ran things it was okay. Now they're making us do this rainbow shit.

— You're telling me.

> Dr. Sathyavagiswaran [Los Angeles Coroner] conceded he could not, without any degree of medical certainty, say how many people were responsible for the murders or whether only one single-edged knife was used in the attacks.
>
> —CourtTV content: Developments in the murder trial of O. J. Simpson from June 12–16, 1995

26

JUNE 12–16, 1995

The Haitian graffiti artist who went by the professional name of Crazy Goat began banging on the walls. Trying to get me to stop making noise. I was screaming. "The gloves didn't fit. The gloves didn't fit." I kept yelling. I had to share this with someone. I ran downstairs. I opened the door upon his half-awake face. The odor of cat manure almost knocked me down. Some naked blonde jumped up from a dirty mattress and ran into the bathroom. Narrow, bony ass. "What's wrong, mahn," he asked.

"The gloves didn't fit."

Marcia Clark looked stupefied. Chris Darden looked as though he were about to burst into tears. He was obviously stunned. He had fallen for F. Lee Bailey's trap and had asked Simpson to try on the gloves found at Rockingham. Nothing that the pro-prosecution networks, ABC and CBS, who tried to play it down, or the *New York Times*, which quoted pro-prosecution legal expert Laura Levinson, who tried to say that the gloves fit, snugly, could diminish my glee. (In 2008, O. J. stalker Laura Levinson says about the

Las Vegas trial of O. J., to some, a legal shame and disgrace like the civil trial, we can get him like the feds got Capone, on a lesser charge like, in Capone's case, tax evasion.) It was clear to people all over the world who watched the demonstration that the gloves didn't fit. Attorney Roy Black said that the gloves didn't fit. If the gloves, which were said to have belonged to the murderer, didn't fit, then O. J. wasn't the murderer. Few in the media recall that when the gloves were first introduced, O. J. Simpson turned to one of his lawyers and muttered, "They look too small."

Stays in Vegas

"Look, Bear, calm down." Crazy Goat was one of these artists who were pouring into New York from the Caribbean hoping to become the next big primitive to be adopted by the uptown galleries. He was wearing the usual dreadlocks. He painted, dressed in a black three piece pinstriped suit and walked around in his bare feet like he'd seen in the picture of Jean-Michel Basquiat, this poor Haitian who gave Andy Warhol's career a blood transfusion, the traditional role of black artists in the United States. Providing white artists with inspiration, like something bred so that its body organs might be donated to someone important, the possible role of blacks and Hispanics in the twenty-first century.

"Mahn, you letting this case get to you."

"But, don't you see the prosecution has lost the case."

"They'll get him, mahn. If it takes a lifetime, they'll get him."

"You don't understand. If he's acquitted he goes free." He laughed.

"You don't know the Jews."

"Come again?"

"If O. J. is acquitted, the Jews—reporters, commentators, and lawyers—will gang up on him. They'll get him for Goldman."

"That's preposterous. They're not even talking about Goldman. He's the forgotten victim of this tragedy. Besides, what about the Italians who were or would be on Simpson's case? Garcetti, Bugliosi, Petrocelli, and the Jews who were defending him? Shapiro, Neufeld, Scheck?" Chris Darden referred to Neufeld and Scheck as "those people from New York."

"That's because they think that the murder of Nicole will be enough to kill Simpson, but if he gets off, watch out. The Jews won't rest until they get Simpson for Goldman's murder."

"You've been reading *The Final Call* too much."

"Oh, is that so? Well, you can't see the light because you're married to a Jew." I approached him. Collared him.

"Okay, Mahn. Okay. Calm down."

"You say another word about my wife, and it'll be me and you." Besides, my wife's not Jewish, she's a Gypsy, I started to say. But fuck it, what's the use. The blonde came out of the bathroom dressed. They had a few words in private. She took some money from her purse and gave it to him. She kissed the Haitian and exited.

"Calm down, Bear. You forget that I'm a Jew, too," he said, without looking away from his canvas. He took a drag from his reefer. His eyes were jaundiced, indicating a liver problem. The black dreads crowded his face. There were White Castle bags on the floor. He didn't look as though he followed a healthy diet.

"O. J. didn't do it," he said, finally. This smoke must have been strong because after inhaling a second time, his legs wobbled and his pupils seemed to sink.

"What do you mean?"

"Nicole sealed her doom when she slapped the Jamaican sister. They'll never find the killers because the killers are dead. Been dead. The killers were undead. Duppies killed Nicole. The Jamaican maid put a curse on her."

There had been a report that Nicole Simpson had slapped a Jamaican housekeeper, indicating that she could give as well as take. I figured that the guy had toked up on too much ganja.

"So, Bro. Bear. How much they paying you for those silly cartoons?" I ignored the dig. I'd remembered that the guy had survived a battle with hepatitis.

"They pay me enough."

"Before long, I'll be bringing in some big bucks."

I looked up at one of his works. A direct rip-off from Basquiat, but only cruder. Big bucks. That's a laugh, I thought.

"Yeah, right. Look, I got to go."

I went back upstairs and spent about an hour e-mailing Bat, Snakes, and Rabbit. I e-mailed the news to Otter. We were all delighted that the gloves didn't fit. We thought that this would be the end of it. We thought.

27

JUNE 10, 1995

Scott Simon and Daniel Schorr praised a U.S. pilot, who successfully hid from some Bosnian combatants, as a hero in a heroless age. Antiheroes for them were O. J. Simpson, Mike Tyson, and Magic Jackson. Simon corrected Schorr. He apparently meant Magic Johnson, but Michael Jackson was on his mind.

Two years later, July 5th, 1997, Schorr and Simon cast Jimmy Stewart as the hero and Mike Tyson the antihero. During December of 1999, Scott Simon and Roger Rappaport chuckled over NFL player Lawrence Taylor's trouble with the law during a review of Oliver Stone's *Any Given Sunday*. They attempted to show how superior their tastes were to Stone's. Simon complained about Stone's problem with women. At NPR, where women were suing over work discrimination.

For awhile in 1995, the first three stories on the news were Commerce Secretary Ron Brown's ethical problems, O. J., and Colin Ferguson. Colin Ferguson was the black man who killed a number of passengers on the Long Island railway.

Snakes wants to know why my O. J. cartoons have been removed from KCAK broadcasts and are only appearing on the station's experimental blog, receiving only about a thousand hits per week. I tell him that they wanted to eliminate my cartoons altogether but my fans called in and complained about their absence. This led Kraal to back down. I'm lying.

The car was taking me to the Kraal Towers, the headquarters of Kraal enterprises. The traffic that day was worse than Madrid's at three P.M. on Mondays. When I reached the office, I was sorry that I decided to go in. It was June 12, 1995, the first anniversary of the killings. Princessa was wearing one of those Nicole Simpson Guardian Angel pins. She was watching the trial. It was being carried on a portable TV set that had been placed on her desk. I wondered how much of the estimated twenty-seven billion dollars in productivity, lost because of the O. J. trial, was traceable to women who have wigged out over O. J. Why do women write fan mail to serial killers and even marry them in prison? Princessa knew that I was standing there but she took her own good time noticing me. I guess this comes under the heading of passive aggression that some whites practice against blacks each day. Like you're in a store and you're next in line after a white customer and it's your turn and the white clerk, instead of attending to you, does some task, or begins a conversation with another clerk, or, sometimes, just disappears all together. By 2009, in New York it got even worse. Colonial-minded African immigrants service whites first no matter what position a black person might have in line. The retail profiling of traditional African Americans was also passed on to them. "Tokina came by." She began to pin one of the things on me.

Get that shit off of me, I started to say, but then I remembered the good butt whipping that her brothers had dealt Armstrong who was still out on disability.

"Ms. Torres, I don't wish to participate, thank you."

Princessa formed a wicked smile. "You of all people should be wearing one—after all, one of your black brothers did it." She looked down at Princessa for approval and the approval was given with a nod.

"Why don't you do something useful, Ms. Torres? Lend a hand to the millions of your fellow sisters who can't afford cable.

"Anyway, why are you mourning some party people? People who spent all day in the gym and all night on the Disco floor. Who leech off of men. Gigolos who leech off of women who leech off of men. I find it insufferably tasteless for you to mourn this party girl after the Oklahoma bombing. What about those forgotten victims? And what about all of the Latinas who get murdered and battered all year around? Why don't you do something for them?" She criticized Latinas for asking for handouts like blacks. She was despised by the Hispanic community. She was in the ethnic pariah business for which there was a lot of white money and support. An ethnic pariah was a person who got sympathy checks and rewards from whites by blaming their ostracism from their ethnic fellows on the basis of their taking brave stands against the prevailing opinions of these communities, before white audiences.

They hold vigils for Nicole Simpson and Ron Goldman at various places around Los Angeles. But this is more than mourning. It takes on aspects of a lynching. Posted to some trees is the sign "Guilty," according to Charles Rosenberg, a commentator on E-Network.

"Nicole Simpson stood for all of us. What happened to her has happened to women throughout the century. What *if* she had sex with other men, and partied? O. J. didn't own her."

"She was a good mother to her children," Princessa said.

"A good mother to her children? Get serious," I replied. "What kind of mother would give some guy a blow—I mean, perform unconventional sexual practices while her children are upstairs? And what kind of mother would have old nasty Faye Resnick in her house? A druggie who used her home to stash her supply." Nicole said that Resnick's crowd scared her. Judge Burt Katz, who, with Ira Reiner and Dominick Dunne, became a media hero for his insistence upon Simpson's guilt, said that Faye Resnick would have made a good witness during the criminal trial. "Look at her body language," he said.

"You don't know that. You don't have any proof of that. Judge Ito isn't even going to let that in. Besides, why are you so disparaging of white women? You're married to one. Are you saying that all of the white women in the world are no good except yours? Your child is half white. Do you hate her?" She really got me there. Over the years I'd received crude, ugly letters from people, mostly black women, about how could I be a black militant and be married to a white woman. At first, I'd respond that most of those who comment about black issues are married to white women: George Will, Pat Buchanan, William Bennett, and even immigrant intellectual mercenaries like Dinesh D'Souza, for example. Are they saying that a white man married to a white woman had more freedom to discuss issues of race than a black, and what did being married to Esther have to do with the facts that I was offering? But that didn't work. Jeffrey Toobin had told his readers that it wouldn't work. After I got diabetes I'd answer such letters with one line, asking the letter writers, "When's the last time that you had your hemoglobin checked?"

"Leave my family out of this."

"Oh, I see. Nicole and Faye are no good, but your white woman is different. What makes her so different?" She was rotating her head like the actress in *The Exorcist*. Princessa was enjoying this. The newsroom was silent as Kraal employees stopped working on their laptops. They were taking it all in.

"What goes on between my wife and me has nothing to do with this case."

"It has everything to do with the case. You and O. J. married white women because you have an Othello complex."

"An Othello complex, huh? Well, there is a theory that Othello was based upon a black Moorish King of Spain. Maybe a distant ancestor of yours." She really went off then. Cussing me out in Spanish. These white-looking Hispanics go off on you when you hint at the possibility that they might have African or Indian ancestors. Victor Cruz and Miguel Algarin, Alejandro Murgia and Rudy Anaya might own up to the black heritage of Hispanics, but many of them don't. They spend a lot of time bleaching themselves and straightening their hair in order to look "fair." Princessa Bimbette was enjoying our argument so much she'd lit up a cigarette and had turned off the television set. Hearing the raised voices, Sebastian Lord slammed his office door and returned to his phone conversation.

"What the hell's going on?" Kraal asked on the other end of the line.

"The usual race and gender clash. If it were up to me I'd fire both of them. Merit should be the only determining factor in our hiring practices. Can't you pay him off? Do we really need his crude cartoons? The one he submitted about O. J. sodomizing America was a stretch. I'm British. And even I'm offended."

"What are you worried about? He'll disappear into a blog, never to be heard from again. Let him cool off. I suggested that he return to doing Badger, this harmless inoffensive, old, cranky pest. It was your idea to have him do the O. J. stuff. Now he's got his hackles up. Coming on like Sharpton or somebody. Sticking with his brother man. Not only that. I'm under pressure to keep him on. You know that."

"But I'm the station manager. I felt that I had the right to—. The old man?"

"Yeah. He insists that I keep him on."

"I'll be glad when he's—"

"So will I. But for now, he controls fifty-one percent of the company. And forget about his disappearing from the scene anytime soon. They gave him six months to live. That was ten years ago. He's ninety-five now."

28

Denise Brown is on Larry King's show for an hour. King protects her from a caller who asks why she sold photos of the Simpson kids to *Life* magazine. King, who has come under sexual harassment charges himself, is very gallant toward women who come on to muddy the reputation of black men. In 1997, he ran interference for Anita Hill, who never brought a complaint of sexual harassment against Clarence Thomas while working for him, and followed the man from job to job.

During a later appearance, Ms. Brown says that the *Life* magazine photographer tricked her family. That she just wants to protect Sydney and Justin. Many of the authors, who've made millions from the murder, express philanthropic attitudes toward Sydney and Justin. Faye D. Resnick, author of *Nicole Simpson: The Private Diary of a Life Interrupted*, says that she's giving some money to the kids. Her book has made thirty million dollars. Marc Eliot, author of *Kato Kaelin: The Whole Truth*, also says he's giving money to the kids. After the civil trial, Tammy Bruce and Gloria Allred, separated at birth from Robin Blake, and Denise Brown begin a drive to recall the judge who gave custody of Sydney and Justin to O. J. Hypocrites all over America pretend to be concerned about the fate of these two black children while the country has cast millions of black children off the AFDC rolls. By 2001, millions are cut off from welfare.

In *The Los Angeles Times*, Chris Darden elicits the sympathy of some of the white media experts with a real lachrymose spiel about how he wants to quit law and how the trial has been a disgrace, but he doesn't mean that the prosecution is a disgrace, oh no, not them, but the other people are a disgrace and one media expert says it's a shame that a black prosecutor can't prosecute a black defendant and black juries are so biased that they can't convict a black criminal, yet the jails are full of black people, making me wonder who's putting them there. A man who breeds unicorns? Upper-class white-male media experts say that Mexican-Italian American Gil Garcetti should have had the case tried in Santa Monica, the implication being that only a white jury can be fair. (With the Civil Trial, they get their wish). Ira Reiner and Gloria Allred agree. In the civil suit, Fred Goldman says that he wants "a proper jury," and Daniel Petrocelli, who is called by the anti-O. J. press the greatest lawyer since Clarence Darrow, when, given the fact that half the jury were white women, and most of the jurors thought Simpson to be guilty, even before the trial opened, his winning the civil case was a simple layup. He instructs the all-white jury to "even the score," yet nobody accuses him of playing the race card. Ron Shipp's lawyer, Robert McNeill, says that presumptions should not have been made about the mostly black jury, nor should there be presumptions made about the Santa Monica jury that might be largely Jewish. That no one is predictable and incapable of seeing both sides. Avoid inflammatory persuasion from lawyers. Understand DNA.

What is the proper jury for the O. J. haters? Maybe the white jury that called some blacks "chimpanzees" during a Florida case which had to be retried because of the white jurors' remarks. Clarence J. Munford, author of *Race and Reparations: A Black Perspective for the 21st Century*, observed: "When a black couple in Florida sued an insurance company in 1992, after they had been hurt in a car accident, the all-white jury compared them to chimpanzees with drug dealers for children." Maybe this is the kind of proper jury Mr. Goldman, sometimes heckled as a gold digger, had in mind.

29

I'm really angry tonight. I'm having evil thoughts about the media. Forbidden thoughts. I turn on the TV to KCAK and there is Princessa Bimbette, and Simon Fansworth, and this weasel carries on about how he had to leave Hollywood in disgrace and how now he's called upon to give the gossip about O. J., much of it of a sexual nature. Dominick Dunne said that Nancy Reagan and Elizabeth Taylor, women with raging libidos, requested that he brief them weekly about the case. Even the Pope and Boris Yeltsin were interested.

Princessa is screaming and yelling at a caller and saying that O. J. should have the autopsy pictures rubbed into his face to show him the horrible crime that he has committed and Simon Fansworth agrees with her. Her face becomes one big set of teeth. She totally wigs out on the caller, who says that it might be more complicated. The Britisher, Fansworth, wears a smirk. His face features some big space-creature eyes. He is an "extra man" for New York's old money crowd, someone to sit next to a billionaire at one of their parties, or be a walker for a society dame.

Their show is broadcast during the hour when Jerry Bareheart, former station manager, used to have something uplifting on, John Cage, Meredith Monk, James Baldwin or an interview with Joe Heller or Kurt Vonnegut, or some Alvin Ailey dancers, or some Pueblo dancers from the Southwest, Jim Pepper, the Neville Brothers, or Carla Blank discussing early Judson. This was when the station was viewer-sponsored. But now KCAK has to pay its way. Must subject itself to free market forces. Free market. That's a laugh. Corporate Socialism is what we have here. The government bails out Wall Street from its bad loans to third-world countries and in 2009, as a result of Wall Street greed, the country is on the verge of bankruptcy and just as black mayors were elected when the cities became broke, a black man is elected to rescue "white America," an almost impossible task. The taxpayers have to pay a trillion. The free marketers demand that their congressional whores provide them with tariffs and protection. I wonder how long the black president of KCAK, Renaldo Louis, can take it. If things continue the way they are now, he'll soon be out hustling cigarette and liquor ads. When the blacks ask him about Virginia Saturday, and the constant interviewing of blacks about teenage pregnancy and dope and crime and drugs, he says that he sees his mandate as that of raising capital for the station, now that it needs more corporate underwriters in order to survive. Again, he says that editorial content is none of his business.

30

The defense scores some big points during the week ending June 3, 1995. Barry Scheck, whom Ito despises, is able to draw out the fact that the blood on the back fence at Bundy is less degraded than that found earlier on the path leading away from the scene. This might buttress the defense's theory that the blood was planted. The media still ridicules the defense's theory. These middle-class men who dominate MSM find it incredible that the police would plant evidence. As William C. Thompson, Professor in the Department of Criminology, Law & Society at University of California, Irvine wrote in his article on "DNA Evidence in the O. J. Simpson Trial":

> O. J. Simpson's blood was planted on the back gate. Most of the blood samples from the crime scene were collected on June 13, 1994, the day after the murders; but the three blood stains on the rear gate were not collected

until July 3, 1994. According to the prosecution account, these stains were simply missed during the initial collection and were only noticed later. According to the defense account, these stains were not collected the day after the crime because they were not there at that time. The defense offered a powerful piece of evidence to support the planting theory. A photograph taken the day after the crime shows no blood in the area of the rear gate where the largest and most prominent stain was later found.

Princessa Bimbette is on the defense's case every night. The ratings for the O. J. show—during which she makes sarcastic remarks about the defense and calls O. J. a butcher and other loathsome names—have soared, to the delight of Kraal and his stockholders. Her voice is just as flaying on the nerves as her opinions. High-pitched, and laced with an offensive nasality. She sounds like Laura Ingraham.

D.A.'s office, Los Angeles County:

— Those fucking idiots. Fell right into that slick tricky nigger, Cochran's trap.

— Is that why you didn't invite Marcia in on the meeting called to decide how we're going to regroup after Cochran and Shapiro made fools of us—? She's pissed.

— Let her be pissed. If only Hodgeman hadn't gotten sick. We wouldn't have had these two yo-yos trying the case.

— Did you see Simpson as he approached the jury? Swaggered right up there and put those gloves right in front of their faces. They're too small, he kept saying.

— I'd like to put his ass on a stick and slowly revolve him over a hot flame. Rotisserie that black nigger. He made a fool of us. The niggers on the jury are bound to acquit him now.

Princessa tries to make light of the gloves not fitting O. J. She spends the rest of the show ignoring this development and instead lambastes Michael Jackson and his new record. When she's not doing Jackson, it's Mike Tyson, Clarence Thomas, etc.

31

Fred Graham, courtly, silver-haired commentator for Court TV, says that O. J.'s affluence may have led to his undoing. He has assumed that the Italian shoes whose prints were found at the crime scene belonged to O. J. Simpson. Graham's themes throughout the trial are whether a defendant who is not as wealthy as Simpson could have gotten such a trial and his disbelief that anybody would buy into a conspiracy against Simpson. Commentator Robert Pugsley says, sarcastically, even after the Fuhrman revelations, that the defense team seems to want to blame everybody for engaging in a conspiracy against Simpson, even the president. Commentator Robert Pugsley also has a thing about Marcia Clark having bodily contact with Johnnie Cochran, who another commentator says is more villainous than the killer, by whom he meant O. J.

Pugsley doesn't say anything about the back massages that Marcia gives to Chris Darden. In his book, Dominick Dunne complains about Marcia Clark's flirting with Cochran. After the case is over, San Francisco columnists report that Clark and Darden checked in at the same hotels, apparently to soothe each other from the emotional scars that had been inflicted by the trial. A few days later, we discover that a salesman from Bloomingdale's can't verify whether O. J. bought the Bruno Magli shoes, size 12. There is no receipt for the purchase of shoes that O. J. called "ugly-assed."

The defense claims that all that the prosecution has established is that both the killer and Simpson wore the same size shoe, 12, which is the size that fits nine percent of the population. Millions of people. On February 13, 1999, Marcia Clark appears as a host on Geraldo Rivera's show. She says of the Clinton sexual harassment case that suspicions are aroused when someone comes forth with evidence late. She's talking about Secret Service agent Louis Fox, who tells a newspaper that Monica Lewinsky and President Clinton met alone in the Oval Office. Mr. Fox comes forth late with this eyewitness. Well, isn't that what happened in the O. J. civil case? Someone coming forth late to show Simpson photographs of him wearing what are purportedly Bruno Magli shoes? She also says on the same show that if a witness is caught in one lie during a case, then the jury has a right to reject the witness's entire testimony, under California law, but she has ridiculed the jury in the criminal trial for doing the same thing, rejecting Fuhrman's testimony because he lied.

32

One night we found out why Louis stalked out of the restaurant after having been shouted at by Kraal. The two guys were hosts of *Nigguz News*. The network had provided them with cameras and audio equipment with which they recorded all of the activities among African Americans that sent their ratings soaring, the way O. J.'s alleged murder of a blonde had. Charles Grodin had confessed that because of poor ratings he was badgered into doing O. J. shows by Roger Ailes, an ex-Bush campaign manager and one of the authors of the infamous Willie Horton commercial. The O. J. coverage was inspired by how the Willie Horton campaign had played, the latter having contributed to a dramatic rise of twenty percent among southern voters for Bush, just as O. J. had snatched millions of eyeballs for CNBC. And so the viewers of *Nigguz News* had been treated to the dreary interviews of black people down on their luck. Poor unwed mothers, crack addicts, people living in abandoned buildings, and the whole tangle of pathologies. It ended with a black teenager boasting about how many girls he'd gotten pregnant. (At NPR there must be a prize for the producer of the smarmiest story about black life. In February 1998, the prize went to a NPR station in Wilmington, Delaware. They discovered a black mother with five out-of-wedlock children.) His interviewers, Jagid and Jagan, snickered through their gold teeth and their laughter showed some kind of metal object on their tongues as the teenager produced his narrative, guaranteed to massage suburban vanity and give yuppies an opportunity to practice their Ebonics. These stories also stimulate the nucleus accumbens of white blue collar people: I may be a miserable cipher, a wage slave who can be downsized on any day, with very little by the way of savings and capital but at least I'm not black. But Richard Wright had been among those writers who'd made this observation before. The scene in his great, underrated book, *The Outsider*, when Cross Damon transforms himself into a minstrel black in order to obtain a dead man's identity. He amuses the white clerks with his dullwittedness, in that way achieving his ends while boosting the egos of these run-of-the mill white supremacists. Members of the Master Race.

3 3

Everybody in the station could hear Renaldo's raised voice coming from Kraal's office. It was the morning after the second installment of *Nigguz News*. This segment included the testimonies by black men convicted of rape. They were interviewed by Jagid and Jagan. Some were shown in prison, others were still at large, and unlike whites who are interviewed under similar circumstances, their voices and faces were not pixilated out in order to disguise their identities. Special emphasis was placed upon those rapists whose victims were white.

It even angered Renaldo whom we all felt would drink a glass of pus if Kraal requested. He was one of these nonconfrontational blacks. He didn't want to sound too '60s. He was moderate and quiet-spoken. He, unlike Rabbit, Snakes (well, maybe not Snakes), Bat, and me, wasn't used to bopping people over the head with a whole bunch of angry rhetoric. He strode calmly into Kraal's office.

"Statistics show that most rape victims are assaulted by members of the same race. *Nigguz News* argues that rape is exclusively a black male problem. It's a canard." Sebastian Lord sat on a sofa alternately smirking and sneering.

"There you go again with your fucking statistics. You sound like that opportunist Al Sharpton. You saw the newspapers this morning. These men scored higher on the Neilson's than any show in this station's history. Our stockholders and advertisers are happy. Why can't you get with the program, Renaldo, for crying out loud? Besides, your job as president is to sell the station to advertisers. Not to interfere with the editorial part," Kraal said, glancing at Sebastian and winking.

"He's jealous," Sebastian replied. "He knows that with these guys and others like them that the days of Bryant Gumbel, and these other rich showcase Negroes, are numbered. These kids represent what blacks really are like. He's being defensive. Trying to blame us for telling the truth about African Americans. What do you want to do? Kill us because we're the messengers?"

Both Lord and Kraal laughed. "Besides," Lord continued, "blacks use the word *nigger*, yet when we use it we're accused of racism. I've heard Jagid and Jagan refer to each other as 'my nigger.'"

"The pickets outside don't see it that way. They booed me when I entered the station this morning. I was embarrassed," Renaldo said.

"You let those hotheads bother you. OK. I'll tell you what. We'll issue . . . a statement." Kraal rises from the chair behind his desk and begins to pace the room as he begins to think out loud. "Something like, we're sorry that people misinterpreted the title of our show,

Nigguz News, and were offended. It wasn't our intention to offend anybody. As for those race-card blacks who seek to put whites on a guilt trip, no apology is necessary. Think that's enough?"

"Thanks J. K. I was sure that if I came in here and reasoned with you, you'd take action. I just think that we ought to have standards," Renaldo said. Lord and Kraal exchanged some sarcastic smiles.

"Don't worry about these guys, Jagid and Jagan. They're no threat to you. We'll try to tone down the future episodes of *Nigguz News*. Feature more middle-class Negroes. Like yourself. We know that it's all about class. That you and middle-class blacks like you have more in common with Sebastian and me than with those over-breeding underclass people in the inner city." Renaldo is mollified.

Kraal reassures Renaldo about Nigguz News

Lord rose and began to escort Renaldo from the room.

"Anytime you have some problems or something that you want to get off your chest, just drop in. By the way, is everything all right? How's your mother? Maybe she can come here and work for us one day. We can always use another good lawyer."

"I'll pass the message on to her, Jonathan. Listen, I'm sorry that I lost my temper at the restaurant."

"Forget it, Renaldo. We all have our off days." Escorting him from the office, Kraal had his arm around Renaldo's shoulder, while looking back at Lord, who winked. After the door shut, Lord and Kraal roared with laughter. Lord even mimicked Renaldo. "I'm sorry that I lost my temper at the restaurant." They laughed louder.

34

On June 26, I spent the weekend at the Sheraton Miramar in Santa Monica. The black concierge guy insisted that I get a room with a view of the ocean. He said that they were always assigning blacks to rooms in the corner. There was some business I had to attend to and I welcomed the opportunity to be near the Pacific. I also dug walking along the boardwalk and Santa Monica Boulevard. For a guy like me, standing on the mountain in Costa Rica, from where you could see both the Atlantic and Pacific, would be my idea of a lifelong ambition. I arrive at LAX on the day that the *New York Daily News* had been given a scoop by either the prosecution or the police. Ever since Michelle Caruso, abandoning her journalistic objectivity, said that she was glad that there were nine women on the jury, meaning that she thinks O. J. should be convicted on the grounds of domestic violence, the LAPD had been leaking to Caruso like a sieve. Her paper says that O. J.'s hair is on Goldman's shirt, and on the knit cap, Nicole's hair is on the gloves and the knit cap fibers from the Bronco are on the knit cap, and Goldman's hair is on both gloves. Everybody forgets that the black hairs in the cap were dyed and that O. J.'s barber reported that she didn't dye his hair. The hair found at the crime scene was also full of dandruff. O. J.'s hair was dandruff-free. Besides, a blonde hair belonging to none of the parties was found at the murder scene. These are among other unexplained hairs—none of which belong to Goldman, Simpson, or Nicole—that were found at Bundy and at Rockingham. But the defense has explanations for this, too. They say that the LA police department's crime lab is a cesspool, therefore all of this forensic evidence that seems to incriminate O. J. is a matter of garbage in and garbage out.

I'm sitting in a restaurant called Ralph's, located on the Third Street Promenade in Santa Monica. The clams and linguine are swell and the waitress, having forgotten my wine order, gives me one on the house.

I want to be away from O. J. but as with millions of Americans he has his hooks into me, I can't help myself. I watch some of the proceedings on KTLA TV Channel 6. Their expert is Al DeBlanc, who is so biased against the defense that it ain't funny. KTLA itself is so pro-prosecution one suspects that its feed originates from the district attorney's office. Unlike the other pro-prosecution experts and reporters, at least he owns up to his connection to the LA police. He was a former sergeant.

Michael Knox, a juror, has published a book about his experiences. It follows the publisher's line that O. J. is guilty. Says that he'd made up his mind about O. J.'s guilt even before the DNA was introduced. He plays to feminist sales by saying that it was the domestic violence evidence that did it for him, even though he was ousted from the jury as a result of his having abused a woman. His testimony gives the CBS morning show an excuse to titillate the audience with that 911 tape again. Plays to the white lynch mob theory that if blacks don't come in with a guilty verdict, it doesn't mean that O. J. is innocent. It means that the races are divided. What about all of the whites who say that O. J. is innocent? Have they defected to the black race? And what about the blacks who believe in his guilt? Have they discovered Dr. Junius Crookmore's formula and become white? On March 18, 1998, O'Reilly, one of Rupert Murdoch's attack pundits, of "The O'Reilly Report," puts former ambassador Andrew Young through some grilling about O. J. and Clinton, "the O. J. president." (In March, Mary Matalin refers to O. J.'s lawyer F. Lee Bailey when discussing Clinton's reaction to "allegations of sexual misconduct.") O'Reilly uses Young to chastise African Americans for their irrational and "emotional" responses to the O. J. trial, many of them holding him innocent of the crimes. O'Reilly says that he knows that O. J. is guilty because he covered the trial. In 2009, O'Reilly is accused by some of having encouraged the murder of a doctor who performed abortions.

His colleague, Glenn Beck, turns up as a reference used by a white supremacist, Richard Poplawski, who murdered three Pittsburgh policemen. (Weeks before his deadly shooting spree, Poplawski uploaded a video clip of Beck ominously referencing the FEMA camps on Fox News.) He wanted to protest the Zionist Occupation Government, language right out of the ultraright's playbook, *The Turner Diaries*, yet none of the "mainstream" journalists notice this source. Gossip has it that O'Reilly likes golden showers.

The late Dr. Paula Gunn Allen wanted to know why Native Americans weren't being polled about Simpson's guilt. (Good idea. O. J. certainly looks Native American to me; his family comes from Shreveport, Louisiana. Home of the Caddo Nation. Could be. Why doesn't Geraldo insist that the Hispanic Race be polled? Dr. Bruce Weir, the prosecution witness, said that the concept of race is nonscientific. This in a trial during which Hispanics are referred to as a race.) I had to think about that one for a minute. Ira Reiner says that people who believe that O. J. is innocent are limited to those who cheered him as he rode in his infamous Bronco chase. He calls people who support Simpson's innocence "funny" people. For this attitude, Ira Reiner is rewarded with unlimited TV time on the O. J. prosecution panels.

35

The day after my arrival in Santa Monica, a black Mercedes limousine driven by a bald man with a European accent takes me to Young Brothers Studio in Burbank. We drive through the familiar neighborhoods of ticky tacks and palm trees. I meet for about half an hour with some black producers, who are about half my age, who say that they're really interested in doing *Attitude the Badger* as an animated cartoon. Nothing comes of it. I'm not surprised. *Huffington Post* blogger, Trey Ellis, says that though the media has reported a renaissance of young black male filmmakers, the whole operation is being run by fifty-year-old white men. But it was nice to get away for a few days.

The night before I leave L.A., I have a pizza at the Mezzaluna (now closed), the restaurant where Nicole had dinner before walking off into myth. The waiters are very courteous, which I didn't expect, thinking that O. J.'s trial might make this a hostile place for black men. I say that I want everything on my pizza, even though it isn't on the menu, and the waiter accommodates. I could see this as a druggie hangout. I then walk to other places frequented by O. J., Nicole, and their entourages. Starbucks and a yogurt place.

The next morning, before I headed for the airport, I heard on the news that the Unabomber has threatened to blow up an airplane departing from LAX. My flight was delayed. I remained in the hotel and caught some of the trial. They have another criminalist on the stand. She admits under questioning that the gloves didn't shrink, one of the theories used by the anti-O. J. crowd to explain why the gloves found at O. J.'s estate didn't fit. She says that they measured the same on June 14, 1994, as they did on the day of her testimony. Little is made of this information by the shows that have argued that the gloves shrank. During the noontime news, the newscaster doesn't even mention it. Nor does David Margolick mention it in the June 29 edition of the *New York Times*.

The prosecution tries again to dirty Simpson's reputation by placing a mug shot with other photos on an exhibit. Darden admits that this is the prosecution's purpose. In one exchange, Darden approaches the defense table when the defendant is trying on the pair of gloves. O. J. says, "Go away." His defense lawyers laugh. Darden shoots back, "I'll laugh when the jury comes back," yet, later, Darden says that he knew he'd lose the case when the composition of the jury was determined. Who played the race card? The defense? Or the DA who hired a black lawyer when they found that the defense would have black lawyers on its team?

July 31, 1995—Blood expert Herbert MacDonnell testified for the defense Monday that there was blood on the inside of a sock found in O. J. Simpson's bedroom. He said, in his opinion, the blood got on the inside of the sock when blood was pressed through the fabric on the opposite side with no foot in the sock.

36

Upon returning to New York, I decided that I'd stay for a few days at our uptown condo. I would have to brave the glares and contempt from my father-in-law who not only rejected me but his daughter when she married me. I was reminded of a black World War II veteran who said that some of those people in Europe, devastated by the war, would pleasure you for a quarter, but when they came over here, they'd call you a nigger. Karl Marx called some of these people "ethnic garbage." When Esther opened the door, I had prepared some remarks, but I was so astonished by the way she was dressed that I forgot what I was going to say. What the—? She'd been to their favorite beach in the Hamptons and had gotten a suntan. Instead of the usually tasteful blacks-and-spare jewelry, she was weighed down with large earrings, jangling bracelets, and rings. She was wearing some kind of head scarf and a long gaudy dress with some sort of busy decorations. I looked over her shoulder to see some packed luggage. She was heavily made up—mascara, eye shadow, etc.

"What's going on?"

"I've contacted my surviving relatives. I'm flying to Spain in three hours."

"What?"

"You're always talking about your fucking roots. Now I'm going to find mine."

"You're going to do what?"

"Look, I don't have time to argue."

"Your roots—" I began to laugh. I couldn't stop laughing.

"Oh, it's OK for you blacks to have your own separate nation and even a national anthem, your red-green-and-black flag, but as soon as we white ethnics try to sort out ours, we're met by ridicule." I embraced her. "Look, I didn't mean—where is your dad?"

"I put him in a nursing home."

"Why?"

"One of Hibiscus' friends stopped by. I wasn't home. She wasn't aware that Hibiscus had gone to California. I came back from shopping and found them together. They were on the couch, fucking. She couldn't have been more than twenty." We both laughed.

"So this means, we're through? I—"

"I just need to find myself. I still love you." I embraced her again. One thing led to another. I hadn't had sex since the trial began. Like the women who were polled by Entertainment Network, those who'd rather watch the trial than have sex, the O. J. trial was my sex. When I concluded, I trumpeted like an elephant. Esther drifted off to sleep and was soon snoring. But I couldn't sleep. I woke up. I turned on AMC. The movie was *Harvey*. It was about a man named Elwood P. Dowd and his imaginary friend Harvey, a six-foot, three-and-a-half-inch-tall rabbit. I saw the movie when it was released in 1950. But I was too young to understand the sharp satirical barbs at psychological theory that was becoming the vogue in the '50s. The psychologists at the institution where the character Dowd's sister is attempting to have him committed are fastened to Freudian dogma, and there's an orderly who roughs up his patients. They can't tell the difference between the person who desires to commit the sane relative and the sick relative. And so they commit his sister, temporarily. *His* sickness? He thinks that people should be pleasant to one another. A cab driver warns of the side effects of antidepressant drugs! (In September of 2009, Eli Lilly & Co., a dealer in antidepressant drugs, is convicted of running a criminal operation. They knew of the toxic effects of the drug Zyprexa.) In a film that reached the screen in 1950! Though from a family of means, Dowd betrays his class by inviting working-class people to dinner. And the final irony: the head of the institution begins to see the rabbit, too.

3 7

July 4. No O. J. today. The country's celebrating the Fourth of July. The Declaration of Independence created by those slaveholders and womanizers.

(Do you suppose that historian Jeff Rosen considered the response of the black listeners of KPFA radio when he discussed "The Majesty of Thomas Jefferson's 'Legacy?'") I'd always wondered what his contemporaries meant when they said that Hamilton was a debauch and, maybe, the illegitimate son of George Washington. I had smoked a half pack of cigarettes already even though I had sworn off cigarettes. By noon, I'd downed six cups of coffee. The diabetes instructor said that caffeine constricts the blood vessels. Does caffeine hamper the sugar control of people like me with type 2 diabetes? Yes and no.

> When the patients ingested caffeine, their average daily blood sugar levels went up by 8 percent. After meals, their

blood sugar levels rose even higher, shooting up as much as 26% after dinner.

However, the data don't necessarily mean that people with diabetes or at risk for it should stop drinking coffee. Several large observational studies have shown that coffee drinkers have a lower risk for diabetes. Researchers speculate that other compounds in the coffee have a beneficial effect and may blunt some of the negatives of caffeine.

—*New York Times*, January 30, 2008

But what the hell? It finally occurred to me that I can't do without O. J. That I need O. J. to get me through the day.

Coffee too. (I'm like Dominick Dunne, who, interviewed on MSNBC, June 28, 2001, said that O. J. had overtaken his life.) I had finished reading the newspaper. All about how Kraal's security had been tightened ever since the kidnapping of Lim Burger. I go down to a coffee shop where some of the old '60s people hang out. It's called The Golden Sardine, named after the title of one of Beat poet Bob Kaufman's books. Had my earphones on, tuned to O. J. commentary. Like methadone instead of heroin. Among all of the beards, I see my friend Jerry Bareheart, a man with an Ojibwa mother and a Celtic father. The former manager of KCAK, who was replaced by Kraal. He's one of the few bald-faced men in the establishment. As clean shaven as Dali's Christ. He'd received the hatchet like some of the other employees. Rumor had it that he read about his dismissal in the *Anglo-Saxon Explainer* and that when he arrived at work, all of his belongings had been placed on the sidewalk, and the security people barred him from even entering the building when he attempted to get an explanation about what had happened. That seemed to be Kraal's modus operandi for telling unwanted employees that they were through. He was dressed casually. A black sweatshirt, draw-stringed cotton pants and moccasins. There was a graying about his temples. Bareheart had spent twenty-five years of his life at KCAK. Thought of himself as a composer, but wasn't original. I sat down at his table. We shook hands. He seemed to be uncomfortable.

"Listen, Jerry, I'm sorry that they let you go. The station has gone to the dogs." The waitress brought the espresso that I had ordered. He looked disdainfully at my espresso, to which I had added milk. He would be that kind of guy. Down on people who put milk into their espresso. Otter once told me about ordering espresso in a Greek-run restaurant in Hanover, Germany, called the Moor. Had this sign with a black-skinned Moor with curly hair and thick red lips hanging above the entrance to the establishment. Otter said that the owner had refused to bring him milk for his espresso. The owner told Otter that the milk would ruin it.

"How are you getting on?"

"I'm broke but I'm getting on. I'm doing some light composing. I've been offered a job teaching music at the University of New Mexico at Albuquerque. Might just go back home." He seemed to really be annoyed with me. Strange, because my experiences with him in the past had been pleasant. His hands were trembling and his skin was unusually whiter than usual. Everybody thought of Jerry as having an extra sense. The kind of guy who showed up just as someone was mentioning his name. Was able to tell who was in the room by that person's odor. His opera, *Winebojo Enters the World,* had received critical praise but was a box-office failure. It closed after a week Off Broadway.

Some said that Bareheart's days were numbered at KCAK anyway. He had really offended some subscribers by devoting a series to the work of Gerald Vizenor, a Native American who couldn't be reasonable. The kind of Indian who in the movies can't bring himself to sit down and smoke the peace pipe with the white man. Who refused to avail himself of an all expenses paid trip to Washington to pose for pictures with the great white father. A man who made war whoops in academia. An Indian, who when approached by courteous and polite whites, would say "sorry, I don't do wampum." A rogue. A renegade. A maverick who even annoyed his fellow Indians. Listen to the experience of someone who tried to teach one of this tricky red man's books. Louis Owens said that his Indian students, mixbloods, complained about the contents of one of this hothead's novels which included "homosexual and transsexual Indians." Indians "who were lustful, bestial, violent, sadistic, greedy and cowardly." As for the humor? "Undeniably sick, including a gratuitous amount of truly shocking sexual violence" and "more serious yet, making fun far to often of 'Indianess.'"

"I'm thinking about leaving New York. After I've cleared up some unfinished business."

"That's too bad. Can't you find another job?"

"Not for what I want to do. Everybody has become a commercial whore. That seems to be the trend. Did you know that in a few years, ten to twelve companies will control what Americans see and hear? It's all Westinghouse, G.E., and Disney."

"What about WNYC?"

"Giuliani is talking about privatizing it."

"Well, what about going into another field?"

"Too late for that. Nobody's going to hire somebody in his fifties."

"Damn. It's depressing."

"Yeah. Listen, what happened to your cartoons?" he asked.

"I was suspended by Sebastian and then he asked me back. Said he wanted to limit my cartoons to something called a blog with which they're experimenting. They misinterpreted one of my cartoons. They said that I had O. J. sodomizing America. What I intended was O. J. calling the plays for the media. Later, he called and said that he wanted me to continue. It's getting confusing. This fag—this Lord hates my guts. He seems to have a strange hold on Kraal."

"Yeah. The station has definitely taken a right turn. I've heard Bimbette, and Fansworth. They're using O. J. to get you guys. Once they start calling you savages, it's not before long that they start making lampshades out of you."

"You're talking about Hitler and the Jews."

"No, I'm talking about Andrew Jackson and the Indians."

"Never heard of it."

"One of those incidents that slipped through the cracks of American history."

"This Indian group in Long Island is still up at Kraal's. They're protesting your firing and they're still pissed off at the naming of the Geronimos and the mascots, the two monkeys, Sitting Bull and Geronimo. Maybe the Indian Wars haven't ended. Look at what's happening in Mexico. Indians are still fighting for space in the Americas. Look at the protest over some liquor company naming a beer Crazy Horse malt. Crazy Horse was a teetotaler."

"Yeah, well some are saying that the Bush administration is a disaster because his grandfather stole Geronimo's skull."

"Well some blacks are saying that it's failing because of the curse of the cruel slave master."

"Go on."

"There's a legend that a slave master who was unusually cruel towards the brothers and sisters suffers a terrible fate. Vines and mildew creep into his mansion. Maybe an alligator crawls in. Terrifying spectral shapes appear in the house at night. Hellish dreams afflict the man. Wooooooo!" We laughed.

"Like your boy O. J. His is an old story, too. A legend."

"What do you mean by that?"

He looked at his watch. "The Captivity Narrative."

"The what?"

"White women get kidnapped by Indians and are rescued. A story as old as American literature. Since *The Sovereignty and Goodness of God*, by Mary Rowlandson, published in 1682, the notion of a captured white woman under the management of an Indian or black man has earned billions of dollars for publishers, Hollywood, and television from that time to a film called *Righteous Kill* in which Robert De Niro and Al Pacino rescue Carla Gugino (in real life a brunette but in this movie a blonde) from the evil clutches of 50 Cent, or *Brooklyn's Finest* . . . in which a cop played by Richard Gere rescues white women from black pimps who hold them in sexual bondage, but on many occasions, when the settlers rescued white women from the Indians, the women escaped, preferring life among the Indians to living in settler communities where they had less freedom. Buffalo Bill used the captivity theme in his show. Had Indians attack a cabin full of white women and when there were no white women available, he'd use Indians to play white women. Some of the sales pitch for this kind of thing is aimed at the prurient. Long before Hugh Hefner, you have that painting by John Vanderlyn done in 1804. It's called *The Death of Jane McCrea* and it shows a kneeling Jane McCrea about to be tomahawked by two half-naked Indian men. Her right breast is exposed."

"And so while you and your friends are debating about O. J.'s guilt or innocence they're going to ensnare him whether he's innocent or guilty. While you might have thought that O. J. was married to Nicole, for them she was a captive who had to be rescued. Notice how some of the commentators refer to her as Nicole Brown. By her maiden name. The only question left is who will do the rescuing. They can't lynch him, but they'll hunt him down until they catch him. The coyote's tail will be trapped."

Somebody at the next table had been listening in on our conversation and began butting in. He was bearded and his hair was unkempt, his clothes disheveled. I recognized him from a photo I'd seen in one of the downtown papers. His Loisada apartment had been raided by the F.C.C. and the F.B.I. He was operating a radio station without a license. He was one of a growing a number of radio pirates. Only they weren't seizing ships on the high seas, they were seizing radio bands which they said were being sold to the rich. Sitting with him was. What? Virginia Saturday.

"The media are fomenting hate crimes against Indians, blacks, and Hispanics," he intruded. "To take action against the media is an act of self-defense. Remember that incident in Mogadishu. The Americans claimed that this radio station was broadcasting hate mongering. They had the Air Force take it out. If that's a good idea over there, it's a good idea over here. Also in Bosnia. The United Nations troops closed down a station because its political commentary was biased." The guy was really hyperventilated. Wild-eyed. Virginia was nodding. I'd heard that she'd been offered lucrative contracts with other networks but had spurned them. This was odd because black women were disappearing from network television. The white boys were finding it easier to deal with Asian women. Indian women from the subcontinent. Less confrontational. Glad to be there. Ben said that one night he'd remained late and went into the coffee room for some java. He found Kraal there. His pants were around his ankles. And one of the women, an FOB from India, was on her knees servicing him. She was working her head up and down and Kraal was leaning against a wall, smacking his lips, his eyes closed. He was really enjoying himself. Next thing he knew, she was made head of their London office, and broadcasting international news. Black newsman Bob Teague in his classic book *Live and Off-Color*, an exposé of the media, wrote about some of the sexual compromises that women had to make in order to succeed in the media.

"You advocating terrorism against the networks? What good would that do?" I asked. Bareheart was giving the man an indulgent smile while sipping his cappuccino.

"It would get their attention. Boycotts don't work. Protests." This guy who butted in on our conversation was obviously one of these conspiracy theorists. The pirate and Virginia began to speak some kind of manifesto language about how the rich were taking over communications and using them to make the American public even dumber.

"You're wasting your time, talking to him," Virginia said. "When those cops arrested me and manhandled me, he didn't raise a finger. The brother is in the pocket of the corporate media." How come Virginia was talking like this? What had come over her? She was dressed like one of these "postblack" people. Hair cornrowed. Jewelry on her tongue, her nose, etc. "They fired everybody, but him. Shows where his head is at." The white boy who was with her smirked. "Come on Mark." She and Mark got up and left.

"Talk. Talk. That's all you hear down here is talk." He stared after the two contemptuously. "Look, I got to go down to the unemployment office. I got about five hundred dollars between me and a shelter," Bareheart said. I reached into my back pocket. "I can lend you a few bucks."

He waved the money away. I was surprised. The way that Kraal treated him and he wasn't bitter. Commendable, but I wasn't listening to him. My mind was on O. J. A few days later, I read that Bareheart had been questioned about the kidnapping of talk-show host Lim Burger.

38

The O. J. trial was off for the day. One of the jurors had a dental appointment. I took the opportunity to visit the Kraal Towers to check my mail. Since Louis's announcement that I had been suspended, people at the station had had different reactions. Some were sympathetic, but others were pleased and showing it, as Judge Katz said of Faye Resnick, with their "body language." Rafiki's Lincoln appeared and soon, we were on the way uptown. Rafiki was going on about how Olajuwon withstood the assault of an aggressive offense by merely standing in front of a basket and knocking down the opposition's balls. His lifetime record of 3,830 blocked shots has not been surpassed. As we pulled up, we saw Kraal's car double-parked in front of the building. The two black guys who hosted the show *Nigguz News* rode into the building on these scooters that have become such a fad. They were followed by photographers and reporters. "What the hell was that all about?" I asked Garfield on the way up to the receptionists who held my mail. Garfield said that the men were being put up in a suite at the Plaza Hotel.

39

O. J.'s "Dream Team" was up against not only the prosecution in the courtroom but all of the white lawyers sending in faxes to the DA's office, advising them on their strategy. All of the talking heads on TV who are advertising their law practices and saving money for outfits like CNN and MSNBC, the lead eye poachers for cable. Even Burt Katz eventually got a show. The Dream Team were even up against Dick Cavett, who was sending in helpful faxes to the prosecution while hosting all-white TV panels about the case. He said he'd leave the country were O. J. acquitted in the criminal case. Sigh.

But *Seinfeld* mirrors the '90s zeitgeist. In their last show, the characters are sent to jail for violating the Good Samaritan Law, for refusing to come to the aid of an obese man who is being mugged. A few days later, a hospital denies aid to a black kid who lay dying in the streets located near the hospital.

Marcia Herskovitz, a Chelsea collagist of the middle '60s, compared the situation of us black men, which includes Rabbit, Snakes,

Bat, and me, to that of dwarfs, in chains, railing at giants. From our vantage point, the giants are the cannibals, though Roth discusses Zulus and cannibals in the same sentence. But they're not smelling the blood of an Englishman, they're smelling our blood. The networks are Beasts with A Thousand Eyes. But instead of preying upon human flesh, they prey upon our image, and distribute our meat to the hyenas known as the general public. We're the favorite meal. They're fascinated with us. They can't do without devouring and regurgitating us. On the day, in 1997, when Hungary and Poland are admitted to NATO, and the Senate hearings about campaign finances are begun, the lead stories of MSNBC are Tyson, Cosby, and O. J. Even Coz, everybody's favorite father, is tossed out to cannibalistic eyes. There's a sick audience for this stuff. They've even taken our victimhood. At least we had that. You know, our four hundred years of oppression. The slave ship quarters. The chains. The whips.

Everybody is a victim, these days. You can nowadays exhibit your emotional sores carnival-like. The Barnum & Bailey bigtop has been replaced by all-day with O. J., Ramsey, and Monica. Bat, Snakes, Rabbit, and I form just another demographic group. Blacks felt that their oppression had been filched by other groups. Like some gays calling themselves the new blacks, because the old blacks, after the election of a Celtic black president, had reached the Promised Land.

Gays and blacks didn't always see eye to eye. Gays began the process that would gentrify black neighborhoods and remove blacks from cities like San Francisco. And when a black man, Willie Brown, ran for mayor against a gay man, Tom Ammiano, gay commentators on stations like KPFA sounded like ex-Confederate colonels discussing Reconstruction black politicians. Calling Brown "arrogant" and "vain." The gay campaign against Brown had racist overtones, even though Brown had supported gay rights for twenty years prior to the election. Marlon Riggs of *Tongues Untied* wrote eloquently about vanilla racism among gays. Barbara Smith said that when she joined the gay and lesbian march on Washington, the leadership told her to get lost.

That they wanted to go mainstream and weren't interested in Civil Rights.

And then, during May 1998, a big fuss was made about this millionaire comedian, Ellen DeGeneres. She said that gays and lesbians suffer more than blacks because at least their families accept them. Bat complains that other people use the strategies that the brothers invented and get over in places where we have setbacks.

The Beast with A Thousand Eyes is under the control of people like Ted Turner and Mort Zukerman. They want to raise their money by breaking O. J. like you'd break a bull, or a wild horse. But, by the fall of 1997, O. J. is still playing golf, raising his kids, and going about his business, to the frustration of O. J. haters like Dan Abrams who, in an exchange with O. J. and F. Lee Bailey, wants to know why O. J. isn't concerned about his image (after Abrams and others have destroyed his image). They want to see O. J. break some rocks, or be Fred Goldman's slave for the rest of his life. They want to take him into the toilet and stick a plunger up his ass. Symbolically. They want to know how O. J. does it.

A December '98 MSNBC panel made up of white men and black women grouse and fume over pictures of O. J.'s new home. This comfortable-looking home with a swimming pool. When I see this house at the top of a hill I think of the Beatles song that includes the line, "the fool on the hill." I draw O. J. with a coxcomb on his head. He taunts them. While being interviewed by English television, he pretends to stab the host with a banana, while mimicking the soundtrack music from the shower scene in *Psycho*. His pretending to stab a white woman with a banana sends out a whole bunch of signs. *Critical Inquiry* would fill an entire issue with this image. O. J.'s father, one of the tabloids said, was a female impersonator, which brings me to an observation by the eminent Puerto Rican poet, Miguel Algarin, that Kato Kaelin was both O. J. and Nicole's sex slave. In my cartoons, I draw O. J. helmetless in the football game of life (so to speak).

But a British woman, because she has given what she deemed a fair interview with Simpson, is regarded as a race traitor. Her interview is subjected to some mean criticism from a MSNBC reporter who questions her loyalty to the white race and complains about her journalistic standards. (This encounter occurs during a week when MSNBC broadcasts a man blowing his brains out on the Los Angeles freeway.) The British interviewer takes her hits a few months after another white woman gives what is considered by Geraldo Rivera to be a too friendly interview with O. J. in *Esquire*. (This is the Geraldo Rivera who gave a softball interview to slothful-eyed Mark Fuhrman. Told him he was welcome on his show, anytime.) Though it's been O. J. on trial, the media and its followers derive a great deal of sadistic pleasure from rubbing the case in our faces as though it were the big behind of a hog. We spend a lot of time on O. J. as a matter of self-defense. Because when they do O. J., Tyson, C. Thomas, and Latrell Sprewell, they're signifying on us.

They force us to rally around the flag of black brotherhood (so to speak). They are annoyed by our "identity politics," yet they are the ones who rounded us up, drag-netted, and profiled us into "identity politics." Brother. Next time you're stopped by a black-male-hating cop like Fuhrman, who said that if he saw a white woman in a car with a black man he'd stop the car (yet dated black women), tell this cop that race is a social construct.

Race loyalty, for the media, is another element in the Simpson case they magnify. They write a lot about how the brothers and sisters defend O. J. After all, according to Jeffrey Toobin, voice of the white mainstream, we don't have the necessities to think logically. In January of 2000, he appears with Chris Matthews, a bona fide hysteric who kisses up to older powerful white men, especially those of the World War II generation. A freak. He could have been the model for the book about the authoritarian personality (later he congratulates Giuliani for his "little Fascism"), and he says that black reaction to the O. J. Simpson verdict in the criminal trial set race relations back fifty years. Yet race loyalty among whites isn't discussed. Not even by rational, clear-thinking, Toobin. Why haven't the hundreds of cases over the last two hundred years (during which whites got off for killing blacks or not even charged, as in the case of lynchings,) set race relations back two hundred years? Why is it that only when blacks do something that offends whites, their actions set race relations back fifty years? Is it because Hispanics, blacks, Native Americans, and other "ethnocentrics" must audition for white acceptance, behave themselves and fink on one another in order to be welcomed into the mainstream? Take Philip Roth's suggestion that blacks get there by reading Euripides? Not in the original Greek but the same Victorian translations that Roth reads.

When F. Lee Bailey, who began Fox News's "O. J. Outburst" week by discussing O. J.'s performance on a polygraph test, went to jail, white prisoners gave him a hard time. They said that they could understand why Cochran defended O. J., but not Bailey, a white man. After all, whites are objective. Rational. Subjecting everything to scientific scrutiny. They think, therefore they is. Any one of them could have invented the automobile. The Internet.

40

Faye Resnick's publisher says on television that anybody who believes in O. J.'s innocence had a low I.Q. She's a genius. Mark Fuhrman's lawyer, Robert Tourtelot, says that if the jury votes for acquittal they're brain dead. When the mostly white male jury of media experts are not signifying about the intelligence of the black jurors, they chastise Johnnie Cochran and the members of the defense team. In September of 2008, after O. J. is arrested in Las Vegas, Pat Oliphant does a cartoon in which the late Johnnie Cochran is calling O. J. from hell. In 2010, Vice President Cheney and his daughter get into trouble for claiming that anybody who defends a person accused of terrorism is a member of Al Qaeda. Legal minds from the left and right condemn the Cheneys and insist upon the right of a person's defense no matter how heinous the crime. They cite John Adams's defense of the British soldiers involved in the Boston Massacre, ignoring the fact that Adams's argument includes some racist digs at the blacks and Irish who battled the British soldiers. For Pat Oliphant hell is a place for lawyers who believe that a defendant, no matter how heinous his crime might be, should receive his rights under the Constitution. White reporters and correspondents covering the trial are full of contempt and ridicule when discussing the defense's conspiracy theories. On February 26, 1999, Burt Katz, a former judge, takes it upon himself to decide whether O. J. should maintain custody of his children. Later on MSNBC an all-white panel, including Victoria Toensing with the built-in sneering lip and others, join in.

Colonel Fred Graham of Court TV comes back to the defense strategy obsessively, expressing disbelief about why anybody would believe that LA policemen would be engaged in a conspiracy against Simpson. He's also concerned about Simpson's ability to hire expensive lawyers. The pro-prosecution commentariat can hardly conceal their glee when they report, during May 1996, that O. J. is about to run out of money and might have to get a credit line on his estate. They'd love to see him lose his estate. (The media always provides those whom they regard as their prime customers the spectacle of a prosperous and impudent black man brought down. They loved it when M. J. lost Neverland and the targets of the mobs in both the 1900 New York riot and the 1921 Tulsa riot were prosperous black men. In 1900, a New York mob shouted, "Let's go get those Williams and Walker Niggers," meaning successful entertainers, Bert Williams and George Walker of "The Two Real Coons.")

When the IRS put a lien on O. J.'s home, Eliot Spitzer, a guest on Geraldo's show, laughed out loud. He was having fun. When it looked as though the all-white jury in the civil case was going to do what it was picked to do, break this nigger's back, commentator Joe DiGenova began to toy with a small brown cigar, which, whether we knew it at the time, becomes a link to the next O. J.—Clinton, the white O. J. He does this while appearing on Geraldo Rivera's show. The brown cigar and a soiled dress are synecdoche for the Clinton impeachment.

41

"The camera is needed to give the public the clearest, most accurate depiction of what occurs in court," said lawyer Floyd Abrams, who represents Court TV. "This case, because of its history, is filled with suspicions, doubts and bewilderment on how the system works."

In the civil case, lawyers for the families of murder victims Goldman and Nicole Brown Simpson want a jury to find Simpson responsible for the June 12, 1994, killings and make him pay damages to compensate for their losses.

Simpson's criminal trial, which was widely televised, ended in acquittal last year. Legal experts fear if people are not allowed to see the civil trial, and it has a different outcome, the public may be baffled even outraged.

"There is a concern that if the plaintiffs win, some people will say: 'They moved the trial to white Santa Monica, closed it down and railroaded O. J. Simpson.' They will say there's a two-tiered system of justice," said Southwestern University law professor Robert Pugsley.

"If the Goldmans win, people will think it all went on behind closed doors. The only way is for the public to see it," added Abrams.

> —Michelle Caruso, *Daily News,* Friday, August 23rd, 1996

SIZE OF AWARD SHOCKS EXPERTS

By Wendell Jamieson and Jane Furse, Wednesday, February 5th, 1997, 2:01 A.M.

The damning civil trial verdict against O. J. Simpson and the massive $8.5 million damage award stunned legal experts last night.

"It's truly amazing. It seems like they are saying, 'We not only find you liable, we find you liable with a vengeance,'" said Robert Pugsley of Southwestern University School of Law in Los Angeles.

"The fact that they voted straight yes down the ticket means they firmly believed in Simpson's liability," he added.

The decision finding Simpson responsible for the slayings of his ex-wife and her pal elated former Los Angeles prosecutor Christopher Darden who failed to win a conviction against Simpson in his criminal trial.

"We said all along that O.J Simpson committed these crimes and all we asked . . . was our day in court . . . a fair hearing on the issues. And I believe that we've done that, that that's been accomplished," said Darden.

But former Simpson Dream Team lawyer Alan Dershowitz warned that the verdict is vulnerable to an appeal especially because a juror was booted during deliberations.

"There will have to be an investigation into whether the other jurors were tainted by the panelist who was dismissed," said Dershowitz, who is expected to be involved in the appeal.

O. J. JURY STARTS ALL OVER LONE BLACK PANELIST THROWN OFF THE CASE

By Michelle Caruso in Los Angeles and Jere Hester in New York, with K.C. Baker and Austin Evans Fenner in Los Angeles, Saturday, February 1, 1997, 2:01 A.M.

The all-white Santa Monica jury will carry out the mandate of the television commentators by holding Simpson liable for the deaths of Nicole and Ron, without anyone accusing the jury of arriving at a decision based upon race, which is how the decision in the criminal case was regarded. Toobin said there would be days like this. This white jury is rational, clear-thinking and "the black jury," which existed in the minds of the commentators, was prone to primitive thinking. Tribal thinking. Nonsentient.

While the white jury is unsequestered, the commentators, unpaid agents for the Goldman family, introduce what they regard as incriminating evidence against Simpson, while hosting Detectives Tom Lange and Phillip Vannatter, who are promoting their book, *Evidence Dismissed*, which garnered a $150,000 advance. Vannatter says that with this cash "he will improve his lifestyle." (What was Vannatter doing carrying around vials containing both Goldman and Nicole's blood?) Vannatter and Lange aren't the only ones who are doing a victory lap while the white civil trial jury is still out. Mark Fuhrman is hailed by Robert Novak of CNN's *Crossfire* program as one of the few people in the case who behaved rationally and is given sympathetic treatment by interviewers who obviously admire this man who boasted of a police station in Los Angeles where, he says, the blood of black police victims cake the walls. A baseball player in tolerant Seattle even invites Fuhrman to be his guest at an opening game. He gets redeemed quicker than Nixon. And later, when a real baseball player, John Rocker, makes bigoted remarks about blacks and gays, his white fans cheer him. Our perception of reality is, er—skewed.

42

TUESDAY, MAY 14, 1996

The media bounty hunters have bad news and good news. During a debate at Oxford, Simpson receives an enthusiastic reception, after a group of anti-O. J. commentators had predicted that the Oxford audience would give O. J. a hard time. They didn't. That's the bad news. The good news is that the IRS put a $600,000 lien on his home. A sit-in host for Geraldo Rivera and two white male guests laugh aloud while O. J.'s difficulties with the IRS are being discussed. Simpson's reception is good in Europe.

Why is there a racial divide in the United States, yet no racial divide in Europe, about the Simpson case? Aren't the Europeans white? Could it be that Americans, who receive all of their news about the case from Dominick Dunne and from the prosecution-friendly Larry King and Charles Grodin, are informed by a media that has been lynching black men and women for a few hundred years? Now we're getting somewhere.

In a settler society, when one of the settlers is murdered, the nearest native has to be burned. Anyone who gets in the way of the mob is murdered too. John Singleton's *Rosewood* shows the power that any deranged white woman might have over black men. A white woman accusing a black man of raping her sets a mob on black women and children. In *Rosewood* the white men even kill their beloved Mammy, though Paul Mooney doubts that white men in the South would murder their beloved Mammy. He speculates what would have happened had Aretha Franklin's breast been exposed instead of Janet Jackson's, whose exposed breast nearly stopped the Super Bowl and sent a panic throughout the country (while the National Geographic channel regularly shows the breasts of women regarded as "primitive"). He has white men stepping over their wives to get a smack of Ms. Franklin's breasts.

43

Ben was sitting in a very comfortable white sofa and having a glass of white wine. He was wearing a Roland Martin ascot and a smoking jacket, and seemed very relaxed. He told me to go to the cabinet and pour myself one. Ben Armstrong had called that morning and asked me to come to his place. Said he had something to tell me and didn't want to do it by land phone. Rumor had it that he'd be returning to work soon. He was watching the Bulls play the Sonics. I fixed myself a drink and sat on the couch opposite him.

"What did you think of *Nigguz News*?" I asked. Without looking away from the game he said: "A piece of crap. I understand that Renaldo was so angry after the third installment that he took a few days off. Said that Kraal had promised to drop the name and issue an apology. Man, these Caribbean blacks are really naïve." Some say that he was appointed president of KCAK alternative TV because he was a fence mender. The station had come under attack for its hiring practices, there being too many white males and white women and not enough minorities. After two years, white women were over fifty percent of the employees at KCAK, there still were only a few blacks, but there was a growing number of Latinos. The 'right' Latinos. Those who were opposed to Latino Studies, bilingual education, and who were not offended that the only consistent stories about Latinos KCAK broadcast involved girl gangs and Mexican immigrants.

"I'll bet it was Lord's idea. Jagid and Jagan are harvesting the eyes for them. You know how white folks love things that show black people screwing up so that they can feel good about their own miserable lives." Snakes said that he tuned in on some Hip-hop station and all that he got were songs about oral sex, a trend that had been begun by a former president of the United States.

"You sure that's all?"

"What other explanation do you have? There must be a market for this stuff. Why else would Kraal be interested? All he thinks about is money. I think that it has something to do with depression. You know . . . and . . . ," he mentioned the name of two mass media magazines. "They're always putting black gangstas on the cover, but once in awhile they'll have long articles about depression, which must be a big problem among their white subscribers. Half their ads are from pharmaceutical companies. Things to make you sleep. Stuff that will calm you down. Stuff that will get you hard. I think that the two are connected. The showing of black people as the nation's uglies and the depression of white people. Dissing blacks is like a kind a stimulant for the pleasure centers of their brains. White supremacy is social morphine. A thrill, a high." Interesting explanation, but one that lacks depth.

"Why can't Renaldo do something?" I was hardly listening.

"The guy has no power. They gave these two guys offices. It's bigger than his. They stay in there all day gettin' high. Blasting that goddamn music and sampling the office fucks."

"What? Why doesn't he quit?"

"He's drowning in debt. His secretary says that credit card companies call the office. He gets harassed by bill collectors."

"But, isn't his mother a lawyer?"

"A very good one. It's expensive living in New York."

I felt better talking to Ben. The guy had to act like a bubbling frenetic idiot on television. A real motor mouth. But in private, he was serious. Thoughtful. Philosophical. Well-read.

"So what did you call me up here for?"

And then, out of the blue, and not taking his eyes from the basketball game, he said, calmly:

"O. J. killed that girl and Goldman, too."

"What are you saying, Ben?" I began to experience shortness of breath. I started to pull out my little monitor. Check my blood sugar. But momentarily I recovered. I started to review the evidence that pointed to reasonable doubt. I was feeling weak. I had to go to the refrigerator and fetch some orange juice. A well-stocked fridge. Steak, ham, frankfurters, a lot of red meat, a lot of protein. Loaves of Wonder Bread. Fried chicken. The freezer contained cartons of ice cream. When I returned, I had recovered.

"But what about the blood on the back fence at Bundy being less degraded than the blood found three weeks before?"

"Guilty."

"What about the fact that the sock has EDTA and so has the Bundy blood?"

"Guilty."

"What about the coroner's testimony that two knives were used in the murder and that the hair found in the knitted cap were not consistent with O. J.'s."

"Guilty."

" . . . and what about the fact that O. J.'s blood wasn't found on the victim's clothes. The blood underneath Nicole's fingernail that didn't belong to any of the parties, the fact that Fuhrman lied about the time that he discovered the bloody glove."

"He's guilty."

The Sonics beat the Bulls. I was beaten and O. J. was beaten. But what was wrong with Ben? Why had he changed his mind? Why didn't he identify with O. J. as other black men had? And then taking a sip of the wine, he said, "Why are you so hung up on O. J.? What has O. J. ever done for you? What has any of them ever done for you? Before O. J. it was Michael Jackson, then Mike Tyson, then Wilt Chamberlain, then Marion Barry, then Clarence Thomas, Magic Johnson. Mel Reynolds. Where will it end?"

Was this the same man who had argued with Raquel about O. J.'s innocence?

"Why can't you race artists get behind a good guy instead of backing these millionaire losers. Somebody like, like—Scotty

Pippin, Doug Fisher, San Antonio's Admiral David Robinson, or Hank Aaron."

"You know what the black man is up against in a racist society—"

"Look. Did it ever occur to you that these guys might be guilty? Besides, race had nothing to do with his murdering that girl. The tip-off came when those two guys, who checked his luggage, when he was about to depart for Chicago, said that he dressed young. He was an old man and she was taunting him with that. Fucking these young guys and associating with young studs like Goldman. She let Goldman drive his Ferrari. She was fucking with his image of himself as this virile satyr-like cat. You remember what Nicole told Faye Resnick. She didn't want to be wheeling him around in a wheelchair when he was forty-five. He was jealous."

"Jealous. Look, if O. J. were jealous, why didn't he get upset with Marcus Allen for fucking Nicole? What does he do? He lets the guy get married at his estate."

"Aw man, you know that a brother don't get upset when his old lady is knocked down by another brother, it's the white boy. This guy Keith what's his name?"

"Keith Zlomsowitch."

"Yeah. Slamsandwich. It's one thing to have your old lady snatched by a brother—but by a white boy, now that's humiliating." When black feminists exposed the brothers as being bad lovers, regardless of the song lyrics that boasted otherwise, the brothers thought that this would end the curiosity.

Some speculated that Zlomsowitch wasn't called because his appearance would enable the defense to push their drug theories about the case. O. J. always maintained that the key to solving the case would be found in the circles that Faye Resnick moved in, but in neither the criminal case nor the civil case was this avenue explored. Nicole had said that Resnick's crowd "scared her."

"You haven't been following the testimony. O. J. saw them making love on the couch and didn't do anything. If he were jealous, he would have killed them then." Louis Menand didn't take this into account when he scolded Toni Morrison for her doubts about the O. J. case. He says that O. J. killed Nicole and Ron out of jealous rage. This theory was shot down even by the anti-O. J. commentators. Menand forgets that it was Nicole who wanted to reconcile with O. J., not the other way around.

"We don't know. But look at you. Look what this thing is doing to you. Do you think it's worth losing your family over whether every black male celebrity is guilty or not? They don't care anything about you. All they want to do is flash and fuck young girls. Look at Mel Reynolds. Rhodes scholar. Harvard. Everything going for him. Let his peter bring him down over some young pussy. Last I heard, his wife and kid were living in a shelter. Do you think that you could get through Mike Tyson's entourage, or into O. J.'s Rockingham estate? There you are, backing loser after loser, like that idiot Marion Barry. Led around by his dick like a fucking zombie." Otter once told him about a poster he'd bought at a museum in Munich. Showed a woman with a tiny grinning devil peeking through the slit of her vagina. An open-mouthed rattlesnake. The rattlesnake that would bite even a holy man like Jesse Jackson. That's right. During January, Jesse Jackson is exposed as an adulterer like Bill Clinton. This is what you get when following King David's example.

"I'm not defending them, I'm defending myself. Because when they're trying O. J. and Marion and Mike and all of the rest, I'm on trial, too. So are you."

"Says who?"

"The larger society."

"Look. Forget about the larger society. Those people will always be looking over their shoulders at black people. That's not your problem. They're paranoid. They're worried about extinction. They're worried to death about darker-skinned people taking over from them. White women are killing millions of their fetuses. The birth rate in Europe is so low that for the first time, Europeans aren't replacing themselves. Soon, Europe will be known as the Dark Continent despite the efforts of the Europeans to exclude them. Turks, Ethiopians, Moroccans, Nigerians, Dominicans. That's what this European unification thing is all about. Keep brown and black people out. The man's sperm count is down all over the West, due to the poisons leaked by his technology that he holds over everybody's head as proof of his superiority. They see themselves engulfed by angry colored people who want to pay them back for their crimes. Right now you're taking up half your waking hours wondering what white society thinks about you. Waiting for the next brother to fall. To be indicted. So that you have to choose sides. The brothers against the world. These people feast on race. That's all you hear about or read about? Besides, these whites created O. J. Just like they always create black leaders. This communist guy Levenson had such a hold over King that he was able to veto James Baldwin's participation in the movement. Where would DuBois and Booker T., and even King, who was backed by powerful whites like the Rockefeller family, have been without these patrons? Blacks don't create leaders. They're just asked to condemn them when they mess up. Whites loved O. J. Hell, how many black people do you see at football games? The crowds are as white as the Marine Band. He fell for it. Thought that color didn't matter and that he'd be viewed for his merits. For his abilities. But you see what happened when he killed that girl. His fans turned into a lynch mob. White people who pretend to admire blacks can turn into a lynch mob just like that. One minute they're asking for his autograph, next minute, they're stringing him up. You remember that Rutgers game?"

"What about it?"

"This white crowd is cheering the brothers who are dribbling up and down the court and doing slam dunks, alley-oops, and jump fakes, etc. when all of a sudden these black kids pour out onto the floor and stage a sit-down. They're protesting the president of the college who said something about low black IQ's. These white fans, who had been cheering the black athletes before the demonstration, begin calling these kids niggers. White people get bipolar about black people. One minute cheering them on, the next minute they're dragging some black man from the rear of their pickup. White people love blacks playing basketball, because in their minds, it's a kinetic sport. For white people, the basketball court is like blacks' natural habitat."

"That's some speech coming from a guy who makes his living as a sports announcer."

"Not anymore."

"What do you mean?"

"I'm not going back to the station."

"I don't get it. Why?"

"I'm sick of sitting there like some kind of grinning idiot and making small talk with people I despise."

"So what are you going to do?"

"Law. I'm going into law. Man, I look at Johnnie Cochran and Carl Douglas and Leo Terrell and Johnny Burris and Star Jones. Don't those people make you feel proud? And my favorites Al DeBlanc and Chris Darden and Melanie Lomax. People who are braving black opinion that wants to let the brother off because he's black."

"What?" I couldn't believe what I'd heard. He ignored me, so engrossed was he in his narrative.

"Look at all of the heat coming down on Johnnie from all of these crackers on TV and phoning in. You look at them and you see what the media's been keeping from us all of these years. How they define us in terms of characters like Mike Tyson. They love them guys because they fulfill their fantasy of what a black man should be, an irresponsible naked brute. But Cochran and Burris and these other cats . . . cats like Howard Moore, Jr. They're playing mind basketball with this man. Dancing all around him and doing reverse layups on his head. Naw man. I'm not going back to some sports desk. I'm enrolling in Fordham Law School this fall."

"What?"

"To law school."

"What about your book, 'The O. J. That I Knew'?"

"I returned the money to the publisher. It was blood money. Besides, a year from now, everybody will have forgotten about the case. The book would have gone right from the printing plant to the remainder warehouse. While I've been laid up here for the last few weeks, I've been thinking. Thinking about my life. Thinking about how I want to look five years from now when I'm fifty. I have somebody in my life now. Somebody very precious to me." The buzzer rang. He pushed a button.

"Who is it?"

"Raquel."

"Tokina?"

"Don't call her that." He shot me a scowl.

"But her brothers did a Fuhrman on you, and you're receiving her in your home."

"She's sorry for what they did. She hates this machismo shit. Blames it on the Arab influence on Spanish culture. On the other hand, I had it coming. I shouldn't have addressed her in the manner I did. Man, we have to start respecting women, like the Khan is always saying.

"She's been coming over here ever since the day I came home from the hospital. Helping out. Building up my confidence. I don't know what I would have done without her. She's very contrite and she made her brothers apologize. Why I'm going to one of these Day of the Dead festivals that these Mexicans are always having. You got her people all wrong."

"Boy, are the sisters going to be upset with you. You and a Mexican woman. They're going to accuse you of having Enchilada fever."

"That's their problem. Besides, Mexicans have the same background as us. They're Indian and African. Ain't got nothin to do with Europe. The way I look at it, we share the same gene pool. Some black, some red, and some white." There was a knock on the door. I opened it. Unlike the cross look she carried around the office, she was smiling. She walked into the room and kissed Ben on the forehead. She greeted me warmly. Warmly! He beamed. They began to chat as though I wasn't even in the room. Now I'd seen everything. I said goodbye and went back downtown to my studio. Ben Armstrong had defected to the other side. Now there was only Rabbit, Snakes, Bat, Otter, and me who believed in Simpson's innocence. That wouldn't last long. Bat defected the next day. Called me and said that the white girls who worked at his literary factory had convinced him that the blood evidence was overwhelming and that he, O. J., was guilty. Besides, they said that they would go on strike if he continued supporting O. J. I called him, going over the garbage-in-garbage-out theory. Of the disappearing and appearing blood in the Bronco. Of Fuhrman lying about the circumstances under which he found the bloody glove. I argued persuasively about how the leaves surrounding the glove didn't indicate that someone had jumped over the fence and dropped them there. I repeated one of O. J.'s lawyer's assessments of the LAPD lab as a cesspool of contamination. I told him that the DNA results were based upon the sampling of just two Detroit black men. But Bat wouldn't budge. In fact, he was interrupted by an incoming call and one of these white girls whom I called, in a fit of frustration, "always seventeen," wanted some money for their magazine *Getting Along*.

44

THURSDAY, APRIL 23, 1996

I wonder whether the producers of the *Today Show* play this tape in order to embarrass and rattle Bryant Gumbel and Al Roker. The story is about a McDonald's in Houston, where they play classical music in order to discourage "riffraff" patrons. The "riffraff" are shown outside. All young black males. But the effort isn't entirely successful, suggests a sneering sarcastic voice. The visual depicts two black males fighting.

Bryant Gumbel's days are numbered, and the quiet, well-mannered Bernard Shaw is let go from CNN, though they tell the press that he wants to retire and write books. Greta Van Susteren said that one of the reasons she left CNN was over the treatment of Bernard Shaw (*New York Times*, January 28, 2002). He's been replaced by a manic Wolf Blitzer, who's like a kid in the toy section of Macy's when the Pentagon tried out its new high-tech weapons on an army that was equipped with 1917 Soviet rifles. Both black men—even those who are understated are getting the shaft, like our Pulitzer prizewinner who got hassled by police who didn't know who he was. Shaw's last day at CNN is awkward. They lavish him with affection. Judy Woodruff praises him silly. She is absolutely giddy. You could tell by Shaw's snappish and curt responses that there's a hidden scene being enacted here. Ted Turner says that while the other networks had white anchors, he congratulates himself instead of Shaw. He'd hired Shaw. Nothing about Shaw's cool professionalism. Bryant Gumbel gets upset because NBC denied his request to interview O. J. They want Katie Couric to do it.

During the O. J. trial a controversy arises about whether one of the voices heard at Bundy, seconds before the murders, is a black voice. The media turn this into ignorant mush as usual, with mostly white commentators debating the issue. Later, during the civil trial, witness Robert Heidstra says that he never heard a black voice, which had been the subject of so much media speculation. His lawyer said that this claim was made by anonymous callers who phoned in during the lunch hour on the day that Heidstra was testifying in the criminal case. Anonymous callers who couldn't be cross-examined.

The decision in the civil case is influenced by mob opinion, stirred up by mob leaders who sit in warm studios and fire up white passions with their rhetoric, but nobody accuses them of bopping people on the head with a whole lot of angry rhetoric or going way over the top about race. Daniel Petrocelli, the Goldmans' lawyer, sees that no black jurors are selected for O. J.'s civil trial, and in his arguments relies upon the blood evidence, much of which has been challenged by the expert forensics team that represented the defense in the criminal trial. The judge refuses to allow evidence that Nicole's murder might have been a drug hit, perpetrated by some of those people of whom she was so scared. Sixty-eight percent of the whites chosen for the jury believe in O. J.'s guilt, yet the judge seats them anyway. In view of these facts, a verdict that held Simpson liable for the deaths of Ron and Nicole was inevitable and after the verdict was handed down, an ugly white mob greeted O. J. as he left the courthouse. Like the one that greeted Lucas Beauchamp in *Intruder in the Dust* (1949).

> Rural Mississippi in the 1940s: Lucas Beauchamp, a local black man with a reputation of not kowtowing to whites, is found standing over the body of a dead white man, holding a pistol that has recently been fired. Quickly arrested for murder and jailed, Beauchamp insists he's innocent and asks the town's most prominent lawyer, Gavin Stevens, to defend him, but Stevens refuses. [IMDB]

The appeal argued by O. J.'s lawyers amounted to one hundred pages, but the appeal was denied by a Court of Appeals that yielded to mob pressure. Those who participated in this marathon lynching won't be satisfied until O. J. is dead, but history will note that two verdicts were rendered by all-white juries in Santa Monica and Las Vegas and that two legal teams saw to it that no blacks would be impaneled, a fact noted in the Simpson lawyer's appeal of the Las Vegas legal debacle.

During the criminal trial not only does Simpson have to face a biased commentariat, an FBI whose scientists are charged with corruption, and Mark Fuhrman, but thousands of armchair prosecutors who can't be cross-examined, as well. A British observer says that opening the trial to deliberators outside of the jury box would never have happened in England.

After the trials, the mob raised by the white press is still looking for revenge. Defense attorneys Barry Scheck and Carl Douglas are fined by the California bar "because we got so many complaints," yet Robert G. Kardashian, who posed as O. J.'s friend, and betrayed attorney-client privilege, is neither fined nor disbarred.

PART 2

45

DEC. 1996

I turn on the Larry King review of 1996. Except for Colin Powell, all of the heroes are white. When it comes to the villains, we get Mel Reynolds, Mike Tyson, and Colin Ferguson.

Dominick Dunne, this Truman Capote wannabe, is on Larry King later protesting O. J.'s receiving money from an infotainment video in which he tells his side of the story about the murders. TV critic John O'Connor uses the adjective "slimy" when writing about a trashy send-up about a relative of Ethel Kennedy, who allegedly murdered a young woman, a miniseries that's run on network TV, of which Dunne is the author. It's called *The Season of Purgatory*.

Former district attorney Ira Reiner is on too. He says that O. J. got away with murder. He's clearly angry. He's the man who prosecuted the MacMartins for a number of years, only to lose the case, which cost the California taxpayers more than thirteen million dollars. This case, about child molestation, was the costliest trial in American history. I switch channels. On *Hard Copy*, Charles Manson prosecutor Leo Bugliosi is rebutting O. J's video without having seen it. A tabloid show says that it has too much class to advertise the 800 number on behalf of O. J's video sales. OK?

46

I called for Rafiki, but a voice came on the phone saying that the party was unavailable. First time that happened. I hailed a taxi. When I reached the Kraal Towers, Goodwill was there carting off furniture that had been set in front of the building. I entered the elevator; Garfield was not in his usual good mood.

"Why so glum?"

"Haven't you heard?"

"Heard what?"

"They fired Renaldo."

"What?"

"Took out all the man's furniture and put it on the sidewalk. Didn't even give him a notice. I'm leaving next week. It's about time I retired. Things ain't the way they used to be around here. I should have left when Kraal took over from that hootenanny crowd that ran the station for years. Something is wrong with that man. The way he treats people. And that Lord. He's just as bad."

When I reached the floor, I found a scene of celebration, not gloom. But of course, there were no blacks around. People were drinking champagne and snacking on hors d'oeuvres. Two waiters were refilling the drinks and trays. Some were surrounding Jagid and Jagan. Lord came up to me. He was a little tipsy.

"What's going on?" I asked.

"Haven't you heard? We've been nominated for a Peabody."

"A Peabody for what?"

"*Nigguz News*, silly."

"That piece of—" I started to say, but Sebastian staggered off to another clump of the staff, all of whom looked like high-school students. Children born in the '80s who believed that the United States fought on the side of Germany in World War II and that the Civil Rights Movement was a movie: *Mississippi Burning*. In this movie, J. Edgar Hoover is found in his office, sobbing over the murders of Schwerner, Goodman, and Chaney. He dispatches agents to Mississippi to, in his words, "Bring those cowardly racist murderers to justice." I got drunk and of course I paid with neuropathy all night. Pins and needles shooting through my legs and feet and toes. I took my prebreakfast One Touch reading. 220.

47

MAY–NOV. 2001

May 2001. Rabbit e-mails The Rhinosphere about an O. J. movie, *Firepower*, a 1979 movie that includes O. J. Simpson, James Coburn, Anthony Franciosa, Eli Wallach, George Gizzard, Vincent Gardenia, and Victor Mature. A top-heavy Sophia Loren strides through the movie exhibiting her protuberances and in one scene throws off a Caribbean black, who has been hired by the wealthy villain, Stegner, to follow her, by pretending that he has attempted to rape her, and steal her purse. She tears some of her clothes in the market in order to create this effect. O. J. plays the manservant (at one point he is referred to as "Eddie," the Coburn character's "man"). James Coburn plays an ex-gangster who has been hired to bring Stegner to justice in the United States. Simpson does all of the heavy lifting in the movie. Drives the car during the car chases, does some football rushes, kills a dog—one of those protecting the beautiful Caribbean estate of the villain, uses his welding skills to open a bank safe, acts as Sophia Loren's bodyguard. Coburn gets to cut a dashing figure, make love to Loren, and gives the Simpson character orders. At one point, he tells him not to drink "because I want you to be bright-eyed in the morning." When O. J. shows up for a party, Coburn says of his tuxedo, "You look like a waiter from an Alabama chicken restaurant."

In the criminal trial, the different demeanors of O. J. are discussed. In this movie, O. J. is constantly changing demeanors. He robs a bank by disguising himself as a bank guard. Later, as a fireman. He is so clever that the white men who protect Stegner say, in admiration, "Whoever that black is, he's not local." They tell the local blacks, who are employed by Stegner, "Find out who that black is and feed him to the sharks." But O. J. is the one who gets to pour blood on a local black and tease the sharks by using him as an offering, suspending him on the side of the boat and threatening to drop him unless he reveals the whereabouts of Stegner. He grins as he tells the poor man that sharks can smell blood a mile away, and sure enough we see the black fins heading toward the boat. O. J. delights when his pursuers "take the bait." Finally after the O. J. character is killed, while trading fire with Stegner's men, who are firing from a plane, one of the villain's men says, "he was expendable." A week before this movie is shown, a man on CNN, commenting on The Boer's conclusion that more studies are needed, before it can be decided that human behavior influences global warming, says, "that's like saying you're hunting for the real killers." He's not the only one who makes a comment about O. J. when O. J. isn't even the topic under discussion, a classical case of an obsession. As professors say, "They were *decontextualizing* O. J."

48

REACTIONS TO 9/11

You would think that one of the greatest catastrophes to hit United States would take the commentators' minds off of O. J. Not on your life. Previously, they coupled O. J. with Tom Sawyer trickster Bill Clinton. Now it's bin Laden whom the posse is hunting. Don Imus says that he hopes that they capture bin Laden and that if he has to stand trial, let him be represented by Chris Darden and Marcia Clark (laughter). Appearing on *This Week*, George Will, who believes that in comparison to whites, blacks are a backward race, wants military tribunals, lest bin Laden be represented by the O. J. Dream Team.

I had flown in from Santa Fe and was in my hotel room in Santa Monica after yet another meeting with the brothers about the prospect of their doing "Attitude, The Badger." My cell phone played the first few bars of Randy Weston's classic "Hi Fly." It was Bat. He told me to turn on the television. "It's here," he said and hung up. I grabbed my cup of coffee and pressed the remote. There were pictures of people running through the streets like you see in the "Hulk" movies, only this Hulk was a towering cloud of smoke filled with little black specks of debris, rolling through the streets with people fleeing from its path. A man wearing glasses came on and said that two planes had hit the World Trade Center causing the buildings to collapse. Then they showed photos of the planes crashing into the buildings. They must have shown the pictures a million times during the next week. Later they said that security was tight below Fourteenth Street. I hung around Santa Monica, visiting bookstores, and strolling along the boardwalk. Later, some talking heads predicted that because of the "terrorist" attack on America, some civil liberties would have to be curtailed. They were right. The Boer gets through a sleepy corporate-financed Congress some measures that some consider fascist. For me, Bat, Rabbit, Snakes, and the rest of the Rhinos, this was nothing new. Blacks have been living in a police state ever since we got here. Check out this *Times'* editorial: "Lingering Questions About 'Stop-and-Frisk'" (February 18, 2010).

> Civil rights groups and some criminologists are understandably troubled by new statistics showing that police officers stopped a record 575,000 people last year—nearly 90% black or Hispanic—and that the number of stops is growing as crime falls. Instead of dismissing such complaints, the police department should re-evaluate the program.

And check out page 4 of *Slave Patrols: Law and Violence in Virginia and the Carolinas*, by Sally E. Hadden, where this interesting passage appears:

> In the South, the "most dangerous people" who were thought to need watching were slaves—they were the prime targets of patrol observation and capture. The history of police work in the South grows out of this early fascination by white patrollers with what African American slaves were doing. Most law enforcement was, by definition, white patrolmen watching, catching, or beating black slaves.

I spent the afternoon chilling, and channel surfing. The one-eyed beast that had recently been dining on O. J., Chandra Levy, and the Ramseys had turned its attention to bigger game. Islam. Raising lynch mobs against Arabs and Arab Americans. Some of the footage reminded me of how the same people demonized blacks after the decision in the O. J. criminal trial. Some Palestinian children are shown celebrating the destruction of the World Trade Center buildings just as the black university students were shown celebrating the acquittal of O. J. Simpson. That's because in a society in which collective blame is cast upon the many for the alleged crimes of the few, his acquittal meant theirs. Those Palestinians who burn candles for the victims, like the blacks who disapproved of the O. J. verdict, are virtually ignored. The media are after the Arabs and prosecutors, yearning to become famous and are still after O. J., Jeffrey Toobin, and others who began "The Racial Divide," ignored the white patrons in a Buffalo bar who cheered when O. J. was acquitted.

After a minor traffic incident during which both O. J. and a man named Jeffrey Pattinson exhibited outbursts of road rage, Simpson was accused of "running a red light and yanking a driver's glasses off his face." His lawyer, Yale Galanter, said that they were treating this minor traffic incident like a death penalty case. Abbe Rifkin was the prosecutor. She'd promised the Simpson haters that she'd try to get put him away for sixteen years, were he convicted. She missed. The jury acquitted Simpson on October 24, 2001.

An elderly white woman was removed from the jury when a black member overheard her saying that "If they'd gotten that bastard in Los Angeles, we wouldn't be here," reflecting the sentiment of the Santa Monica all-white civil jury, most of whom had decided that Simpson was guilty, even before they were impaneled. They ultimately decided that Simpson was liable in the deaths of Ron Goldman and Nicole Simpson.

Now you would think that the progressive community would express outrage at the bold and obvious attempt to bag Simpson by sentencing him to sixteen years for a traffic incident and handing him over to the tender mercies of the Florida prison system, but what is their stance? Laura Flanders is one of these progressives who believes that the plight of middle-class white women is worse than that of black men and women; she's always complaining about the lack of "women's" voices in the media, when every time you channel surf you see a blonde, or turn on NPR or Pacifica you hear a white middle-class woman. The *St. Petersburg Times* reported on December 11, 2006, that:

> Bill McLaughlin, a former *CBS Evening News* correspondent who teaches at Quinnipiac University in Connecticut, said that the network's problem stretches across the industry.

"The bench is now attractive, fairly young white women," he said. "My specific quote to *Newsweek* on this was that they look like the front line of the Ziegfeld Follies. Maybe they figure the 18 to 35 audience they're trying to reach is (obtained) by using good-looking young white women.

Ms. Flanders said that O. J.'s situation was amusing. I don't know about these liberals and progressives. (The *Times* reports that one of these oppressed women was so upset about the World Trade Center that she couldn't return to her studio in Tribeca and had to travel to Santa Fe to paint.) Explain this. As soon as things get tight, as a result of the World Trade Center bombing, Alan Dershowitz, a liberal, calls for a national ID card. While Bob Barr, considered a backward thinking politician, questions legislation that might curtail their civil liberties. A national ID card? For Bat, Rabbit, Otter, Snakes, and me, our skin color is our national ID card.

Bat makes a comment on Rhino about a young subcontinent Indian woman, a Tribeca maven, who had complained about the odor from the World Trade Center ruins, and how these fumes she was inhaling might affect her in later years. She was worried because she couldn't get white men up to her apartment because of the fumes, Bat had written. Talking to Bat on the telephone, I noticed that he ended remarks like this with a curious cackle. Too bad he couldn't get that cackle down on paper.

She was luckier than many. Some residents of downtown Manhattan had found body parts in their homes. Two hands tied up, with no body. This young woman with her face contorted into a cosmetic mask was one of those who didn't get it. Who thought that she could assimilate into white society.

She was naïve, like Ms. Arundhati Roy, the Indian novelist. As long as she aimed digs at Indian society, the U.S. media welcomed her observations. But when she criticized American foreign policy, she couldn't get her opinions printed in the magazines and newspapers which had been open to her views up until then. *The Boondocks*, a cartoon strip by Aaron McGruder, was pulled by the *Daily News* because one of his cartoons discussed the covert funds and training supplied to Osama bin Laden by the Reagan administration. But he made out better than Julio Briceño, a cartoonist in Panama. He was facing a defamation trial over a cartoon that upset a former vice president of Panama. But when Kobe came up for his turn at the gauntlet, McGruder gets back on board, playing to the obsessions of his syndicators. A cartoon about how O. J. tells Kobe not to give up on white women just because of his entrapment.

49

2000

"I'm not going to be some dancing monkey for you guys," O. J. says. During Fox's "O. J. Lashes Out" Week, moderators ask, how do we get O. J. (how do we bag this coon)? And one nerdy-looking Fox broadcaster wants to know why O. J. is still allowed on public golf courses and accuses him of dancing to spite Fred Goldman. How does the public express its "animus" and "angst" about O. J., asks a frustrated Fox commentator. Can't we get him on perjury? Why can't we skin this coon? One moderator says that O. J.'s outburst is the "Talk of the Country." Others term it, "The Talk of the World," but nobody seems to be talking about it outside the frantic faces on Fox television where O. J. called in to challenge Denise, on Thursday, June 8, 2000. They even bring in some blondes who are as indistinguishable as most of the poetry in *American Poetry, Vol. II,* another book that I brought up here to read. Ho, hum. "Doesn't take much to get O. J. worked up," says Salon.com. The Salon writer goes on to say that the spats between O. J. and his new girlfriend are beginning to resemble the relationship between O. J. and Nicole.

"The trial of the century" has spilled over into the twenty-first as the cable networks, whose ratings have gone south since the O. J. civil trial, when the all-white jury found him liable. (During the first week in June, 2004, the commentators substitute the word "guilty" for "liable," but why would we be surprised that the American tabloid media, which now uses the *National Inquirer* as a credible source, takes the prosecution's side?) They served as little more than a procurer for The Boer and his fake premise that Saddam had weapons of mass destruction, and CNN's White House correspondent is so devoted to the Boer administration that when he leaves office, she would accompany him to Crawford, Texas, like Diane Sawyer accompanied Richard Nixon to San Diego.

Fox is trying to drum up some business by using O. J. in a twenty-first century version of a slave auction. O. J., during his "outburst," says that he will take a lie-detector test for money, but not for free. "I'm not going to be your dancing monkey," he says, but he is, isn't he? He's earned the networks a few billion and allowed a whole bunch of corporations to make a killing, so to speak, while he has to survive on a modest football pension. It was Chris Matthews who credited O. J. with the rise of cable television.

Geraldo Rivera is as happy as he can be. His ratings had plunged so that on some nights his only sponsor was Cowboy Don Edward's *Saddle Songs*. And so the O. J. phenomenon is like this diabetes-related toenail fungus I received recently. No matter how much cream one applies, it's bound to flare up again. Jeff Cohen of FAIR (Fairness & Accuracy In Reporting) is barely tolerated by a Fox host of a media show. Cohen says that Fox is just trying to make some money, because they weren't around when CNN and other cable channels made their money off O. J., and so Fox is trying to make some money now, and lo and behold, during the commercial break for this O. J. show, which includes four white men and one white woman, the racial makeup of your typical anti-O. J. TV panel, Fox does a promo for their upcoming O. J. shows. The dancing monkey. A digital slave who earns money for those who despise him while under the threat of a thirty-three-million-dollar judgment, the highest award ever made against an individual in a civil case. Finally, a Fox suit asks a Fox blonde who interviews O. J. whether she didn't feel that she'd come in contact with "slime." At Fox, they must be experts on slime. Roger Ailes, Fox president, nixed the story about the dire consequences to consumers from a Bovine Growth Hormone which another mad scientist has invented. It may make cow's milk warm, but it promotes tumor growths in mammals. So let's say that O. J. did murder Nicole and Ron. Who is responsible for more murders? O. J., or somebody who gives consumers cancer by injecting Bovine Growth Hormone into cows, or drug companies guilty of mass murder by making billions on drugs whose harmful effects they tried to hide, like Avandia, which was no better than Actos, and riskier to the heart. The *New York Times* showed this on July 13, 2010:

> But instead of publishing the results, the company spent the next 11 years trying to cover them up, according to documents recently obtained by *The New York Times*.

The company did not post the results on its Web site or submit them to federal drug regulators, as is required in most cases by law.

The O. J. ratings at CNBC are orchestrated by Jim Welch, of General Electric. Well what about the corporate murderers who get off because they are able to afford wealthy law firms? The corporate murderers who are able to buy presidents. The day after the Scalia coup, pharmaceuticals, tobacco, and oil stocks rose. These companies own The Boer, a white dancing monkey.

Monsanto's Heifer

50

Esther and I are back together. As a matter of fact, we celebrated the last eclipse of the millennium, taking turns photographing each other with a Minicam, the moon in the background. She'd gone to Spain to track down her Gypsy relatives. At first it was exhilarating, but after a while she became tired of their singing songs asking why people disliked them and wondering why they were despised all over the world. She decided that she could get that kind of discussion around the house listening to me and the Rhino group. At first they were standoffish because they noticed that her Gypsy clothes were designed by Yves St. Laurent, but as they began to know her, my Esther, they accepted her as one of their own.

My most recent show was held at the Kenkeleba (spelled correctly, whew!) Gallery in New York with the critics raving about my Santa Fe style and its elements of negritude. After the closing of the opening, we returned to our Tribeca apartment to relax.

Esther went into the bedroom to lie down and read a book. She walked past the doorway to take the mail out of our mail slot. After about fifteen minutes, Esther came out of the bedroom. She was clearly upset.

"What's wrong, baby?"

"It's Hibiscus."

"What?" Hibiscus had been living in Africa for a year on a Fulbright. She had broken up with Karisha and had gone to Africa to get over it.

"Something wrong? She hurt or something?" She handed me the letter.

"She's getting married. He's what they call an Oba. He's very wealthy."

"That's great. And so you're so happy that you're crying."

"He has thirteen other wives."

"What?" She read the letter that Hibiscus had sent.

"Dear Mom and Dad. I have good news. I'm becoming the 14th wife of Oba—. Please don't be shocked. My fellow wives are so thrilled that I, a foreigner, will join their number. Unlike the western and Arabian marriage, in which the woman has no respect, the polygamous marriage guarantees that a woman will have autonomy, which is why many women find polygamy attractive, even educated women like me. They're preparing a wonderful ceremony next month. Of course, both of you are invited. I'm so excited. It might even be carried on satellite." I thought for a moment. Esther was distraught. I went into the kitchen and made her some green tea. It always calmed her down. I handed it to her. "What are we going to do?" she asked. *What are we going to do?* I started to say, *you were the one who condoned the idea of Karisha and Hibiscus getting married, starting her down the slippery slope.* I had an idea. I called up Karisha.

"Hello." Grumpy.

"Karisha?"

"Yeah." Real sullen and unfriendly.

"This is Hibiscus' father, Bear." She hung up. I called her again.

"What do you want? Last I heard you were supporting that evil dog, O. J. Simpson. How do you feel about your hero now. Ha!" I had to ignore this jab if I were to make peace.

"Karisha. I'm in New York. I'd like to come to New Hampshire and meet with you." She had become one of those feminist professors who was using the curriculum as an excuse to vent her rage against the men in their lives. Especially the dads.

"You know how much Hibiscus cares for you. I mean, you've been separated for a year and that happens to a lot of people, even Esther and me. You know she went to Europe to uncover her roots after her father confessed that they were gypsies."

"What's that got to do with me?" she grumbled.

"I think that you and Hibiscus should give it another try."

"What? After all of the hassles you gave us with your homophobia."

"I know. But I've developed a more enlightened attitude—" She really got a big laugh from that remark. I put the phone down for some seconds so that I wouldn't hear her scornful laugh.

"You, enlightened? All you did to defend that acquitted scumbag, O. J. Simpson. You—"

"Listen, there's no need for us to argue on the phone. I can take a bus to Hanover tomorrow. We can talk and then we, hey I got an idea, we can call Hibiscus in Africa, that would be fun—"

"Keep talkin'."

"What you say, I can bring a couple of bottles of cognac and we can all have dinner and—"

"Keep talkin'."

"Hibiscus would love to hear from you; we get letters from her. She's missing you." I lied. She paused for a moment.

"I'll be waitin'."

"The Dartmouth Coach will be arriving at two P.M. We can have dinner at The Hanover Inn." She hung up. I didn't want to discuss O. J. with her. I mean, the fact that none of Simpson's fingerprints was found at the crime scene.

Would the mystery of June 12 ever be solved? Was I the only one who had questions? Fred Goldman said that he would forget about the money if O. J. would describe how he killed Nicole and Ron. I thought that Petrocelli had described how it was done. Why didn't that satisfy him? Why did he need Simpson to explain? And how will the all-news networks make money now that O. J. is done? As Henry Lee said. Something Wrong. "Is something wrong?" I asked Esther. She gave me a generous smile. She'd overheard my conversation with Karisha.

"I now realize how much I love you. I married a man who can change. All of the gay bashing that you used to do was so, so Ashcroft. So backward. But now you're asking Karisha to reconcile with Hibiscus. You're so creative." She gave me a hug. I was feeling like a protagonist in one of those novels which have been written fiftymillioneleven times. One who grows in the course of the novel and by the end has changed. A character with whom the reader and critics could identify. I'd had my Road to Damascus event.

Otter had married a Japanese dancer and moved to Kyoto. Esther and I were aging gracefully, as they say. When it came to O. J. we had to agree to disagree. This was also the agreement I'd made with my daughter and her partner, Karisha, for whom O. J. represented worldwide male evil. They got back together, lucky for her, because shortly after she left Nigeria to be with Karisha again, this Oba was assassinated for taking bribes from Big Oil. They moved to San Francisco. Once in a while, I saw the two of them marching in a Gay Pride parade. Those who thought that the O. J. story would go away were wrong. It's O. J. Forever. Take the end of the year 2000, for example. There are people who can't get O. J. off their minds. The country is still obsessed with O. J. I'm not the only one. If there were an O. J. recovery group, I'd sign up. Bill Maher would lead the recovery sessions. But given my history, I will survive this. So will Paul Mooney, the comedian. He's had his ups and downs because he failed to follow the directive that art by African Americans be quiet and should not make those who can afford seventy dollar tickets for a play about how blacks are given to "self-sabotage" anxious people who can afford satellite. (I took the hint, though.)

He's anything but quiet and his act leaves white people so uncomfortable that very few show up at an Oakland club, called On Broadway, for his December 2000 show. Mooney's take on O. J. is that O. J. is suffering from what Bill Clinton, whom some have called President O. J., calls AGD: Attention Getting Deficit. According to Paul Mooney, O. J. calls 911 because he wants to make the newspapers. "I'm not your dancing monkey," O. J. told Fox.

Mooney says that with his deftness with knives, O. J. could get a job at Benihana's. He says this to say that O. J. would have had to be superhuman to have done all he did within the prosecutor's timeline of ten minutes. Drive from Rockingham to Brentwood, murder two worked-out young people, drive home, dispose of the murder weapons, change clothes, summon a limousine, and catch a plane for Chicago. Mooney goes on with his routine about white people, whom he represents with a frightened, weak, and cowardly voice. Says that *The Blair Witch Project* didn't surprise him, because white people are always missing. The club owners don't realize the talent of this man, asking him to leave the stage after two hours. "I'm making money for these brothers and they ask me to leave the stage. I bet you wouldn't ask Bob Hope to do that." Without missing a beat, he says, mimicking an imaginary club owner, "Nigger, what you doing interrupting the great Bob Hope. Nigger, you fired." Paul Mooney is a survivor. Me too. I thought the performance was a little raunchy but was delightful in spots. Mooney has a little better material than Pryor, but Pryor had depth.

51

It's 2008. Ben, Bat, and Snakes, had deserted the brother. Snakes writes in one of those eloquent e-mails he always sends in which everything is spelled out:

> My fellow Rhinos. It is with regret that I tender my resignation as a Rhino. I've enjoyed our exchanges over the years which registered our grievances about black men, whom we likened to Ted Joan's rhino, galloping through the rainforest looking for some leaves to munch on only to be poached by his enemies, but I think that we are all preaching to the choir, so to speak. In other words we're at risk of becoming a cult instead of finding some way to reach the outside world. We are at risk of being hoisted on our own petard. We must ask ourselves whether our support for O. J. Simpson, an arthritic has-been football player with knee problems and bad feet, isn't counterproductive. Besides, we're entering a phase in our lengthy struggle where

our brightest people are beginning to place race in the background. Any other position would be counterproductive.

The next day, we read that Snakes, as we called him, had been appointed to the presidency of a small university. Part of his getting the job depended upon the result of a very thorough screening. Otter was still on board and so was Rabbit. In fact, he had contacted me and I was to meet him for the first time. He told me to meet him for a drink. Said that he had spent the day meeting with film producers at the Plaza. He had something to discuss with me. Though we communicated almost daily by e-mail, we never saw each other in person. Come to think of it, it's doubtful that we would be friends were we to associate with one another frequently.

I met him the next day at the bottom of Central Park, across from the Mayflower Hotel where Esther and Hibiscus once had their jewelry stolen. There was a little white appearing in his beard. I was upset about how *TV Guide* had put Elvis Presley—this rhythmless, nonsinging cultural imperialist who had ripped off black music—as the entertainer of the year. I was pissed about how "I Can't Get No Satisfaction" by the Rolling Stones was placed as the number one Rock and Roll piece of the century. How can that be? Fats Domino was still alive. I was bitching like a Gypsy.

"Warm, huh?"

"Yeah." There were people seated on benches, joggers, roller skaters. I thought I'd begin the counterpunching. "Did you see where Jim Brown is challenging this judge who sentenced him to community service? And what did you think about Elvis Presley being named entertainer of the year by *TV Guide*? And how about the all-white male roster of achievers for the millennium by the mass media?"

We sat down on a bench. An old man was sitting across from us. He was wearing a fedora, a long coat that reached his ankles, dark glasses and his coat collars were covering his face. He was reading a newspaper, but from time to time he peered over the top of the newspaper at us.

"I've been asked to do a TV script on O. J. and Nicole," Rabbit said. I thought about that one for a moment.

"Well, that's good isn't it? I mean you'll have an opportunity to set the record straight. Tell the brother's side of the story."

"Not exactly," he said. I turned to him. He looked away.

"What do you mean, not exactly?" I said, my brows furrowed.

"They want me to write a guilty ending." We were silent for a moment.

"Just like the all-white jury."

"We all have to give up some ass from time to time."

"Some more than others."

"Sorry you feel that way. But this book, *If I Did It*—"

"He did that book in order to raise money for Sydney and Justin. Doesn't mean that he's confessed."

"That's not the point."

"What's the problem, then?"

"I got to have a triple bypass and my insurance has a $25,000 deductible."

"Oh, I didn't know."

"Look, we're not getting any younger. Let these young people carry on. You know, back there in the '60s we were all full of vim and vigor, but now I can hardly get up in the morning."

"You try vitamin D? That's to help with the aches and pains." He rose from the bench and began to hobble away.

"Rabbit?" He turned to me.

"Do you really believe that he could have driven to Bundy, killed two healthy people, a man afflicted with football injuries, returned in a Bronco whose floor wasn't covered with blood, and disposed of the knives in ten minutes? And then these all-white juries backed up by an all-white commentariat—it was a lynching like in the Old South."

"You got to get this O. J. thing behind you. He got it behind him. Maybe jail is good for him. Let him cool out. He was a constant embarrassment. You're still trying those cases in your mind. I told you that this diabetes came about because of your obsession with this O. J. thing. It turned you into a gazer and starer. Sitting in front of television and going to bed on a belly full of chocolate chip cookies. French fries. Fried okra and snapper. Fried catfish burgers. Alligator popcorn. Praline candy. Banana pudding.

"As a matter of fact, Esther called me once and asked me to intervene. She was concerned about your weight. She said that you were sneaking over to Big Fat Chickens and using coupons that allowed you to get two Big Fats for one. You saw how your weight ballooned up."

"That's far-fetched. It's hereditary. Both my aunts on my father's side had it." How did she know about Big Fat Chickens, I thought.

"That's what you say. But others hold diabetes as being the result of stress. That's you all right. You're not going to convince these white people that he didn't do it. You're not going to prevent them from mixing you, me, and a whole bunch of other guys up with O. J. So what? Get over it. Don't let them control you the way that One Touch monitor controls you. Telling you when to have a snack, when you haven't given enough blood. You'll never give up enough blood to satisfy these people." We shook hands. Formal. Cold. Rabbit disappeared into the West Side. I was getting hungry. I walked downtown, thinking, aimlessly. I stopped in front of The Big Fat Chicken.

I was so depressed that I needed to abandon my bland diabetic diet and get ahold of some mother food. Plus it had a jukebox that featured James Brown, M. J., George Clinton, Rick James, and Prince. There was a picket line outside. Mostly white, mostly young. Women. As I passed the picket line, a young white woman yelled out, "Those are not real chickens they're serving in there." Another young white woman yelled, "They're genetically manipulated organisms with no beaks, no feathers and no feet. They're antichickens." I pushed her out of the way and entered the restaurant. She yelled at me. I went to the counter and ordered.

"Your people should be the last ones to patronize these places. Obesity is a big problem in the black community. Soul food is the second leading cause of death among black men."

I ordered three pieces of this antichicken, with a side order of mashed potatoes and green peas. When I got home I got another jolt. As soon as I opened the door, Esther ran up to me.

"You've won! You've won!"

"Won what?"

"Read this." She handed me the telegram.

"You've been awarded $250,000.00 first prize from the International Society of Cartoonists."

"What. For what?" I was puzzled.

"I was cleaning out your wastepaper basket, and saw this cartoon. Look, I made a copy of it. The cartoon that had O. J.'s face pasted to a horse's behind. I submitted it to this competition."

"Esther. Why did you do that? All of the brothers have abandoned O. J. Somebody has to be on his side. Only me and Otter are left. I drew that cartoon at a weak moment. When the blood evidence was introduced, but now I'm convinced that the blood evidence was planted. Dr. Henry Lee said that the drops at Rockingham looked as though they came from an eye dropper and Mark Furhman had a history of planting evidence. He was set up by the LAPD which has a history of corruption. I'd read in Paula Barbieri's book that O. J. referred to himself as a black stallion. It's half finished. The horse looks emaciated and I wanted to place O. J's face on the horse's behind, not as something that the horse relieves himself of." *Why would they give a prize to something as sloppily drawn as that,* I thought.

"Besides, the picture is unfinished."

"That makes it avant-garde. Haven't you seen Larry Rivers's 'Dutch Masters'? It's unfinished."

"Who the hell is Larry Rivers?"

"But remember what you said about Billy Strayhorn? He threw his masterpiece, 'Take the A Train,' into the wastebasket. It was Mercer Ellington who retrieved it. This cartoon transcends the simple art of cartooning."

I ignored the simple art of cartooning remark. I wanted to say that this simple art of cartooning had paid the bills all of these years.

"I can't accept that prize. I would be selling out."

"Look, Bear." Even she'd begun calling me that instead of my real name. Paul Blessings. Had something to do with an ancestor who was hidden from slave catchers by Quakers. "Hibiscus and I are tired of this O. J. shit. The guy is a simple-minded idiot, a wife-batterer and murderer, yet he's taken over your life. Besides when I first met you, you use to make fun of athletes. Called them rich slaves."

"Athletics were one of the few avenues open to the brothers."

"The brothers! The brothers! That's all you think about. Goddamn it. I've talked to Hibiscus and she agrees."

"Agrees about what?"

"That . . . that you have to choose between O. J. and your family. Which is it?"

I had to think about it. Sleep on it. Sleep on the couch, because Esther said that she didn't want me in bed with her until I reached a decision. Only me and Otter were left but a letter that arrived the next day changed my mind. It was from Otter.

> Hey, Bear, I'm in a jam here in Japan. I've sent my family on to New York and they will be arriving to stay with relatives until I can get there. I can't leave yet because these nutty Mishima followers are looking for me, but some of the people in the antiroyalist community are hiding me. We're waiting for a boat that will take me to Korea. With hope, not a slow boat. I feel like one of the fugitive slaves in a neoslave narrative, a term coined by Ishmael Reed. Speaking of Ishmael Reed, he's sort of responsible

for the predicament I'm in. In an issue of MELUS a critic named Tsunehiko Kato criticized Ishmael Reed for his sexist attitudes. Well, given that a Japanese critic felt that all of the sexism could be applied solely to black male writers, I figured Japan to be a country where Japanese women have been liberated since he has time to criticize black men and their relationship to women. That there's no need for a liberation movement in Japan because the women have been emancipated and so he can go to the United States and hector the brothers over there.

This gave me the idea for my debut puppet show. "The Liberation of Princess Masako." I felt that given his blaming black men for all of the world's sexism, the Japanese audience would be open to showing crown Princess Masako as a liberated woman. In my script, she's a Harvard and Oxford graduate and has decided that she no longer wishes to be a human incubator for the production of Japan's next Emperor. She hasn't produced a male heir and since Princess Kiko and her husband Prince Akishino have, her child, a daughter, has no chance and the move to change the law so that her daughter can become Empress is now moot. In the denouement, we see Princess Masako shocking Emperor Akihito and Empress Michiko, Kiko and Akishinoa and the old nosey household agency chief Shingo Haketa by announcing that she is leaving the monarchy to pursue a career. She calls the monarchy outdated and a parasitic institution freeloading off the Japanese people who are suffering unemployment and homelessness.

Well, the show didn't even complete the first act before people started throwing things and booing. I had to be hustled out of the theater by the side-door exit. Now these right-wing guys who motor about the streets of Tokyo with their loudspeakers blaring are denouncing me for defaming the royal family. Anyway, you support O. J. I'm trying to save my own *deguchi*. I know now why this Kato guy is talking about liberating women in the States and not here. If he's serious, he'll quit the States and return. Take up the cause of Japanese women instead of living a soft life on some American university campus. Attending faculty teas. All-expenses-paid sabbaticals. In my opinion, this guy is missing in action.

Otter had abandoned the O. J. cause. He said that he was interested in saving his own black ass. Good advice. And as Ben said, why should O. J. and I be the only ones broke?

Hell, the city of Los Angeles made four hundred million dollars as a result of newspeople and others from all over the world showing up for the year-long trial. Hotels, restaurants, etc. made millions. After I finished reading the letter, I went into Esther's office. She looked at me, a look that made me feel like I was a planet covered with ice. I announced my decision. She rose, walked toward me and embraced me for a long time.

52

Get this, their escort called and said that they were ready to depart for the ceremonies. Esther was dressed to the max in elegance and sophistication. I didn't look all that bad myself. Tuxedo. Bowtie. We climbed into the black Lincoln that drove us to the site that the International Society of Cartoonists had booked for the event. When we entered the Waldorf, we were escorted to our suite from where we would descend to the ballroom.

To think, I'd entered the hotel whose history was associated with colorful characters like Mark Twain, Lillian Russell, Gentleman Jim Corbett. As soon as Esther and I entered the ballroom people began smiling at us and some applauded. After some speakers had finished their part of the program it came time for me to receive the award named for one of the country's most brilliant cartoonists, George Herriman. It was a gold replica of Krazy Kat. They announced my name and I mounted the stairs and headed for the podium, my cartoon of O. J. projected onto a screen. O. J.'s face on a horse's ass. The audience stood as one and began to shout my name. "Bear, Bear, Bear."

I began my remarks. I thanked all of the board of directors of the organization and acknowledged the judges who had bestowed the award upon me. I tried to begin the main text of my remarks with a joke. "I've prepared a ten minute acceptance speech, about the time that O. J. was supposed to have murdered two people, driven home, changed, and headed to the airport." A groan went up from the audience. I looked down at Esther. I could see that she was looking for an inconspicuous exit. I got the message. I'd watched many Oscar Award ceremonies so I had some guidance as how to start my acceptance speech.

"My fellow cartoonists. Gee, I'm so overwhelmed. I don't know where to begin. Wow. This is unbelievable. I guess I should thank my lifelong partner, Esther." Esther beamed.

"She rescued the cartoon from the wastebasket. The cartoon that was responsible for my getting here. I want to thank George Herriman, after which this award is named. Where would our profession be without the contribution of this innovative mind? I want to thank some of the African American cartoonist pioneers. Ollie Harrington, E. Simms Campbell, Wilbert L. Holloway, Leslie Rogers, Zelda (Jackie) Ormes, Morrie Turner of 'Wee Pals,' and *Playboy* cartoonist Buck Brown. (As each name was mentioned, one of their cartoons was shown on a screen above my head, followed by applause.)

"And their successors. And now Robb Armstrong, Stephen Bentley, Ray Billingsley, Barbara Brandon, George Winners, Walt Carr, Ramzah and Gerald Dyes, and Robert Gill, Brumsic Brandon Jr. and the great novelist, Charles Johnson. We African American cartoonists have come a long way, but there is still much ground to cover. Recently, black cartoonists protested the omission of their work in mainstream publications. Little has changed since the time of Orrin C. Evans, 'The Father of Black Comic Books.' He was born in 1902 and died in 1971. He exposed segregation in the armed forces in 1944 and won the Hayward Hale Broun award that same year. Imagine the slights that he took he took on our behalf. Charles Lindbergh, the Nazi sympathizer, refused to allow him into a press conference during which he discussed the kidnapping of his child.

"This pioneer, this brave journalist who was subjected to death threats produced All-Negro Comics in June 1947. It was created by blacks and featured an all black cast in lead heroic roles.

"A second issue was planned. The artwork was completed, but was never published. He had trouble getting white vendors to sell his work but with cyberspace, we can overcome this. We can cut out the distributors. I once pooh-poohed the idea of blogs. But now I can see where the Internet can put power into the hands of those who are infomationally challenged."

(*Applause*)

"The 1940s saw other tests for our colleagues, I direct your attention to the screen. (A picture appeared. It showed students at St. Patrick's Academy in Binghamton, New York, making a bonfire of comics.) This comic book burning occurred in 1949 at St. Patrick's Academy. A few years earlier, in 1945, students at Saint Peter and Paul elementary school burned 1,567 comic books, among them classics like *Batman*, *Wonder Woman*, *The Spirit*, *Superman*, *Captain Marvel*, and some as harmless as *Archie*. Have we forgotten these scenes of the burning of cartoonist art? The investigations? The arrest of newsdealers? A nationwide hysteria launched by the mad doctor Fredric Wertham? Comic books dismissed as 'lewd, filthy, indecent, and disgusting'? We survived this witch hunt and now there exists in San Francisco a Cartoon Museum, the brainchild of Rod Gilchrist who, along with others, did much to raise cartoons to the status of an art form; comics are now considered art and we cartoonists artists.

"The Pop artists also did much to introduce cartoons into the most prestigious galleries: Andy Warhol's 'Dick Tracy', 1960, eleven years after the comic book bonfires; Roy Lichtenstein's 'Blam', 1962. And let's not forget Poons and Koons. Larry and Jeff were responsible for elevating cartoon art. Jeff with his famous Popeye and the lobster hanging above the sailor's head. Black, Hispanic, and Asian American artists subverted popular images deemed offensive. Joe Overstreet, Robert Colescott, David Hammonds and members of the younger generation, Paul 'DJ Spooky' Miller. Let's not forget Amiri Baraka and others who based their poems on radio heroes, Hollywood stars. Baraka's 'Jello'. Frank O'Hara's poem about Lana Turner.

"I know that our people have suffered many setbacks as a result of the dwindling newspaper readership, cutbacks, buyouts. But we've faced challenges in the past that we overcame and I'm sure that we will meet this one. As the great David Levine said, 'Caricature is a form of hopeful statement: I'm drawing this critical look at what you're doing, and I hope that you will learn something from what I'm doing.' Let us not forget our role. That of providing the critical look."

I received a standing ovation. I glanced down at Esther. She was brushing away tears. That night I dreamed that Popeye was scolding me for abandoning O. J. In the cartoon, I had big feet.

PART 3

53

YEARS 2008–2010

Gabriel Grasso [Simpson's attorney during the Las Vegas memorabilia case] highlighted several instances where he suggested investigators' demonstrated bias.

Page 193 of the LVPD transcript quotes two investigators as they process evidence in the Palace Station hotel room. It reads:

MICHAEL PERKINS: This is great. Yeah. Uh, John said, he's like, yeah. California can't get him _____ now we'll be _____ got him.

(Laughing)

Grasso said that even with the court's "junky sound system," listeners can tell that crime scene analyst Michael Perkins is actually saying, "California can't get it (expletive) done, now we'll get it done."

He suggested the investigators were talking about Simpson's 1995 double-murder acquittal.

Grasso said investigators had it in for Simpson and were determined to build the case against him.

Later in the transcript, on page 148, Perkins and another investigator, Clint Nichols, talk about Simpson's imminent arrest.

NICHOLS: Uh, he's gonna get arrested.

PERKINS: Who, who's gonna get arrested?

NICHOLS: O. J.

PERKINS: Oh, good.

—*Las Vegas Sun*, September 29, 2008

Rafiki stopped driving for Kraal years ago. He bought a home on Staten Island. Used the equity to purchase two more homes. Finally bought a building in Harlem and rented it out. Hakeem Olajuwon Arms. Sebastian Lord was offered a job with a London newspaper and returned to England to the relief of American journalists who found themselves competing with journalists who were hired over them solely on the basis of an English accent. Every word they uttered, no matter how ridiculous, was considered profound.

KCAK was losing money and in a desperate attempt to appeal to a new younger crowd had hired Virginia's pirate radio friends, who, predictably, left the Lower East Side, moved into Trump Towers, cleaned up and began appearing in the society pages of the *Anglo Saxon Explainer*. Kraal's blog, once experimental, was expanded to a site called The Weekly Carnivore, which was devoted to gossip about celebrities, about which Hollywood actors were getting married, divorced, and having children. Princessa Bimbette became a star with huge ratings at Wolverine, Rathswheeler's anchor TV operation. She created something called *The Kettles*, people who were so disaffected from government that they were on the verge of blowing their tops. She did her show dressed in a camouflage outfit and guns strapped to her hips. She was now urging people to arm themselves for a March on Washington for the purpose of ousting the Antichrist.

Raquel and Ben got married. At the wedding, the Nuyo 'Xicans sat on one side of the room and Ben's black and white friends sat on the other side. The blacks and whites were laughing it up and celebrating nosily. The Nuyo 'Xicans were subdued. At the reception the black disc jockey didn't know any Mexican music and so—what the hell—he played Horace Silver's "Señor Blues." Karisha and Hibiscus found out what many married couples discovered. That married life can be miserable. Both were living alone and joining a growing number of single adults their age.

Naomi Campbell got into trouble in London after a dispute about an airline's handling of her Louis Vuitton luggage. Seeing that she was the most beautiful woman in the world, over this white goddess Diana (Bat once said he imagined Charles had to work all night to get her to come), he couldn't understand why the Queen didn't intervene. But her prediction, that for the media O. J. stood for all black men, was as true in 2008 as it was in 1995 and as it is in 2011. The media even glommed him onto the third black president of the United States. Barack Obama. For example, Bill Maher said that he knew that blacks would come home to Obama because they came home to O. J., one of many references that Maher has made to O. J. over the years. The New Jersey Republican Party had to take down an ad that read "Obama loves America likes O. J. loves Nicole."

I invested my prize money and still held "Koots the Badger" in suspension, not knowing whether I would ever draw him again. I hadn't thought about O. J. in months.

KCAK TV had become the bottom of the bottom line, its cameras scouring the alleyways looking for used condoms to film or taking up whole segments to follow car chases. If cable had become a sewer, it reflected the American mood in the summer of 2008 when one of the top tourist attractions was the men's room at the Minneapolis airport where a senator was the subject of a sex sting. A summer during which Britney Spears invited the paparazzi to join her in the toilet. Project Censored reported that the corporate press also made more of an issue about the death of dogs than about the Iraqi people whose death toll had reached one million. Around the time Tiger Woods was cut down to size for doing what many white male celebrities are admired for. One scandal sheet said that they had retrieved the tampon of one of Wood's girlfriends, after Woods and the woman had left the scene in the parking lot where he fucked her against the car. She warned Tiger that she was damp, but Tiger wouldn't be dissuaded. Focused on that pussy as he would a three-foot putt.

According to Chris Matthews, cable originated with the O. J. trial. People are still cashing in. I got mine. The summer of 2008 saw Ron Goldman's father denounce *If I Did It*. It was penned by a ghostwriter. The money was supposed to go to a trust for his children, Justin and Sydney.

After calling the book "sick" and "disgusting," Goldman decides to cash in on it. Denise, his former partner in gaining sympathy from a majority of the American public for their shared tragedies, breaks with Goldman. Says she finally realizes what the Gold in his name means.

Of course, she's been called a gold digger herself, accused of cashing in on her late sister's murder. Simpson commented about Goldman's hypocrisy: "I find it sort of hypocritical that they talked everybody in America to boycott the book: it was 'immoral,' it was 'blood money,'" he told interviewer Kate Delaney for the Associated Press. "But we now see it wasn't 'blood money' if they got the money."

August 1, 2007. After O. J. is convicted in another public lynching by the all-white corporate media and another all-white jury, the Goldmans go on TV to talk about O. J.'s "ugly face," and to make other nasty remarks. The bloggers, with no advertisers dictating the content of their POVs, which was the case of the pro-Goldman media of the 1990s, are not as supportive of Fred Goldman and Denise Brown as the corporate media. They take note of Fred

Goldman's flip-flop, first calling *If I Did It* sick and disgusting and then trying to make money from the book's sales. Goldman told Larry King, "The fact that someone is willing to publish this garbage . . . is just morally despicable to me. I would hope that no one buys the book." The bloggers let him have it. One blogger for the *Phoenix New Times* writes:

> Anyone catch the Valley's most famous Nordstrom employee on Oprah yesterday? I'm talking about the silver-mustachioed Fred Goldman, father of O. J. Simpson-victim Ron. See, Goldman, who recently had been working in the Scottsdale Nordstrom's men's department, was on Oprah Winfrey's show with Ron's sister Kim shilling for his version of O. J.'s now-infamous pseudo-confession *If I Did It*. You remember, the book Goldman was so pissed about before he won the rights to it in court.

When CNN's ratings sagged, the *Times* headline was "Calling on O. J." They apparently called on O. J. and they got him. First the controversy about the book. Then O. J. is arrested for crashing into a hotel room to retrieve some memorabilia. Even comedy writers get in on the act. Bill Maher brought up O. J. in a discussion with Mos Def and Cornel West. Totally out of context. They were shocked. The morning after the first debate between Barack Obama and John McCain, Joe Scarborough, apparently a manic caffeine addict, and a sweet-tempered Jonathan Capehart discuss whether the lighting had darkened Obama as *Time* did O. J. But even O. J. has observed that he is always "decontextualized." He said something like, they bring my name up in situations that don't even have anything to do with me. During November 2008 Maher proves his point. He does a skit about election scumbags, after which pictures of Bush, Cheney, and Palin appear. And O. J.? Unlike the others on the list, O. J. was not running for anything. Three apples and a plum. Maher doesn't believe that the LAPD were capable of planting evidence because he, like the white men of his class, has a different relationship with the police. He boasts about his marijuana use every week, an offense for which thousands of blacks, Hispanics, and Jerry Springer whites are doing time: The *New York Times* reported on July 20, 2010 that:

> No city in the world arrests more of its citizens for using pot than New York, according to statistics compiled by Harry G. Levine, a Queens College sociologist.
>
> Nearly nine out of ten people charged with violating the law are black or Latino, although national surveys have shown that whites are the heaviest users of pot. Mr. Bloomberg himself acknowledged in 2001 that he had used it, and enjoyed it.
>
> On the Upper East Side of Manhattan where the mayor lives, an average of 20 people for every 100,000 residents were arrested on the lowest-level misdemeanor pot charge in 2007, 2008, and 2009.
>
> During those same years, the marijuana arrest rate in Brownsville, Brooklyn, was 3,109 for every 100,000 residents.

That means the chances of getting arrested on pot charges in Brownsville—and nothing else—were 150 times greater than on the Upper East Side of Manhattan.

Blacks coming home to O. J.? Nothing about why whites left. Why doesn't the media discuss why whites abandoned O. J.? Immediately after the criminal trial, the white disagreement with the verdict was at forty-seven percent according to a *USA Today* poll. But a year later, white disagreement with the verdict had risen by twenty-five percent. Could be that after the jury in the criminal trial voted for acquittal, the all-white media jury had its say? A jury that didn't have to vote on the basis of facts. The distortions about the trial continue. When a guest on the September 4, 2007, Lou Dobbs show pointed to the jury composition in the Jena Six trial as being all white, guest Steve Malzberg of New York's WOR reached back to the O. J. criminal trial to counter that the jury in that case was all black. This was incorrect. The jury in O. J.'s criminal trial included one Hispanic and one white. The jury in the civil trial was all white, because the plaintiff's lawyer challenged the seating of every black juror, certainly a reason for appeal, but how does one find a court that hasn't been influenced by mob opinion?

Chris Matthews said that the black jury that acquitted O. J. was paying back the LAPD for past offenses. That isn't what the black members of the jury said during an interview. Like many white media men, he knows the minds of women, Latinos, and Asian Americans better than they know these minds themselves. The jury claimed that they were swayed more by scientific evidence offered by Barry Scheck. Ted Koppel tried to trip up one of the black jurors on *Nightline*. Turns out that she was an expert on forensics.

But what was supposed to be a two-week story, the Brentwood murders, is still being discussed sixteen years later. Henry Lee's famous comment about the trial, "Something Wrong," is as current as it was in 1995. Simpson's alleged wearing of Bruno Magli shoes, whose prints were supposed to have been found at the crime scene, was proof, according to the lawyers in the civil case, that Simpson committed the crime, yet in 2008, forensics expert Michael Baden, on his show *Autopsy*, said that most of the shoe prints found at the crime scene were made by the police who believed that wearing booties, the proper procedure, was somehow sissy, which refutes the claim made by FBI agent William Bodziak that there were no other footprints left behind on the night of the murder. (In *Big Daddy*, the 1999 comedy starring Adam Sandler, a character says, "If O. J. can get away with murder, why can't Sonny have his kid?" He's a goofy slacker who gains custody of a five year old.) So Hollywood and television through years of propaganda were able to do what the criminal jury, which studied the evidence, was incapable of doing. Convicting O. J. so that when he is convicted for a Las Vegas caper the newspapers admit that those who testified against him were former felons and the evidence was shaky, but argue that he got what he deserved, as one newspaper put it. Was this because the evidence that led to reasonable doubt, the blood type beneath Nicole's fingernail being different from that belonging to other parties, blonde hair on the glove, the sock blood containing EDTA preservative, the missing blood from the vial gathered by the nurse, the confusing testimony of the driver, Allan Park, a key witness, the lack of bruises, and blood on O. J. and the timeline. People forget that, before reaching a decision, the jury asked to hear Park's testimony again.

PART 4

54

Since 2002, federal judges have suppressed guns as evidence in more than 20 cases after finding New York police officers' testimony to be unreliable, inconsistent or false; but the Police Department does not monitor such cases. In 2008, the Police Department declined to pursue 35 percent of the cases in which the independent Civilian Complaint Review Board issued a finding of police misconduct.

—*New York Times,* January 4, 2009

On October 1, 2009, I awoke at about two A.M. They were reading the verdict of the bogus Las Vegas O. J. trial. An all-white jury, nine women and three men did what the previous all-white jury didn't have the power to do. The Santa Monica jury, the one that Ron Goldman's father called "a proper jury," was only capable of holding O. J. liable for the murders of Ron and Nicole. Some legal experts hold that the jury was rigged by Judge Hiroshi Fujisaki. He had to prevent another Japanese judge from seeming to be too chummy with O. J. That would risk having a white mob march on Japantown holding torches. *USA Today* reported on February 6, 1997:

> Simpson may have grounds for appeal, but would he win? . . .
>
> Simpson's lawyers haven't said whether they will appeal, but legal pundits have seen a wealth of errors on the part of Superior Court Judge Hiroshi Fujisaki that could be grounds for reversal. And virtually all of his most controversial rulings went against the defense:
>
> Allowing testimony about a failed lie-detector test and a call from "Nicole" to a battered-women's shelter. Alleged jury misconduct. A ban on testimony by Mark Fuhrman, the former detective the defense accused of a racist plot to frame Simpson. Allowing an undated letter from Nicole Brown Simpson accusing her ex-husband of beating her . . .
>
> "This case is likely to be before the courts for years to come," Lance Ito, the judge at Simpson's murder trial, told the Pasadena Star-News.

Kraal was so excited that O. J. Simpson had been captured (some say poached) that he invited everybody to a party to celebrate at his home on December 6, the day that O. J. Simpson would be sentenced. He called it the O. J. Sentencing Party, and promised that Rathswheeler, the Boss of Bosses of American news networks, would attend. Necktie party if you asked me. But, hey, I have had my fill of O. J. and after receiving money for a cartoon that showed O. J. as a horse's ass, or worse, I wasn't about to get involved, plus I had to obey Esther and Hibiscus's ultimatum that I choose between O. J. and my family.

November 2008 saw the biggest job loss in thirty-four years, 533,000 jobs lost, but guess which story got covered first and was the subject of a CBS special report? That morning MSNBC's *Morning Joe* began with a kind of warm-up for what was to come. Willie Geist, whose idea of humor is to make nasty, puerile remarks about celebrities, began the morning with some ridicule-profiling of three black men, two of whom were former television star Gary Coleman, in trouble for a traffic violation, and Plaxico Burress, a football player who had shot himself accidentally. He quotes Ludacris' dumb line about his having, "hoes in every zip code." (What is it about some black men and the pimp aesthetic? They're as incompetent at that form of crime as the others.) Even Obama is slimed on the same morning. Jennifer Skala of *Hotline* wants to know why Obama isn't doing more to solve the economic crisis. Even the "conservative" black panelist Brian DeBose from the *Washington Times* has to remind her that Obama hasn't taken office. The media allows Sarah Palin to hang around even though she has little support among the electorate. Even Republicans. But the media have decided that they want her as a 2012 presidential candidate.

Sarah's latest smear

Just as P. T. Barnum made money from a black woman who claimed to be George Washington's nurse—her story marking the beginning of the penny press, which featured it—MSNBC and CNN use O. J. to shame black people, their big moneymaker, while ignoring crimes that, in comparison to O. J.'s entrapment, seem small. Case in point: on December 5, 2008, the day that O. J. is shown broken, pleading for a light sentence, he makes the cover of the *New York Times* shackled and humiliated. Tucked away on page B8 of the business section is a story about the problems confronting another individual, the Bank of America, which is technically an individual, according to the Roberts court.

"A federal jury in Manhattan . . . found Bank of America liable in a securities fraud trial." This fraud involved "some of the biggest names on Wall Street." The following Monday workers demonstrated in front of Republic Windows and Doors, which had fired them the week before. The company was in trouble because Bank of America had cancelled its financing even though the bank had received a twenty-five-billion-dollar government bailout.

O. J. Simpson goes to jail because he tried to retrieve some mementos including a photo of him posing with the late FBI chief, J. Edgar Hoover. Bank of America's fraud hardly merits a mention, and of course, like the 1830s, blacks are used by the media as the circus act that diverts attention from the excesses and the greed of the capitalist system.

After the sentencing is rendered by the judge—15 to 33 years— following a verdict by an all-white jury, the all-white media jury, the all-white criminal jury's reliable back up, begins its predictable drubbing of O. J. This includes TV lawyer Jack Ford, who of course sides with the prosecution. Rick Sanchez leads with O. J. over the economy and so does Chris Matthews who at least mentions the racial composition of the jury but nothing about the fact that the FBI was in on the sting set up by Thomas Riccio that lured O. J. into entrapment. But even the FBI couldn't vouch for the audiotape that Riccio recorded without O. J.'s knowledge. This suspicious tape was the basis for the all-white jury's conviction. And then O. J. came on to deliver his plea. Of course when I heard that the seating of African Americans had been challenged by the prosecutors, using a strategy of Petrocelli, the old Southern strategy, in the civil trial, I figured that O. J. was sunk. Broken. Humiliated. Trapped. O. J. asked the judge, a white woman, for mercy.

Yes, your honor, I stand before you today. Sorry. I'm somewhat confused. I feel apologetic to the people of the State of Nevada. I've been coming to Nevada since 1959. I worked summer jobs for my uncle in 1960 and 1961. I've been coming here ever since. I have never gotten into any trouble. People have always been fine to me. When I came here I came for a wedding. I didn't come here to . . . I didn't come here to reclaim property. I was told it was here. When he told me that Monday that my stuff was in Nevada . . . he was going to be in Nevada. I talked to my kids, I talked to my sisters, and I even called the Brown family. I told them I had a chance to get my property back, property that over the years we've seen being sold over the Internet. We saw pictures of ours that were stolen going into the tabloids. We called the police to ask them what to do. They told us what to try to do. But you could never find out who was selling them. This was the first time I had the opportunity to catch the guys red-handed who had been stealing from my family. I knew these guys. I did think that Mike Gilbert would be there, and I know as they told me of the two guys who were there, he was the one who did it. I have no hatred of Mike Gilbert. In the past, as we know, you heard in the tapes, Mike Gilbert tried to set me up in the porn video, tripped me up into a room with hidden cameras, and still in the newspapers and tabloids, they still had cover stories that O. J. did it, even though there's no porn videos, even though I didn't participate in it. I forgave Mike. I yelled at him, but I forgave him. I yelled at him like I did Bruce and Beardson. I've forgiven them. We talked about it, Beardson and I, the next day. Bruce and I hugged and talked about it. His kids have called me since then. We've apologized to each other. The only person I asked . . . I requested to help me here was Mr. Stewart. I did request. I needed his car. I asked him if he had some guys to help me remove these things from the room. I didn't ask anybody to do anything but to stand behind me, allow me to yell at these guys and ask them to help me remove these things, and if they didn't help me remove these things, we would call the cops on them, 'cause I thought that they were wrong. They had to turn over some of these things that were both garnishable and things that were not garnishable. I didn't want to yell at them. I think that {Mr.?} from the previous trial said that I didn't ask them to yell at anybody. I didn't ask them to yell at anybody. I believe it was my fault because I brought them there, and I knew the character of a couple of these guys who were there, and it was my fault that they were there. But in no way did I mean to hurt anybody, to steal anything from anyone. I spoke to Bruce before I left the room, and he told me what was his, and I called him when I got to the car and said, "Say exactly what you had and I want to send it back to you." I talked to the police officers. I volunteered immediately to come back, show them what was taken, and to tell them what took place. Before anybody talked to the police, I was the first guy to volunteer to do it, and I heard on the tapes that they thought I was stupid for doing it. But I didn't want to steal anything from anybody. I don't think anybody said I wanted anybody else's stuff, just my own. I wanted my daughter . . . Mrs. Brown . . . her mother's wedding ring, stolen. My kids' picture . . . my oldest son has his own family now. He wanted the picture from the oval office with Gerald Ford when he was five years old. Stolen. All of these things are gone. My family knew what he was doing. We didn't want to hurt Bruce. We didn't want to hurt any of these guys. I know these guys. They have eaten in my home. I've done book reports with their kids. I sung to their mothers when they were sick. I wasn't there to hurt anybody. I just wanted my personal things, and I was stupid. I am sorry. I didn't mean to steal anything from anybody and I didn't know I was doing anything illegal. I thought I was confronting friends and retrieving my property. So, I'm sorry. I'm sorry for all of it. All the other guys, except Mr. Stewart, volunteered. They wanted to go. Mr. Stewart is the only one I asked to help me. All the rest, when they found out, volunteered. "Come on, let's go." One wanted to be the security guy. He said he was a security guy. But I didn't mean to hurt anybody. I didn't mean to steal from anybody. Thank you.

We got him for California

Pitiful. Pitiful. They made him crawl. Kiss their feet. Allow them to sit on him. A week or so after the decision it turns out that O. J. was correct after all. The property, that memorabilia, did belong to him and not to the collector. Why else would he have to turn an O. J. ring over to Fred Goldman? I remember when Denise Brown said, "Now I understand what the word gold means in his name." For his part, Fred Goldman says that he's glad that he doesn't have to look at O. J.'s ugly face. Since he and his son Ron didn't get along, Ron, whose murder has brought millions to Fred Goldman, perhaps, had problems with his father's face. Didn't even speak to his mother.

Esther came over, gently removed the remote control from my hand, walked to the window and threw it out. I ran to the window only to see the object shattered on the pavement below.

"Hey, what the—" She didn't know that I had prepared for such an emergency, hiding about twelve remotes. Would I reveal their hiding place? Never. They were located right next to my Big Fat Chicken restaurant coupons.

"Hibiscus and I are not going through this O. J. shit again and so don't get any ideas." Her arms were folded and she was tapping a foot. I told her that I was going out for a walk but what I really wanted to do was to stop by the Sentencing Lunch.

55

B. S. Rathswheeler sat in the middle of his newly acquired property. It belonged to the grandson of a man so rich that he is cited in a song written by Dorothy Fields and set to a tune by Jimmy McHugh. It was located across the street from Central Park and housed in a building designed by Rosario Candela. The army of painters, carpenters, plumbers, and other repairmen had just left. The former owner, an old-old money billionaire, was more devoted to financing investigations of UFOs than keeping up his twenty-room apartment. So when Rathswheeler's wife Yum Yum came to inspect the place, she found holes in the floors and in the ceilings. Yum Yum, the porno star he'd met during a conference in Bangkok, Thailand. He'd divorced his wife of forty years and at Yum Yum's insistence had disowned his white children. He was known about town as "The Man From Down Under," which for some of his enemies meant hell. He was enjoying one of his all-day "explosions of flatulence," laughing and slapping his thighs.

"Good one. A good stinky one. Where's Yum Yum. Got to make Kraal's party.

"Sentencing Party. Finally caught that chimp bastard. We'll get their chimp president, his monkey wife, and his orangutan children.

"Imagine. The old money crowd invite him to their highfalutin parties and won't invite me. A white man. I'm too new money for them. The way they treated me when me and Yum Yum entered one of their restaurants. Looked her up and down. I thought if I bought this place Lady Astor's crowd would invite Yum Yum to play bridge with the ladies. Maybe we should join that uptown church they all attend. I could almost understand why me and me first wife were outsiders in England. Over there they have these establishments and me being Aussie and all— well I didn't go to Eton. But over here? Who are they to put on airs? A bunch of second generationers who think they're better than the chimps. And that chimp president. He comes to town. They're kissing his baboon rump and won't give me the time of day. I'll show him. I'll destroy him. I sent that memo out. When we get through with him, he'll be like a dead chimp laying on the sidewalk. Where's that Yum Yum? She's been out all night again with Jagid and Jagan. Going to those player's clubs. I don't mind. Jagid and Jagan saved Kraal's ass. That *Nigguz News*. CNN, Fox, and MSNBC are really jealous. So as Jagid and Jagan say, they can party hearty. Of course, there was a lot of jabber about me at seventy-five marrying a woman from Thailand who was twenty-five at the time. But hell, I'm having a good time. She got me dyeing my hair pink. She's added years to my life. She's made me feel young again. Thought that I'd be impotent after that bloody prostate surgery. But she said, Don't worry. All you have to do is lay there. I'll do the rest. (Loud booming from a boom box can be heard). There they are now."

56

The party was held in an uptown building. Three top floors were owned by Kraal. The very top floor was a penthouse. I arrived about a half hour after the proceedings began.

We were treated to a pretty fancy buffet composed of an assortment of pizzas, a reference to the cuisine featured at the Mezzaluna restaurant, the hangout of O. J., Nicole, and their entourages. There were waiters passing through the crowd. A new crowd. Kraal thought it amusing for the waiters to wear O. J. masks. He also served Starbuck's coffee and Ben & Jerry's ice cream.

I recognized some of the celebrity newspersons who dominated the TV news and talk shows and Sunday morning Meet the Presses. But mostly it was a right wing crowd from think tanks and heads of faux grassroots organizations. Ben came over. I hadn't seen him in a few years. He'd lost some weight and his hair was completely gray. He and Raquel now had two kids. They were attending a bilingual academy. He was now a top entertainment lawyer and spent a lot of time commuting to Los Angeles. I spotted Princessa Bimbette. Rathswheeler had given her a prime spot with her own show.

She ran up to me and put her arms around me and started smacking me on both cheeks. Her breath smelled of alcohol which was being served by the gallons at the bar. I pushed her away, gently. I had heard some of her broadcasts. Especially the series she was now pushing. Rousing a bunch of the disaffected, The Kettles, to March on Washington armed and dangerous "to finish the job that Timothy McVeigh began," as she put it. The demonstrators, who all of a sudden were against big government now that a black president had been elected, were mostly retired over fifty-five white males on Social Security and Medicare and quite a number of them were on disability.

"Princessa, what's the matter with you? You're on preaching sedition every night. Why do you hate Obama so?"

She reeled a bit. "Hate Obama? I voted for him," she said.

"Then why—"

"Rathswheeler. He directs Kraal and Kraal me. I need to keep my job, I have bills. Sorry." Somebody tapped me on the shoulder. Princessa smiled at the person before a famous right-wing broadcaster came up and asked her to dance. He was drunk, too.

"Bear. Goddamn. Look at you—" The usual way that small talk begins. He gave me a well, bear hug.

"How's Esther? Hibiscus?"

"They're fine. How's your family?"

"Raquel is fine. So are the kids. She's sorry she couldn't make it. She wanted to see you. Looks like they got your boy. Nine years. Maybe they'll give O. J. a rest."

"Maybe," I said.

But of course they won't. On January 9, 2009, Dave Shuster and John Ziegler were having a back-and-forth on a show called *1600 Pennsylvania Avenue*. Under some tough questioning, Ziegler was defending a film whose subject was the rough treatment that the networks gave Sarah Palin, a woman who compared herself to a Mama Grizzly, yet who demanded gentle and courteous interrogation by Katie Couric and others. Out of nowhere, Ziegler compared the questioning by Shuster with O. J.'s Dream Team's interrogating the cops. Not to be outdone, on March 20, 2010, Roy Sekoff, a contributor to the Huffington Post, compared the hypocrisy of those Republicans who were criticizing President Obama's stimulus bill to "O. J.'s saying that he's going to get the real killers." He says this fifteen years after the Brentwood murders!! Where did that come from? Out of earshot, Ben moved closer to me. Almost a whisper.

"You see, if the motherfucker had been cool like that Van Bulow, you know, the dude who put his wife into a coma. He stayed out of sight and went on about his business. But O. J. He had to flaunt it. Shoving that young white pussy into their faces which is like a red flag to these people. Doing coke and partying. And that episode where he pretended to stab that TV interviewer with a banana while humming the tune from *Psycho*. Looks to me like he wanted them to catch him. Why else would the guy maintain such a high profile?"

"The trial was a travesty."

"Man, so what? I agree with the newspapers. He got what he deserved."

"It may not be that simple," I said.

"What is the matter with you? These white people give you all of this money for that cartoon showing O. J. as a fool and a horse's behind. You better not let them hear you complain about that trial. You remember what happened to August Wilson. All he did was mention Elijah Muhammad and he was deemed ungrateful. Never got a play on Broadway again during his lifetime."

"Well. The cops in Nevada said that they got him for California. They admitted it. That the trial was just a way to do that. Like Laurie Levenson said in the *New York Times*, it's like they got Capone for taxes as a way of getting him for larger crimes."

"Look, Bear. You better let this O. J. thing go. You almost lost your family once behind this piece of turd. I'm afraid for your mental health. I mean, before, you remember, you collected all of the minutiae you could find about this guy. Now that you have a little money, get back to painting those Southwestern scenes. Besides, he said he was going to devote himself to finding the real killers. I guess he thought that they were hiding in one of those eighteen holes."

"Oh, I see. Break the guy and then ask him to finance the search for the killers, something that LAPD was obligated to do, but didn't because they judged O. J. to be guilty from the very beginning."

A famous network sports announcer came up and he and Ben began to talk about basketball, whether Kobe Bryant or LeBron James would succeed Michael Jordan. The place became quiet. I looked around. Entering the party was the man known as the Boss of Bosses of the News. B. S. Rathswheeler.

It was said that soon he would own all of electronic and print expression. Accompanying him were the two hip-hop stars, Jagid and Jagan. Jagid was carrying Rathswheeler on his back. Jagan and Yum Yum had taken a cab. The cab driver said that he could only accommodate Jagan and Yum Yum because of Jagan's weight. Three hundred and fifty pounds. Rathswheeler, known throughout the industry as a problem-solver, made Jagid run alongside the cab while carrying him on his back.

Yum Yum was wearing short shorts, spiked high heels, and a fur jacket. She had lips like Angelina Jolie, which Paul Mooney said was responsible for Brad Pitt tolerating her adoptions. Mooney said that her lips were such that if she brought home a chicken, he'd adopt it. The skin on Rathswheeler's wrinkled face seemed to sag. He had the face of one of those undead creatures in the old comic book series *Tales from the Crypt*. They greeted Kraal and Lord. Both of them bowed so before their boss that their faces almost scraped the floor. The party resumed.

Somebody tapped me on the shoulder.

"Mr. Kraal wants to see you downstairs." It was a woman. A nurse. The nurse escorted me into an elevator that descended to an apartment downstairs. I could hear the sounds of Ornette Coleman and Don Cherry coming from behind the door. When she opened the door I was almost knocked over by the odor of marijuana. Dominant among the room's furnishings was a hospital bed. A man sat in a chair next to it. He wore a robe over his pajamas and slippers. He was bald. The nurse had taken up a position behind his chair.

"Sit down." He directed me to a chair that was located near him. I sat. He offered me a huge bong, which I declined.

"You're a spade and you don't like reefer?"

The old man laughed heartily, slapping his thighs but then began to shudder from coughing. He pointed to a glass of water placed on a table. The nurse fetched it for him. He held it with both trembling hands. He spoke from a box that was implanted in his throat, giving the sound of his words a robotic quality. He pointed to his throat.

"Cancer. My name is Jimmy Kraal. I'm the asshole's father." I shook the old man's wrinkled, hairy hand. He winced.

"Asshole?"

"That asshole. His mother, God bless her, would turn over in her grave if she could see what has become of this man I used to call my son. I stay in my apartment rather than mix with the people he brings up to the house."

"Look, I don't think I should get in the middle of a quarrel between a father and his son."

"We quarrel a lot about your drawings."

"What?"

"He wanted to fire you a long time ago, over the police cartoon. The one about Simpson." He was laughing.

"Then the one about Simpson giving the USA some Juice?"

"Yeah. He said that your anger was turning off these upscalers whom he saw as his main subscribers. You know those young white people who are taking over Manhattan, and now even Harlem. He dismissed your ideas about the police. He said that police brutality was an urban myth."

"Urban myth, my ass." I muttered.

"You don't have to tell me. The number of times I got beat up by the bastards." A white man beaten up by the police. What kind of white man was this? I thought. I had to take a long look at this white man. As rare as a quagga.

"Back there in the old union days, they used to bust our heads every time they got a chance. But no matter how hard they tried, they couldn't stop us. There were some hellish strikes in those days. Working conditions were abominable." Somebody talking about the rights of workers. What a throwback this guy was, I thought.

"We didn't know what to do with the kid. He barely made it through Columbia. He bummed around from job to job until he asked me for some money to start up one of those top forty radio stations. He's got his nerve complaining about affirmative action. Then he takes over KCAK. Turns into a right-wing shill. So he listens to this queer whom he brought in. This guy Lord. He listens to him and he's the one who tried to get him to fire you, but I overruled him. I made him keep Garfield on, too."

"How did you do that?"

"I still have a sizable amount of shares in the station. He had no choice but to rehire you. As for that Lord. He's always complaining about blacks getting places without merit. He wouldn't be working with my son if he weren't a fag. Gore Vidal said the same thing about Andrew Sullivan. Some writers resigned from *The New Republic* when Sullivan supported the Bell Curve arguments about the intellectual deficiency of black people. For someone interested in the intellectual shortcomings of people, why did Sullivan support The Boer for president? Why does Leon Wieseltier accuse him of dividing Jews between good Jews and bad Jews? Later, like many tough lovers of black people, he was exposed as being a hypocrite. Advertised for 'bareback' unprotected sex on the Internet, after admonishing gays about their reckless behavior."

"But why?"

"Look, I used to do some cartoons myself." The old man asked his nurse to bring him a book. She presented him with a scrapbook. It was huge. He handed me the book. I began to turn the pages. He was obviously pleased with the content. His cartoons. They were from a 1930s newspaper named *Demand*. The Worker's Bulletin! The drawings were done in charcoal and demonstrated how far the art of cartooning had come. Given today's cartoons, sophisticated and subtle, the use of Adobe, Photoshop, these were heavyhanded. Obvious. Hokey even. One was typical. It showed a figure with the body form of a grinning John Bull, shaking coins from a worker whose ankles John Bull held with his hands. Across Bull's breast, in case you didn't get it, there was a sign that read "Capitalism." He had a tie clip shaped like a dollar bill and the coins were being dropped from the worker's pockets to the bags, which were marked "Greed," "Graft," and "Profits from child labor." There were others like this. War was represented by an unshaven Mars, or the Grim Reaper. The upper classes were always prosperous-looking and well fed. The masses, gaunt and angry. Shaking their fists. Marching on the bosses who were always shown wearing expensive rings and extended bellies. We talked some technical talk. The difference between using brushes or pen-and-ink or color pencils. He then began to talk about his father, a German Marxist who had migrated to the United States and become a union leader in Pittsburgh. He told me something that I didn't know. That most of those killed during the Haymarket Massacre were Germans. He then played me some Utah Phillips and Pete Seeger, Josh White and some songs by Paul Robeson. Afterwards, I took the elevator, which opened to a scene that left me shocked. Some of the leading anchorpersons, talk show hosts, producers, and owners of corporate media were tied up and gagged. The two waiters wearing O. J. masks were guarding them. One was on a cell phone in a conversation with police officials surrounding the building. Even B. S. Rathswheeler, cocaine residue under his nose, seemed shook up and Kraal and Lord who were so full of themselves were as quiet as an audience at a concert of chamber music. Rathswheeler's girlfriend was flirting with one of the kidnappers.

"What the hell's going on here?" I asked Ben. Ben was tied up on the floor. One of the waiters, who was apparently the leader, removed his O. J. mask. Renaldo! Both Ben and my mouths dropped like Dominick Dunne's when he heard the decision in O. J.'s criminal trial. He was the ringleader. Unlike the impeccably groomed Renaldo of the KCAK television station he was sporting a scraggly beard. His eyes were red and they were wild like those of Hollywood's version of John Brown, played by Raymond Massey. "Renaldo!" exclaimed his former colleagues, people whom he partied with, played golf with, attended media conventions with, and even fucked. They said it almost in union.

"Yes, it's me, Renaldo. And since you all are interested in O. J., let me deliver one of his lines: 'Nobody leaves this room.'" Jagid and Jagan were a mess. Before they arrived at the party they had done some cheese heroin. Their agent told them that their record producer didn't have a check for them even though their latest hit, "The Players Club is Bombed," went gold. They were angry at first but then he gave them some heroin and they quieted down. They had joined B. S. Rathswheeler and his girlfriend in one of the penthouse's rear rooms to do some lines. So they were totally unprepared for Renaldo's actions. After Renaldo told Ben and me to leave, Jagid pleaded with Renaldo to call 911 because Jagan was flipping about the room, foam covering his mouth to the fascination of the hostages. This was a better show than *The Wire*, and *The Corner*. Renaldo's response was to go over and slap Jagan. Turning to me and Ben he said, "you two can go."

I hesitated.

"I said go!" He insisted. "The rest of these sons of bitches can't leave this room."

Princessa staggered to her feet. "I object to the term *bitch*."

Renaldo opened his coat. "Bitch this bitch. Bitch this." Both the men and the women emitted cries of shock. He was dressed up like a suicide bomber. What looked like sticks of dynamite were strapped to his waist. Ben and I left the apartment. When we exited the building we were rushed away by the police. It was like the movies. Members of SWAT stationed on the tops of surrounding rooftops. Helicopters hovering near the penthouse where the hostages were being held.

Ben and I left the block and headed downtown. We passed a famous Irish bar, the kind with a four-leaf clover on the front and the simian-faced leprechaun hanging above the entrance. Some words written in Gaelic. "Let's go in here and have a beer," I suggested. So stunned were we that we had walked about twenty blocks in silence.

We entered the bar. It was on the corner of Forty-Fifth and Third Avenue. Faces were turned up to a basketball game. It was interrupted by a bulletin. The reporter stood outside of the Kraal residence. The scene was crawling with the police and detectives. Crowds were craning their necks behind rope lines. The black chief of police was there exchanging messages with Renaldo and the rest of the hostage takers. Since most of the white anchormen were being held back, people were relying upon alternative media and cyberspace for news. One of Renaldo's demands was that the corporate press be banned from the scene.

"Did you think that Renaldo had it in him?" Ben said as he reached for some peanuts that were filling a bowl on the bar. The bartender came over and placed the beer we ordered before us. Raquel's cooking had done him some good. He had lost his globular shape.

"The guy's career hit the skids when he was fired by Kraal and Lord. Last I heard he was one of those squeegee guys. Running up to cars and wiping windshields for a dollar. Had to declare bankruptcy. Lost his apartment. He was living under some cardboard boxes, too proud to ask his mom for assistance."

"I'm as surprised as you. What do you think came over him? Now they're going to give him the O. J. treatment."

"You just won't leave this fucking O. J. thing alone, will you?"

Heads turned as Ben's voice rose. "O. J. O. J. O. J. O. J. crazy. I'm sick of it. And I'm sick of you. You think that you can get by giving white folks the jump fake. You done lost your mind over this fucking loser. O. J. Simpson is the reason we're having this 'bear market.' I've lost about fourteen percent of my portfolio because of this creep."

"How do you figure that?" I asked.

"He started the Bronco craze. Had millions buying these oversized utility wagons. That's why the American auto companies are going broke. He's caused thousands of people to lose their jobs.

"We got Obama in office and people like you are still complaining and whining and—You fucking idiot. They give you these honors and money and you still trying to raise hell. Still giving

298

white folks the old possum tricks. Still on your soapbox of grievances and complaints when for the first time we have somebody
who looks like us in the White House. I know what I'm going to
do. I'm going to stay as far from you and your kind as I possibly
can. You and that crazy Renaldo. He has to go and exhibit his
black behind. Go '60s on the black people in the White House.
Embarrassing Obama and Michelle, their mother-in-law, the two
children, and the dog Bo, who represent the best of us. Sometimes, I'm beginning to think that you're in love with O. J. You
and all of these sick people who won't let go of O. J. Like all of
you want to have a mass orgy with this sucker and then have him
behead all of you. You're like those Japanese who didn't know
that the war had ended. You and the Bill Maher fuck are into
some kind of strange erotic snuff shit about O. J. I'm beginning to
believe that you and this Bill Maher fuck have a gay thing about
Simpson." He angrily chug-a-lugged his beer, flung some dollars
onto the bar and left the establishment before I could reply. The
bar was filled with customers. I looked up at the portraits of Irish
heroes. I wondered whether they were dismissed as last standers.
People who were told that the war was over, yet remained in the
trenches. I ordered a double scotch with predictable results.

57

The standoff went on for three days. Then a bulletin came on the tube announcing that Renaldo's lawyer-mom was about to bring her son out of the Kraal building. Momentarily, his mother led a sobbing Renaldo Louis out to the applause of some hotheads, cranks and others who had not gotten the message that this was a postrace period. They were waving flags that were green, black, and red. The television stars who'd been held hostage followed. They were looking exhausted. Haggard. Some of the women were weeping. Without the heavy makeup required by their bosses, they looked ordinary. Some of them looked better. Rathswheeler and Yum Yum followed. Some of the reporters rushed toward him, and he angrily pushed them away. The two, accompanied by Jagid, climbed into a cab for the ride downtown.

One of the SWAT members was about to fire on the mother and son when the black chief of police lowered his shotgun and glared at the trigger-happy fuck. The reporters rushed the two but the police chief intervened.

Both were escorted into the chief's car and driven away.

On television they were debating Renaldo's actions. B. S. Rathswheeler appeared on Rathswheeler Network, a rare appearance because he had decided to remain in the background while his underlings did all of the dirty work, raising militia activity against the government, promoting Kettle parties and encouraging a secessionist movement. One of his highly paid babblers had concluded a discussion about April as a possible month to celebrate Confederate History Month because, after all, blacks had a Black History Month.

Interviewer: It's an honor for me to interview B. S. Rathswheeler, the head of our network, who found himself held by Renaldo Louis in a bizarre kidnapping attempt. Mr. Rathswheeler, when you attended the party held by Kraal, who is president of one of your subsidiaries, did you think you'd be there for three days?

Rathswheeler: First of all, G'day to ya. Well from the reports that I got from Kraal I thought that guy was a sook, but he turned out to be a real freckle. I was gobsmacked. Me and the Mrs. was having grouse time with the two hip-hoppers but then one of these yobbos in an O. J. mask comes into the room where we were hittin the turps and asks us to come into the front room. Then . . .

I changed the channel.

Virginia Saturday was being interviewed at her downtown five-watt radio operation, which reached listeners within a half a mile of their basement headquarters. The moderator asked her why there had been such an outpouring of affection for Renaldo who, after all, had become a sort of folk hero to those who believed that the media were their enemy. But lest one think that blacks were the only ones who supported Renaldo, he had support from white

American commentators and reporters too. They were weary of the British taking their jobs solely on the basis of their having an accent that wowed their American cousins and were happy that the British were following Sebastian Lord back to England. As a result of their English accents, Christopher Hitchens, Tina Brown, and Andrew Sullivan could make the most inane observations and be taken seriously. As for Hitchens, the atheist, Christianity influenced Duke Ellington, Handel, Michelangelo, and James Baldwin among other great artists. Name a great sculptor, composer, or writer who was influenced by Christopher Hitchens.

"I don't condone what Renaldo did. But they did treat him pretty bad at KCAK. I guess he just exploded after they turned the news over to those two hip-hoppers, moved them into his office and put his belongings out on the sidewalk. I know that a lot of the black employees were unhappy, but nobody listened to them, as long as the ratings were high. But you asked me why the outpouring of sympathy? What do you expect? African Americans, Latinos, Native Americans have been demonized by the media for as long as there has been one. But of course we don't advocate extreme measures like the kidnapping of Lim Burger after his remarks about two of their heroes, but one can imagine how things would have turned out in Germany among the Jews if someone had snuffed Goebbels." Boris Yefimov, Russian cartoonist for *Krokodil* and *Izvestia*, had depicted Goebbels as a rat.

The blonde white woman, Cookie Boggs, who was interviewing Virginia, blinked her eyes with annoyance.

"How long did you think that blacks and Latinos were going to tolerate this media that encourages hate crimes against them? People who see the First Amendment as a hunting license, a permission to target black, brown, red, yellow people, Muslims, abortion doctors and other unpopular movements and individuals. It was the press that has inspired riots, and civil disturbances, and backed unnecessary wars that have robbed trillions from the American treasury. It was a newspaper that printed a full-page ad calling President Kennedy 'a traitor' on the day that he landed in Dallas. You recall the Asian campaign contributions that were such an issue after the reelection of President Clinton. The Asian Americans say that the press made no attempt to distinguish between Asians and Asian Americans. This journalism, which has yet to integrate its personnel and where not only do blacks get slammed, but these Asian Americans don't have anybody to represent their interests. I get so mad when I view some of this propaganda that I want to shoot somebody. Of course, I'm not giving my approval to the actions of Renaldo. But look at the angry ignorant mobs raised by Fox News. People coming to Washington and showing their (bleep). Brandishing guns. Breaking into the offices of their opponents."

"Virginia, that's so overblown, such a bizarre overstatement, after all you have a job."

"Oh, yeah, down here in a basement with little pay and a tiny audience. David and Goliath. But I predict that we'll be around longer than you people uptown." Virginia's interview was interrupted by a bulletin. A voice said:

"We take you to the home of Josephine Louis, mother of the crazed kidnapper who held some of the most important television anchormen and women commentators and reporters at the home of Jonathan Kraal. The incident occurred while Kraal was holding a victory party celebrating the sentencing of O. J. Simpson." Renaldo's mother appeared on camera, standing in front of her townhouse on Edgecombe Avenue. She was got up in Edo fashion: a Buba, with an Iro slung around her shoulder. She was wearing a Gele. With considerable confidence, she read her statement.

"I will be representing my son Renaldo Louis in the coming court case in which he has been charged with several felony accounts, the most serious of which is kidnapping. Of course we reject these charges," she said, crisply.

Reporter: How can you reject the charges when all of the evidence points toward guilty?

Josephine Louis: We'll examine the evidence in a courtroom, not on cable.

With that she turned around and entered the townhouse, followed by members of her staff.

58

I had spent years thinking about O. J. Now I had left Badger and the O. J. cartoons, which some had seen as scandalous and caused me to be suspended and then rehired. I was fulfilling my other ambition. I was doing Southwest art without a single reference to O. J. or to any of the events that had transpired since the Brentwood murders of 1994. Esther's father fell in love with a patient in the assisted-living home. Both of them had Alzheimer's. One day they disappeared from the home, never to be found again. Esther and I took in the cultural resources that New York had to offer. Plays. Museums. I spent many of my afternoons at Dizzy's at Lincoln Center. Then one day I was walking past the United Nations toward home when I got the funny feeling that I was being followed. I looked around and indeed there was a stooped-over man who was walking with a cane. He was wearing an overcoat and had his hat drawn down over his eyes. Dark glasses. His face, what little I could see of it, was very black. I got home and thought very little of it. But the next day, as I was walking cross-town, I noticed the same figure. He seemed to be shadowing me. Later that evening, after dinner I was looking out at the boats on the East River and happened to glance down at the street and there was the same figure. Standing under a street lamp. Like in the movies. I went and got Esther and asked her to come look, but when she came to the window the figure had vanished. Like in the movies. She gave me a strange look. At three A.M. that night the phone rang. I picked it up.

"Hello."

"Ehhh, what's up, Doc?" the person on the other end said and hung up. Esther was aroused from her sleep.

"Who was that?"

I was doing Southwest art without a single reference to O. J.

"Wrong number," I said. The voice was deep and seemed to hiss. The next day, I went down to my studio and found that it had been ransacked. When the O. J. trial was going on, I'd become interested in forensics. Plus I'd become a *Dexter* fan. Dexter worked in the forensics department of a Florida police department. He was also a serial killer. I combed the room carefully to find whether the intruder, or intruders, had left anything behind. I found a mashed cigarette. And then some hair. I put some gloves on and deposited the hair in a plastic envelope and sent it to a lab for analysis. I made up my mind that I was going to set a trap for the man who was following me, and now emboldened, had trashed my studio. I left the studio to go down to the Golden Sardine for some espresso and sure enough I spotted the figure about a block away. I pivoted and began my pursuit.

Seeing this, the figure began to hobble away. He disappeared into an alley. I caught up with him and was about collar him when he bit me and scampered away. I was shocked. My hand was bleeding. I found a clinic on Rivington Street and after waiting for an hour, I was attended to. The doctor told me that the bite was not made by a human. It was made by an animal and that they would have to require more tests.

"Surely you must have made a mistake," I said. "It was a man, he was wearing a raincoat and had his hat pulled down over his face," I insisted.

I went home and had dinner with Esther in silence. But before doing that I went to a hat store and bought a fedora. It looked cool on the man who had bitten me. Noticing the bandage on my hand, Esther asked, "What happened to your hand?

"Cab driver slammed the door on my hand." I didn't want to worry her.

"Well, did you complain to the cab company?"

"No. It's not serious, just an accident," I said, sinking deeper into a lie.

"Bear, is something wrong? You're acting strangely these days."

"It's nothing. Just lost in studying different Southwestern artists' approaches to color. Really concentrating. Right now I'm checking out Georgia O'Keefe's use of landscape colors: a rust brown for hills, purple for valleys, dark blue for mountains nearby, a lighter blue for mountains in the distance, an even lighter blue for skies— How are things at the gallery?" I asked, changing the subject.

"We got a big break today."

"How's that?"

"Crazy Goat, the Haitian artist. He's asking us to represent him. His work is worth millions." I choked on my broccoli.

"What? Crazy Goat? That below-Fourteenth-Street loser? That's not art. That's graffiti."

"Well, you're a cartoonist, he's an artist."

"A cartoonist, huh. What about my show at the Ken?" *And what about my paying the bills for three decades with my cartoons,* I started to say.

"Oh, I talked to the curator. They said that they just gave you that show because he admired *Attitude the Badger.*"

"But—"

"Look, I got to go."

59

When I entered my studio the next day, I found a note. "We Must Talk."

It was done in a strange scribble. I was given an address and a time during the next day when I could meet my tormentor. He was living in Drecklyn, a sort of Hooversville for artists who couldn't afford to live in the Disneyland that New York had become and couldn't afford to follow the exodus of other artists to New Jersey and upstate New York. And, because of the economy, couldn't afford painting supplies.

They lived in a series of tents and cardboard houses. During the day, they spent time rummaging through offal debris and finding other materials from which they created assemblages. I made my way through the encampment and finally found the location of his home. It lay beneath a manhole. I bent down and tapped lightly. Number 252 was crudely drawn on it. The manhole was opened by a paw. The paw's owner beckoned me to take hold of it.

I did and found myself being led down a ladder by a MONKEY! A monkey wearing a beret! I followed the animal down a crude ladder. Once on the ground I faced the man who had stalked me. There were books inside of cardboard boxes. Wooden crates were used as furniture. He sat on one and invited me to sit on one. An old Bugs Bunny movie was appearing on a television screen that was about forty inches diagonally, but instead of laughing, the gaze he aimed at the Rabbit was almost solemn.

His library was extensive. There was a small refrigerator that he had apparently picked up from where someone had placed it on the sidewalk.

He turned toward me.

"Oh, it's you," he said in a hissing voice.

"Yeah, why are you following me?"

"I was trying to tell you something, but was too shy to be forward."

"What do you mean?"

"You're my creator and I wanted to show my gratitude by advising you of a situation close to home."

"I don't follow." At that point he removed his fedora hat, dark glasses, and ankle-length raincoat. He removed his shoes to reveal paws. "What the fuck," I said. I wanted to run, but was paralyzed because standing before me was Koots Badger! I was face to face with my tormentor.

"Calm down." It took a while for my heart beat to slow down. I was feeling dizzy and the Badger pointed to a crate and beckoned me to sit on it. The crate had formerly held oranges.

"Don't be alarmed. I'm just one of your pookas. The other is O. J. Against all evidence to the contrary, you still believe in his innocence even though all of the obvious evidence points to his guilt. Don't you listen to Bill Maher? Even though you won all of that money for depicting him as a horse's ass, you won't let O. J. go, extending the conceit, he's got his spurs into you. I'm like O. J. in a way. He made his living seeking out holes that he could rush through and so do we Badgers. He's gotten a bad press. So have we. That poem you read that's made we badgers seem like an embattled species. Actually, we're quite gentle when you get to know us. That was pretty funny, the cartoon you drew of my protesting crows and ravens missing from the California bird book and the one about my picketing a pet store because they don't sell badgers.

Very clever. But it only adds to our reputation of being hostile and paranoid." I wondered where this badger went to school. He talked like David Niven. Said things like, "My dear fellow," and "spot on," and "bloody this and bloody that."

"Listen, I didn't come here to discuss the O. J. case, I want to know why you've been stalking me."

"I wanted to warn you of a situation close to home."

"Please get to the point, I don't have all day. I'm on a deadline to do my Southwest paintings."

"OK. Here it is. You have an enemy who is close to your wife."

"What do you mean?"

Sirs: It has come to my attention that your book, California Birds, *omits Ravens and Crows. Why?*

"Oh, he's not fucking her, although Gypsies are nomads and just as some of their women go from town to town, they are equally capable of going from dick to dick." I started toward him, but he made that hissing sound and bared his teeth. The monkey bared his teeth too.

"I may be an old badger but I'm capable of kicking your weak diabetic ass. You run the risk of low blood sugar and so you'd best go back and sit on that box. Oh, excuse me, my manners are wanting."

He snapped his finger and the monkey went to a small refrigerator and removed a bottle of red-colored liquid. He poured two glasses. The monkey offered me a glass.

"Would you like a twist of lime with that?" Koots asked.

"What is it?"

"Rabbit's blood. A real delicacy." I spat it out.

"No, a . . . no thanks." I handed it back to him. "Okay, what did you want to tell me?"

"Well first of all I wish to apologize for your hand wound."

"Yeah, well you bit my hand."

"That's because you had me cornered and when cornered, we badgers fight to the death. Instinct took over. Of course, Jeffrey Toobin says that your people also suffer from an impulse control disorder. Incapable of rational thought and David Brooks has commented, citing Malcolm Gladwell, that your people lack focus and discipline. And Nick Kristof said that your people lack perseverance." Motherfucking badger reads the *New York Times*! "You are endowed with what your great writer, Richard Wright, calls 'a riot of instincts.' You know, in my opinion, Richard Wright was not an existentialist but an anarchist. He viewed the Soviet Union as practicing left-wing capitalism. Instead of the private sector owning the means of production, they're run by the state and—" I sighed and glanced at my watch. Noticing my impatience, he got to the point.

"Of course, you remember those brilliant Southwest paintings that you submitted to the famous uptown gallery for a show."

"Right." He got my attention then.

"Crazy Goat was fucking the curator and he persuaded her to drop you and present his work. Then the motherfucker persuaded your wife to represent him. He's convinced the whole scene that he is the new Jean-Michel Basquiat. Your wife is getting ready to sell one of his paintings for six million dollars. An ugly derivative thing called *Uncle Ben's Dutch Ears*. He thinks that he's clever. He's always been jealous of you. He complains about how you treated him when he was living like a rat down on the Lower East Side."

Uncle Ben's Dutch Ears

"I knew it. I knew something like that happened. That Crazy Goat. That fucking primitive wannabe. There ain't a bit of difference between his work and the kind of stuff that people scribble on restroom walls. Only he does have a passable knowledge of acrylics, I'll give him that much."

"I agree. Absolutely no standards these days. Neo-Conceptualist consumer art, identity art, portraits of dictators and Hollywood stars. None of these people have the craftsmanship of a Grant Wood or Norman Rockwell. I look forward to your Southwest paintings, when are you going have another exhibit?"

"I'm examining the approach of Chicano, Native American, and Anglo artists to the New Mexico landscape. But thanks for your interest."

"Don't thank me. I owe my very existence to you."

"But aren't you upset because I suspended you?"

"Not at all. You had to do what you had to do, I have to do what I had to do. Besides, how do you think I got this place?"

"How?"

"Well, here being discarded gives you some prestige. I'm artist in residence. The reason I broke into your studio was to retrieve all of the original artwork for 'Koots Badger.' I didn't want you to destroy them now that you've discarded me. But here."

The monkey scampered to a box and removed a large manila envelope. He brought the envelope to me. I looked inside and found my drawings. I thanked Koots Badger and left Drecklyn. I knew what I had to do. Crazy Goat is what I had to do.

When I got home, Esther was about to leave the condo. "Hi, Babe, where you off to?"

"A press conference with Crazy Goat."

"Going to tell about that piece of shit he's selling for six million."

"How did you know?" Un-huh. The Badger was right.

"You represent him, but you don't want to represent me."

"Let's face it, dear. You're basically a cartoonist; nobody takes cartoonists seriously." Of course during the third week in February, 2009, that would all change. Nervous about his career meeting the same fate as a number of cartoonists whose work had been discontinued, Sean Delano hit one out of the ballpark. Drew a cartoon of the president of the United States as a chimp shot dead on the sidewalk. Even Hitler said that blacks were only "half ape."

"Why are you wearing a hat?" she asked. I started to remind her about the affair she had with a Jazz musician before we met. He wore a hat all the time. She didn't complain then. But bringing that up wouldn't be prudent. She shrugged her shoulders, kissed me on the cheek, and left for the press conference.

60

I had gotten the e-vite from the Uptown Gallery to attend the opening of Crazy Goat's show. I was working on a Southwest painting and had gone through a half bottle of scotch. I called Esther and told her that I'd meet her an hour before the show, but she told me that Crazy Goat was picking her up in a limousine.

When I arrived at the opening, I was pretty sauced. Scotch. I had cried all the way uptown and when I arrived, my cheeks were still red. The cab driver seeing my condition asked. "A woman?" I nodded. "Don't worry about it," he said. "There are plenty of fishes in the sea."

Yeah, but none of them like Esther. In comparison to the others, she was like a tuna. Purple, bronze, silver, and gold. Moreover, he was wrong, technically. As a result of man-made dead zones, there has been a decline in the fish supply that some experts deemed catastrophic.

I stumbled into the scene and headed right toward Crazy Goat, who was surrounded by admirers. He was explaining his piece *Un-*

cle Ben's Dutch Ears. Koots Badger was right. He was saying some shit like he had taken a superstition deeply implanted in the Western psyche that blacks were given to cannibalism. He said that by presenting the cannibalistic act in his painting, he was deploring the myth. Turning a stereotype on its head. It was neither original nor clever. It was using ideas and techniques that had been done to death. He had on his pin-striped suit and was barefoot. Dreads tumbling all over his face. British accent heavier than usual.

"Oh my good friend Bear. You all remember him don't you?" he said turning to the crowd of people surrounding him. "He's an unemployed cartoonist." They all laughed.

"Yes you laugh, but prior to the 1860s, cartoonists reigned supreme as illustrators of the best fiction, with Dickens planning the drawings for his novels with a genius of comic art like George Cruikshank as closely as he might have worked with an outright literary collaborator, and a Thackeray filling the pages of his own classic fiction to wide applause with witty cartoon art from his own hand," I said, quoting Bill Blackbeard. I could have also mentioned John Dos Passos's *The Big Money*, which he illustrated. They only laughed louder. I ignored them. I beckoned to Crazy Goat.

"Crazy Goat, can I talk to you for a minute?"

He excused himself. We went off to the side.

"What's the big idea of you telling this woman not to give me a show?"

"I don't know what you're talking about. Who told you that?"

"Koots Badger, I . . . I mean—"

"Koots Badger. Your wife told me that you'd been acting funny. And now you're talking about speaking to cartoon characters. I don't know why she's staying with you. I'm going to suggest that she leave . . ."

But before he could continue, I took him by the ear and dragged him to the painting. All of the arty conversation ceased. I grabbed the painting and smashed it over his head. Some gasps could be heard. He sank to the floor. His admirers rushed to his aide. They started screaming and pointing at me. Somebody called 911. Esther rose from where she was comforting Crazy Goat who was doing what in basketball is called a flop. Making the most of his situation in order to get attention. Moaning and groaning. Over dramatizing the situation. Bawling and carrying on and complaining about nonexistent ailments. I thought that it was funny. His wearing his six million dollar painting like a collar.

Esther said, "What's gotten into you, Bear?"

"I need some orange juice," I said. The police arrived and took me to the Tombs. I was charged with assault. Esther and Hibiscus bailed me out. Hibiscus had flown in from the New England school where she was teaching in the Women's Studies Department. When we exited from the prison, we found a large crowd outside. When they saw us, they let up a large cheer. They carried signs, which bore my name. A reporter rushed up to me. Said she was from *The Anglo Saxon Explainer*.

"What's going on?" I asked.

"These are all of the realistic painters, intelligible poets and level-headed musicians and clear-eyed filmmakers who have been put out of business by trends in the arts that have taken hold since the mid-twentieth century."

One sign read, "Who says naturalism is dead?" Another read "Mr. Bear MVP of the Arts."

"To them you're a hero for smashing that painting over Crazy Goat's head. They see it as a blow against abstract expressionism, pop art, graffiti, and all of the directions that art has made over the decades. Do you have a comment?"

Hibiscus was smiling, but Esther didn't seem all that pleased. She was probably thinking that the destruction of the six million dollar painting killed her commission. I thought about it. "Well, somebody had to strike a blow for the return to common sense in the arts. You have these self-reflexive novels where the novelist interjects himself as a character. Novels like those written by that Ishmael Reed. He's probably out in some obscure hole in California right now, thinking of another way by which he can badger himself into his work having been criticized for introducing himself as a character in his novel *Japanese By Spring*. You have art where the artist thinks that his personal items are of interest to people. Just walk into any of the so-called art schools influenced by the Brillo Box School of art and look at the students' works and you think, 'I can do that.' Though dismissed as the comment of Philistines, the phrase 'I can do that' is the strongest indictment of postmodernist art. That includes everything from pop art and conceptual art to silk screen portraits." I turned to the crowd. "Look at the great artists of the past. Botticelli. Do you think that anybody can do Botticelli?" Members of the crowd yelled, "No."

"Look at El Greco. Do you think anybody can do El Greco?" The crowd yelled, "No." One man said, "No way." Some in the crowd chuckled. "Look at Picasso, Romare Bearden? Henry Tanner? Do you think that anybody can do Picasso, Romare Bearden, Henry Tanner?" Again, the crowd yelled, "No." I turned away from the reporter and mounted the steps. I looked over the crowd. "Aren't you tired of people putting urine in a jar with a photo of Jesus or smearing elephant dung over the Holy Mother?" Cheers were so loud that I couldn't continue for a few minutes.

"Aren't you tired of twenty bar bass solos improvising on tunes like 'Willow Weep For Me?'" The crowd yelled, "Yes."

"With your help, we will return American arts to the traditions out of which they grew. A tradition of hard work, discipline, and craftsman—craftspersonship. After all, it takes two weeks for oil to dry. Thank you. Thanks to all of my supporters for coming out on this rainy day."

Reporters followed us to the car. As I prepared to leave the steps of the courthouse a reporter asked me for one more comment, I said, "Somebody had to stop the nonlinear hold on American arts. History chose me." The crowd applauded and cheered. Hibiscus embraced me. Esther, however, stood off to the side, glaring at me, her arms folded, stamping one foot. We waded through the crowd of well-wishers, many of them reaching out to shake my hand. Especially an elderly white woman who said to me tearfully, "Thank you young man. Now maybe I will live long enough to make sense of a *New Yorker* poem." In the cab on the way to our condo Esther expressed her feelings.

"I don't get it. In your acceptance speech at the International Cartoonists award, you praised the pop artists for bringing cartoons into museums. Giving them respectability. Now you're inciting a crowd. Sounding like Giuliani or somebody."

I thought about it for a moment before answering. "You're right, I got carried away," I said. She was used to me contradicting myself. Before I married her, I told her that I was a Pisces. But what really upset her was her loss of a commission, but that would change when she got some good news. That afternoon a collector of conceptual art paid six million dollars for her photograph of my crashing Crazy Goat's graffiti painting over his head. Some would go to the photographer, some to Crazy Goat, and she'd receive a commission. She treated us to dinner. That night, some linear-oriented college students started a bonfire consisting of Brillo boxes and Campbell soup cans. As one philosopher said, we're hardwired for order.

The next morning Esther announced, "I bought three tickets to Santa Fe, Bear. We can have a retreat for a month. I figured that you had to get away from New York. My treat."

"It will be a pleasant trip for you, Dad." Hibiscus and Karisha had broken up again. Had something to do with black women always having to play the butch part in lesbian couplings. On the last episode of *The L Word*, which took place in a club where lesbian couples took turns exhibiting their dancing skills, even Jennifer Beals had to play the male, leading her white femme partner and in 2010, a minority woman plays the male to the lead ballerina in the movie *Black Swan*. First the black-skinned lesbians revolted against their white femme partners, and then the revolt extended to yellow women, who are always the butt of jokes in novels written by black-skinned women. Being black-skinned, Karisha moved out and joined a caucus of her fellow black-skinned women.

"You can work on your paintings."

"But you said that I was basically a cartoonist."

"You've taught me that I should be open to many forms of artistic expressions no matter how hokey, I . . . I mean . . ."

"It's okay."

"I . . . look I dropped Crazy Goat," she said.

"I hope you kept your commission," I said. We all laughed. That sort of broke the ice. The morning of our departure, I was in the bedroom and I could hear Esther speaking on the phone in a low tone. "No, I don't think that medication will be necessary. Santa Fe or Hawaii seems to calm him down. Talking to the cartoon character? He was just suffering from exhaustion. Something happened to him the night that O. J. Simpson rode around in the Bronco. Not only him, but the whole nation. Just think how many would sign up were there a twelve-step program that would end O. J. addiction. Bill Maher would probably be the group leader. He'll be fine. He wants to paint. It will be good for him. He hasn't mentioned talking to Koots Badger for a few days now. I think that I have convinced him that it was a hallucination." I didn't know to whom she was talking. But it was obvious that she'd gotten some counseling about my state of mind.

61

One evening, a week or so after we had settled in Santa Fe, we were watching television. It was the trial of Renaldo Louis but since no blonde was involved it wasn't being called the trial of the century. The prosecutor had rested their opening argument and Louis's mother began hers. She is the kind of black woman who gets called "majestic." The great Vinnie Burrows could play her part.

"Ladies and Gentlemen we will prove that my son, Renaldo Louis, is not guilty of kidnapping as charged. He actually was performing a service. He was implementing citizen arrests of those who are guilty of hate crimes. As long as they were restrained, blacks, Hispanics, Muslims, and gays were safe from their inflammatory appeals to hatred. Yes, you might consider such an argument far-fetched and I admit they weren't as obvious as those appeals that were broadcast in Rwanda where members of another ethnic group were called 'cockroaches' by radio broadcasters and as a result thousands were murdered. No, their way of egging on ignorance and even vigilante action against minorities is subtle. Yet it is propaganda nevertheless.

"Take a look at Katrina, where the media cast the victims as refugees—these were American citizens, mind you; they spread stories about widespread looting, rape, and murder when such reporting was based on lies. Don't you think that this was used to justify the actions of white vigilantes who went about massacring innocent blacks? Look at the way blacks are shown on television and even worse in the movies, something those blacks have complained about since at least the 1930s when the honorable Marcus Garvey chastised Paul Robeson for his role in *Sanders of the River* which was to British Imperialism what *Gone with the Wind* was to the Confederacy. In the 1940s, Walter White complained about these presentations. Since then blacks have protested, demonstrated, remonstrated at these images that threaten their safety. My son had had enough and he acted." She went on to recount the protests that blacks had held against Hollywood, radio, and television since the 1910s, almost one hundred years ago.

Things looked good for Louis. As she continued her argument, the camera panned to the jury of Hispanics, African Americans, and Native Americans who were nodding their heads. His mother was wise enough to impanel some Italian Americans, one of the white ethnic groups that took a beating from Hollywood over the years. It took them only an hour to come back with an acquittal. Unlike when the civil jury announced its verdict and O. J. Simpson had to face the kind of lynch mob that resembled the ones that formed in the South for a night of recreation and fun, Renaldo Louis emerged from the courtroom arm-in-arm with his mother. He was greeted by a sea of black, red, and green flags.

62

Even walking through the Albuquerque airport I felt calmer. After unpacking, I went out on the patio and began reading a book that I'd brought along. I was intrigued about Ben's remark that me and my fellow Moses types, who had reservations about the new postrace America, were like the Japanese soldiers who refused to believe that the war had ended. They were Kozuka, Akatsu, Shimada, and Onoda.

Convinced that World War II was continuing, they vowed to fight on. Akatsu defected. Shimada and Kozuka were killed by Philippine troops. Onoda, the survivor, outmaneuvered the Philippine police and Japanese search parties until 1974 when he was found. Before the war, Onoda loved to dance. What did his vow to fight on get him? Thirty years in the jungle, polishing his rifle. Given the choice between dancing and going to war, most people in the world would choose to dance. It's the power-mad hierarchies and oligarchies that start wars. They send the poor to do their fighting while they drink forty-thousand-dollar brandy at poolside, sail the world in three-hundred-million-dollar yachts, and build mega-mega-mansions that make the castle of Versailles seem like Motel 6. That wasn't going to happen to me. Invitations to speak were coming in from colleges and institutions all over the country. Even some liberal ones. My photo made the cover of *Art News* under the headline, "Revolt Against The Non-Linear?" I was the talk of the talk shows. One man said that he didn't feel so embarrassed at Upper West Side cocktail parties when he said he preferred *Our Town* to *Waiting for Godot*. I was not the only one enjoying a second act: the *New York Times* reported on March 20, 2009, that "Sugar, the nutritional pariah that dentists, and dieticians have long reviled, is enjoying a second act, dressed up as a normal, healthful ingredient."

My meditation was interrupted by their returning home. They were loaded down with bags of groceries. After Esther prepared lunch, she brought it to me out on the veranda.

"Where's *The Anglo Saxon Explainer*?" I asked. Stuck here in Santa Fe, I wasn't all that interested in local news. I wanted to read something more national. Something less regional. Less ethnic.

"I—I didn't think you'd want to read it today . . ." She handed me the entertainment section. There was a photo of police standing over the covered bodies of Jagid and Jagan and some other hip-hoppers who engaged in a shoot-out *before* a hip-hop awards ceremony. Seems that Jagid and Jagan and members of another posse got into an argument over who had the longest arrest record. Jagid and Jagan argued that they'd been arrested about fifty times each. The leader of the other posse disputed this figure. Jagid and Jagan lost.

"Esther," I said firmly. "Please bring me the newspaper."

It was on the front page. A photo of Crazy Goat and Young Brothers. They were announcing that they'd found funding to do the animated series but instead of *Attitude the Badger*, their backers preferred "Koots Badger," who was more attune to the postrace America. In the photo the three were standing next to Ben Armstrong who was described as their attorney. Esther also handed me a letter. It was from Crazy Goat. He had dropped the charges against me.

Just as people can tell you where they were when JFK was shot, when the moon landing occurred, when it was announced that Celtic African President Barack Obama had won the presidency, I can tell you where I was when I heard that Ron Goldman and Nicole Brown had been murdered. Vacationing near the Pacific Ocean. I'd gone full circle. The desert is deceptive, because, sitting on this veranda, I am sitting at the bottom of an ocean that existed millions of years ago in the region that is now New Mexico. Its shorelines are still visible. There was a theory that we all originated as cells inside of rocks located at the bottom of oceans. An idea that gives new meaning to Bobby Dylan's line, "Everybody must get stoned."

You look at the rock in question and it looks as though it's tinted with gold. Some sulfur. Sulfur is connected to the environment of hell. That's humanity all right. Some gold, like in Tennessee Reed's poem, and some hell.

Esther joined me on the veranda. We spent some time holding hands and watching the stars where on any planet the same process that led to life on earth might be being repeated millions of times at any moment. And who knows, Esther and I might be sitting in a place where it all began. At the bottom of an ocean that existed millions of years ago.

Another theory holds that life arrived on asteroids. One that landed in the Nubian Desert in 2008 was said to possibly contain organic materials, including amino acids. The Old Negro spirituals, which included lines like "this world is not my home," were closer to the truth than one would possibly think.

Our reverie was interrupted by Hibiscus. "Dad," she said, "There's some character at the door who says that he wants to talk to you. He's standing there with a pet monkey. The monkey is wearing a beret. He's so cute." I smiled and rose to greet my guests, but not before glancing at Esther whose jaw had become unhinged, like Dominick Dunne's upon hearing the verdict at the conclusion of the trial of the century, James Orenthal Simpson vs. The State of California.

OAKLAND, CALIFORNIA
JANUARY 2, 2011

APPENDIX

CNN
Reliable Sources

The Media Get Juiced; Rather's Revenge
Aired September 23, 2007—10:00 ET

HOWARD KURTZ, CNN ANCHOR: The media get juiced. Television goes haywire as O. J. is arrested, jailed, and freed on bail over charges of armed robbery. Are journalists rooting for the conviction that never happened in the double murder case a dozen years ago and are they wallowing in yet another celebrity scandal?

(BEGIN VIDEO CLIP)

. . . let's face it —a media fantasy come true. O. J. behind bars, O. J. charged with armed robbery, O. J. yelling and cursing on audiotape. O. J. Simpson, the man whose murder trial launched television into its current fixation with celebrities, crime, and controversy; whose case blazed the trail for the frenzies over Chandra and Laci and Natalie and Anna Nicole and Paris and Lindsay and Britney. Back on our screens, the lawyers and prosecutors and psychologists arguing over the case again. O. J. released on bail—and this was really the case—a news helicopter following his car as if it were another low-speed Bronco chase. It was like a time warp, 1994 all over again, and every program on the planet got juiced.

JULIA ALLISON, STAR MAGAZINE: After 12 years, finally it appears he might be getting what's coming to him, not in the form we expected but in some form. You couldn't create a juicier scenario. This is act three. All the same cast of characters from the past coming back, Marcia Clark, the prosecutor, in court as a reporter. It is like a murder mystery dinner theater except they are coming back for act three in different outfits.

ROLAND MARTIN, CNN CONTRIBUTOR: I think what's driving the story is O. J. Simpson equals ratings. Bottom line is the public watches. Now, take out the arrest. Prior to the arrest, look at *If I Did It*. The book shot to No. 1 on amazon.com, Barnesandnoble.com. It did not get any kind of advertising. The companies initially said they were not even going to stock it on store shelves. But the American public bought into it. Was that driven by the media?

No. It was driven by the story itself. Now when people say, "I am so sick of O. J. Simpson," show me where ratings declined?

Show me where they remain flat. The reality is when these stories come out, the ratings spike. That means people watch.

Look, I don't understand who buys celebrity magazines. But I flip through and watch people buy coffee at Starbucks. That doesn't excite me, but somebody's buying it.

KURTZ: All right, but of course on cable television you only need a few hundred thousand more people to watch for the ratings to spike. It doesn't mean the whole country is transfixed by this.

MARTIN: Right, but they go up.

KURTZ: All right. Julia Allison, O. J. is such a huge story this is going to be on the cover of "Star." Right?

ALLISON: Absolutely not. We're not putting him on the cover of "Star." Our readers don't care about O. J. Simpson. In fact, our readers were in junior high or high school like myself when he was acquitted. And they don't particularly know who he is. I think it's something that perhaps might be spiking ratings for certain demographics, but it certainly isn't something we're concerned with.

ALLISON: It's just not within the purview of my generation. I think also, in addition to that, we're interested in Lindsay, Britney, Nicole, and Paris. We're talking about sexy young girls who are doing random things. And I think that O. J. is just not something we're interested in.

MARTIN: Howard, but the reality there is, I understand what she's saying. But the focus on Lindsay, Nicole Richie, Paris Hilton, that's an offspring of O. J., as you talked about in your open. O. J. was what created this whole notion of celebrity justice, celebrity focus, in terms of in mainstream media. So frankly, without what we went through with O. J., you would you not see the fascination with Nicole, Paris, as well as Lindsay.

VELEZ-MITCHELL: Howard, can I jump in for a second? I think what's really pathetic is that the choice is between Britney, Paris, and O. J. That's what our society has come down to. I'd love to talk about other issues, environmental issues, the obesity crisis. Nobody ever asks me. This is what America's addicted to. We are addicted to crime and we are addicted to celebrity. We need to ask ourselves why are we so obsessed with these two issues?

KURTZ: When you say America is addicted, I think there is a media addiction.

KURTZ: Julia Allison, I know you're too young to remember some of this, but as Roland Martin mentioned, sorry, as Jane Velez-Mitchell mentioned, some of the characters from the trial in the mid '90s have come back to life in other guises, for example, Marcia Clark.

ALLISON: Yes, blonde hair and nose job apparently.

KURTZ: Julia Allison, I know that your enthusiasm for this O. J. story is somewhat limited, but do you see it having legs—are the media going to keep pumping this up for a while or do you think it is going to fade?

ALLISON: Well, I hope it is going to fade. No, I don't. I'll tell you why. As long as it is getting the ratings in certain demographics, I think it will continue until they get justice that they want. The only reason this robbery case is getting any attention is because everyone thinks it was a betrayal of justice in the first place. So no, they're going to wait until O. J. gets his.

KURTZ: It really is true that we've come full circle here. The Simpson trial in the mid '90s, televised by CNN, really was the first television addiction to this kind of celebrity crime. When we ran out of celebrities, television just invented others, like Laci and Chandra and Natalie and now of course, with the B-list bad girls that have been mentioned here, Britney, Paris, Lindsay, keeping us in business.

But the thing about O. J. is it's become a proxy, this bizarre Las Vegas robbery case—it's become a proxy for the original murder trial. That's why the media just won't let it go.

Ishmael Reed's cartoon predicting the media riot that would occur in the event of an O. J. Simpson acquittal was published in The New York Amsterdam News *in April of 1995 by the then editor, the great cartoonist, Mel Tapley. The acquittal verdict was announced on Oct. 3, 1995.*

ISHMAEL REED is the author of over twenty-seven books—including *Mumbo Jumbo*, *The Last Days of Louisiana Red*, and *Yellow Back Radio Broke-Down*. He is also a publisher, television producer, songwriter, radio and television commentator, lecturer, and has long been devoted to exploring an alternative black aesthetic: the trickster tradition, or "Neo-Hoodooism" as he calls it. Founder of the Before Columbus Foundation, he taught at the University of California, Berkeley for over thirty years, retiring in 2005. In 2003, he received the coveted Otto Award for Political Theatre. Reed has also studied at San Francisco's Cartoon Museum, and has been acknowledged by Margo Jefferson of the *New York Times* as a pioneer of the graphic novel.

SELECTED DALKEY ARCHIVE PAPERBACKS

My Life in CIA.
Singular Pleasures.
The Sinking of the Odradek
  Stadium.
Tlooth.
20 Lines a Day.
JOSEPH MCELROY,
  Night Soul and Other Stories.
THOMAS MCGONIGLE,
  Going to Patchogue.
ROBERT L. MCLAUGHLIN, ED., *Innovations:*
  An Anthology of
  Modern & Contemporary Fiction.
ABDELWAHAB MEDDEB, *Talismano.*
HERMAN MELVILLE, *The Confidence-Man.*
AMANDA MICHALOPOULOU, *I'd Like.*
STEVEN MILLHAUSER,
  The Barnum Museum.
  In the Penny Arcade.
RALPH J. MILLS, JR.,
  Essays on Poetry.
MOMUS, *The Book of Jokes.*
CHRISTINE MONTALBETTI, *Western.*
OLIVE MOORE, *Spleen.*
NICHOLAS MOSLEY, *Accident.*
  Assassins.
  Catastrophe Practice.
  Children of Darkness and Light.
  Experience and Religion.
  God's Hazard.
  The Hesperides Tree.
  Hopeful Monsters.
  Imago Bird.
  Impossible Object.
  Inventing God.
  Judith.
  Look at the Dark.
  Natalie Natalia.
  Paradoxes of Peace.
  Serpent.
  Time at War.
  The Uses of Slime Mould:
    Essays of Four Decades.
WARREN MOTTE,
  Fables of the Novel: French Fiction
    since 1990.
  Fiction Now: The French Novel in
    the 21st Century.
  Oulipo: A Primer of Potential
    Literature.
YVES NAVARRE, *Our Share of Time.*
  Sweet Tooth.
DOROTHY NELSON, *In Night's City.*
  Tar and Feathers.
ESHKOL NEVO, *Homesick.*
WILFRIDO D. NOLLEDO, *But for the Lovers.*
FLANN O'BRIEN,
  At Swim-Two-Birds.
  At War.
  The Best of Myles.
  The Dalkey Archive.
  Further Cuttings.
  The Hard Life.
  The Poor Mouth.
  The Third Policeman.
CLAUDE OLLIER, *The Mise-en-Scène.*
  Wert and the Life Without End.
PATRIK OUŘEDNÍK, *Europeana.*
  The Opportune Moment, 1855.
BORIS PAHOR, *Necropolis.*

FERNANDO DEL PASO,
  News from the Empire.
  Palinuro of Mexico.
ROBERT PINGET, *The Inquisitory.*
  Mahu or The Material.
  Trio.
MANUEL PUIG,
  Betrayed by Rita Hayworth.
  The Buenos Aires Affair.
  Heartbreak Tango.
RAYMOND QUENEAU, *The Last Days.*
  Odile.
  Pierrot Mon Ami.
  Saint Glinglin.
ANN QUIN, *Berg.*
  Passages.
  Three.
  Tripticks.
ISHMAEL REED,
  The Free-Lance Pallbearers.
  The Last Days of Louisiana Red.
  Ishmael Reed: The Plays.
  Juice!
  Reckless Eyeballing.
  The Terrible Threes.
  The Terrible Twos.
  Yellow Back Radio Broke-Down.
JOÃO UBALDO RIBEIRO, *House of the*
  Fortunate Buddhas.
JEAN RICARDOU, *Place Names.*
RAINER MARIA RILKE, *The Notebooks of*
  Malte Laurids Brigge.
JULIÁN RÍOS, *The House of Ulysses.*
  Larva: A Midsummer Night's Babel.
  Poundemonium.
  Procession of Shadows.
AUGUSTO ROA BASTOS, *I the Supreme.*
DANIËL ROBBERECHTS,
  Arriving in Avignon.
JEAN ROLIN, *The Explosion of the*
  Radiator Hose.
OLIVIER ROLIN, *Hotel Crystal.*
ALIX CLEO ROUBAUD, *Alix's Journal.*
JACQUES ROUBAUD, *The Form of a*
  City Changes Faster, Alas, Than
  the Human Heart.
  The Great Fire of London.
  Hortense in Exile.
  Hortense Is Abducted.
  The Loop.
  The Plurality of Worlds of Lewis.
  The Princess Hoppy.
  Some Thing Black.
LEON S. ROUDIEZ, *French Fiction Revisited.*
RAYMOND ROUSSEL, *Impressions of Africa.*
VEDRANA RUDAN, *Night.*
STIG SÆTERBAKKEN, *Siamese.*
LYDIE SALVAYRE, *The Company of Ghosts.*
  Everyday Life.
  The Lecture.
  Portrait of the Writer as a
    Domesticated Animal.
  The Power of Flies.
LUIS RAFAEL SÁNCHEZ,
  Macho Camacho's Beat.
SEVERO SARDUY, *Cobra & Maitreya.*
NATHALIE SARRAUTE,
  Do You Hear Them?
  Martereau.
  The Planetarium.

FOR A FULL LIST OF PUBLICATIONS, VISIT:
www.dalkeyarchive.com